ZINA ROHAN

The Book of
Wishes and Complaints

Flamingo
An Imprint of HarperCollins*Publishers*

Flamingo
An Imprint of HarperCollins*Publishers*,
77–85 Fulham Palace Road,
Hammersmith, London W6 8JB

Published by Flamingo 1992
9 8 7 6 5 4 3 2 1

First published in Great Britain by
Hutchinson 1991

Author photograph by Caroline Forbes

ISBN 0 00 654486 X

Set in Palatino

Printed in Great Britain by
HarperCollinsManufacturing Glasgow

For Paul with love and thanks

PART I

One

'Why can't she stay in a hotel?'

'Because she hasn't the money.'

'Then you pay. You can afford it.'

'That's not the point. I can't just dump her in a hotel and leave her to get on with it. She isn't an ordinary tourist. She'll need guiding.'

'Who said anything about leaving her to get on with it? She could just stay in a hotel . . . and I mean, if this house were a real house, there'd be room enough for everyone without turfing me out – after all this time.' Melanie Sansom's voice was almost shrill with displeasure although, being a landscape gardener, she cultivated a harmonious disposition.

Peter Cerny had bought his neat Kentish Town house purely as an investment, had had it decorated for the same reason, kept its gleaming hi-tech kitchen empty and insisted on eating out or buying takeaways. Every fortnight he purchased fourteen pairs of socks; at the end of the fortnight he threw them away. He collected, researched and catalogued earthenware beer bottles going back to the seventeenth century and gave them pride of place in a series of glass cabinets in the main upstairs room which, according to Melanie, should have housed people, not empty vessels.

Peter spoke such faultless English that no one would have thought he had once been a Czech. He made his money – and plenty of it – as an accountant, also buying and selling houses. Nearly forty, he was tall, inclined to overweight, but with a head of curling dark hair which would never grow sparse – a gift from his English mother, recently deceased. Her framed photograph stood prominently on a kitchen shelf, and there was a glint in her eye, probably the freak effect of the photographer's lights.

3

Peter and Melanie were lovers of two years' standing, but by this summer of 1984 they were beginning to ask of themselves, separately, whether it was necessary to go on for much longer. All was well once they were in bed where they understood each other almost perfectly. Out of it there was increasingly little on which they could agree. Melanie was a woman of high principles, whereas Peter abhorred principle – on principle. Both could cite examples, the same examples, to prove their point.

Only that week a notice had been published in the local newspaper inviting comment on planning permission, currently under consideration, to build, on a nearby site, a hostel for the mentally ill who had previously been incarcerated. Reaction from the neighbourhood had been swift and unenthusiastic. A man had come knocking at Peter's door requesting his signature on a petition of complaint. Peter had withheld his name despite the effect on property values the hostel implied. Surprised but gratified, Melanie had whipped out a counter-petition of her own and put it before her lover. 'Yours can be the very first signature,' she told him. But Peter had rejected her document as well.

'If they build it, they build it. If they don't, they don't. I couldn't care less.'

'But you should care.'

'I don't want to "should" anything. Let me care about whatever I want to care about in my own good time. Most people are like me, Mel. Not everybody runs around with causes in their heads all the time. I'm not interested in community action, especially' – pre-empting her – 'when I'm told it's the good and correct thing to do. Okay?'

But it was not okay.

'Your trouble is,' said Melanie, 'you'd never put yourself out for anyone.'

And now came the nub of her trouble, for Peter had then informed her – politely and tentatively, it was true – that, on the contrary, he was putting himself out to play host for a week to an old friend, going back to his childhood, who was coming to stay, bringing with her, unfortunately, her kid, whom he didn't know. And would Melanie please decamp for the duration. If she wanted, he'd pay for *her* to stay in a hotel. Melanie had lost her temper.

Peter knew he was being hard because, if the truth were told, and it would not be, he wished his old friend Hana had not

4

announced she was coming to stay. He had had things planned for the week which this visit would disrupt, he had wanted to work on the layout of a catalogue for his bottles, he had not wanted to be disturbed. He had nothing to say to Hana and he did not look forward to her chatter, her complaining and, no doubt, her demands. He knew about the expectations of visitors from Eastern Europe. 'You're rich, you've done well for yourself, but that's the West. Now if we only had the chance . . . but there it is . . . So what are you going to give me? Look, my son needs this, my son needs that . . .' Peter had kept himself tucked away from the émigré community and their whinesome relatives. He wanted no part of it; he felt at once hounded and ashamed – the more so because Hana's very presence would make him think about his father, about whom he thought only with the deepest unease, with whom he could not agree, from whom he remembered receiving endless instruction, for whom he nevertheless felt a weary sense of dutiful affection, suspecting, meanwhile, that affection made the old doctor uneasy. Melanie had asked, why does she have to stay here? Good question; so she was being punished for it.

Hana was coming – there was no avoiding it – with that kid; no mention of its father. He didn't want a kid around, banging into his glass cabinets.

The kid in question was at that moment down the hill from home playing with friends. He was seven years old, named Milan, and thought he was going for a week's holiday cure at a spa. His friends thought so too, as did his friends' parents. So, indeed, did the entire village, which is what his mother intended.

The village of Bytlice, forty kilometres south-west of Prague, lay on the lazy brown Berounka, in whose polluted waters other children leaped and swam. Milan was not allowed to. He tended to be sickly and knew it, envying his two companions, the Frantisek boys, their robust disregard for the dangerous water. They were older, bigger, stronger than he believed he would ever be. They had a nice mother, Auntie Alena, who was kind but cried sometimes, and a father, big Uncle Josef, who mended and made, drank and sang. Milan, who wished he had a father and a brother or two, had only his mother, whom he loved with all his might because she was strict and warm but no longer quite perfect. And in faraway Merunkov there was Grandad whom, for some reason, he was not supposed to see.

Apart from chickens, the Frantiseks kept brown rabbits, and Milan stroked them even though he knew Uncle Josef killed them for the pot.

Up the hill his mother, Hana, was looking at her watch. It would soon be time to fetch the boy home, get him fed, bathed and into bed. She wanted him well slept for an early start. And the evening to herself.

Her house, Number 64, was the last up the track with only the plantation of young pines behind it and beyond them the forest. It was the stuff of fairy-tales, brown and white, and crisp as a biscuit, rearing up from its garden on a pedestal of crumbling stonework. The garden dropped sharply away, down to the tennis courts where young enthusiasts shouted with every thwack of the ball, emulating the tennis stars who were always abroad. Then the rutted track, stones like marbles underfoot, plunged down between the trees, winding past other houses, down and down to the main body of the village with its supermarket, post office and butcher.

Hana delighted in the steepness of the hill because it kept her in trim. When she went down to the village and returned with two shopping bags balanced as if on a yoke, she would notice, as they passed, the matronly figures of her neighbours. They resented the climb, groaned over it, but Hana, who exercised to music when the house was empty, sometimes took its incline at a run.

She was small and hipped like a boy, with cropped bouncing hair, and if you did not see her too soon after waking, if you allowed her time to press cold water on her uptilted grey eyes, you would say she did not look her age, not with that elfin face and the wide, slightly lopsided smile. Now, as she ran down over the tussocks of her garden, she felt the muscles of her thighs stretching and tensing, and as always she saluted them, but this time with regret, for this was the last time she would take this short-cut to the Frantiseks, trustworthy and trusting, and much deceived.

The track rose, then suddenly dipped down, and from this last rise she could see into the land behind the small modern block where the Frantiseks lived. There they all were: Alena, in the evening sun, still in her bikini on the concrete veranda

Josef had built; Josef hammering roofing felt on to the chicken-hut; and the boys, the two sturdy ones and her pale runt, whom Josef called Twiglet, running in the shadow of the trees where the dry pines, massed together, blocked out the sun and smothered the grass.

A hiker on the track would pause in his march to smile on this distant, domestic afternoon. He would not know that Alena's hair was thin and her cheeks lined with strain; that Josef would not restrain himself from cupping his hands round the buttocks of any woman, so long as she was young, juicy and not unwilling; that the Frantisek boys were raucous in their father's image, but, in their father's image also, generous. Alena was Hana's best friend. She had been Alena's confidante. Josef, the forester with his party card, had systematically poached the deer in his protection to please the palates of his friends. He had many friends and the deer were dwindling. A few steps from the house, Hana stopped. These were people she knew she would miss. How could Josef be such a decent communist and such a shit of a husband?

Two

Milan slept facing the wall with its giant poster of the West German skier who had won the gold last year. The champion's eyes were invisible, his goggles blanking out emotion. His mouth was open in a wide shout – elation or, possibly, terror. His body was flung forwards, legs skewed to the side, one bent double beneath him. The arms with their poles described wild arcs. He was surely winning again. The boy dreamed of skiing like that but recognised, with a modesty and a self-deprecation unsuited to his age, that he'd never make it. He was nervous and inclined to be clumsy, despite his slight build.

On the floor at the foot of his bed was a wooden box filled almost to the brim with the Lego that the man Peter in England had been sending him, birthdays and Christmases. The Lego gave the Frantiseks an extra reason for playing with Milan, and they were much more adept with the plastic blocks than he was. One of them showed engineering talent and made a windmill with cogs and wheels whose sails went round when you turned the tiny handle he had set into the windmill's wall. Milan so admired that construction that he had refused to allow its builder and, subsequently, Hana to take it apart. So it stood on his chest of drawers for months, and when he remembered he gave the tiny handle a couple of rotations as he went by. He would regret the loss of his Lego, his poster, the windmill and the Frantiseks, but as he didn't know that they were going to be separated he slept peacefully.

Downstairs, Hana was breathing heavily, her guts contracting with anticipation. Within the next few days, she would be with Lukas again, actually see him, actually touch him. She would put her arms round his solid and so long-beloved body, and her lonely imaginings, her tired memories, would flee before the reality. But, for now, she must put that old hunger aside.

She was packing her suitcases again, but in a quandary. How much could she take without arousing the suspicion of the customs? Nobody took books in any quantity for a summer holiday. Books anyway would weigh too much. Forget the books. As she had not yet got round to reading many of them, who was to say whether she might begin now? The issue of the books did not trouble her for long. No, it was clothes and treasures. Her son's winter jacket, his padded trousers, his thick pullovers, her quilted coat, which saw her through last year's unusually bitter cold. Clearly they had no place in the baggage of summer tourists, and yet to leave them behind, unclaimed, was like throwing away good food. She wished she could devise some way of passing them on to Alena or the Kralovs, whose lads were smaller than Milan. She wished more that she could have packed them into a parcel that one of her friends could have sent on to her. It occurred to her that there was still no reason why she should not do that even now. Make a parcel. Hide it somewhere. Write to Alena later and ask her, could she possibly . . . but to help herself first to whatever she needed.

She would wear her gold cross on the gold chain and her father's signet ring intended for Milan when he was old enough to wear it and not lose it. If she wound thread round the ring it wouldn't slip off. But how could she take her precious inlaid table or the glass decanter and the crystal glasses that her Aunt Veronika had said were eighteenth century? Her aunt might have been wrong, or making it up, but Hana's devotion to the objects bore no relation to their value or to their beauty, or even to the fact that they were presents from that aunt. She loved them because they had stood, there, on her mantelpiece. She did not know whether she loved the plates, the prints and the mirror for hanging on the walls of her house, or the house for providing the walls on which to hang them. She would pack the house too, if she could, and as she thought this she smiled wrily at herself and said aloud, 'Get a grip on yourself, you silly cow.'

She boiled the kettle, idly opening and closing cupboard doors in the small kitchen. Every item accused her of betrayal. Had they not served her well? she argued for them; if she was reputed to be the best cook in the neighbourhood, didn't they deserve a share of the praise?

Her gaze took in the cumbersome old food-mixer, ugly but as indefatigable as the pockmarked gardener her father used to return to in reminiscence. At six years old, her father had been chided for recoiling from the gardener because of his ugliness, had been taken by the hand to the rose garden. 'Look at these,' Hana's grandfather had admonished her diminutive father (and in adulthood Hana's father, telling and retelling the memory, had wagged an imitating finger, still defiant), 'Mr Broucek may not be good to look at, but he made these grow. And you know what everyone says. They say to me, your rose garden is perfect. It must be the best there is outside England. And that's the highest praise.' Caressing the hump of the food-mixer, Hana wondered whether the rose gardens of England merited their reputation and whether they still existed. Her father, she thought, had never really learned that lesson. He wanted the rose garden to be as lovely as it was, but to his dying day he could not see why gardeners could not be aesthetically pleasing too. How lucky for them all, her mother, herself and her brother, that they were none of them blemished.

Would her stories be enough? At bathtime Milan demanded tales of the family, demanded a past. 'Tell me the funny things I said when I was little.' And then, 'Tell me the things you did when you were small. Tell me about Grandma and the puppet theatre.' 'What puppet theatre?' – stalling from fatigue and boredom. He wanted her to give him grandparents and great-grandparents, he wanted their voices and their smells. He wanted to know what they would have thought of him: would they have loved him, would they have told him stories? He had a great sense of family, poor fatherless boy. Again the wry smile for applying to him the title used by the locality. She knew he was not a fatherless boy. He did not know it, but he would. He would know it, she sensed, immediately, without having to be told, when the moment came. She had pictured how it would be over and over again but kept her pictures to herself, out of superstition first, and only second for fear of Milan's blabbing young mouth. So far as it was possible, Milan knew his antecedents only from Hana's stories and the photographs, but it was her intention that soon he should know them completely.

The photographs! She reached for the Clark's shoebox in which Peter once sent her a pair of solid brogues and in which since then she had kept her photographs. She emptied the contents on to the carpet and sat cross-legged before them, like a child in school. Which was she to take?

June 1943, Karlstejn Castle. Her mother's impeccable hand

gave time and place but no clue to the persons, whose identity was to be taken for granted. Her mother was in the picture – slightly pregnant, Hana realised by the date, but still undetectably so. There were two other women, on either side of her mother and dwarfing her as most people did. They leaned in from the side, flanking her, implying that of course she was the centrepiece. All three wore belted coats. All three smiled wanly for the photographer, who must have been her father. He took most of the pictures and was therefore represented in almost none of them. One she had to find and keep. And he did his own developing in the back of the pharmacy. That she remembered. But what was the reason for the wan smiles? Did the three of them not get along as well as the intimate postures were meant to suggest? Or was it because all people smiled wanly in wartime? Perhaps they were hungry, or tired, or bored by Karlstejn and the requirement to smile against the backdrop of national heritage.

More pictures of her mother, visibly pregnant now but turning away, trying to hide it. So slender normally, she considered pregnancy an unsuitable subject for archive.

Her mother, head back, light brown hair flowing over her shoulders, smiling up at a white bundle she held at arm's length in the air. Hana selected this one and put it aside. Her first recorded appearance. January 1944. At home in Merunkov.

Shots of a baby in a pram. Mostly fat and beaming. Probably they didn't keep the howling ones. Had she really been so podgy? Wrists and ankles braceleted with creases, tiny eyes, gross cheeks. Then the baby was a toddler, dressed stiff and white for church. Her father must have snapped that one in a hurry. More of the toddler in a garden, raking at something. Indoors on an adult lap. The toddler was placed there for the picture but disliked the lap. A hand restrained her from wriggling off and the adult was grinning fixedly over the top of her head. March 1946, her mother had written. Who was the adult?

Then her mother again, seated with a new bundle cradled in one arm, the other round the waist of the standing toddler. Her mother's face was worn, sleepless. The toddler's was sulky. Hana selected this one too. Milan's Uncle Honza had entered the stage. October 1946.

She sifted through more babies in prams (these showing an infant less waxy fat than she had been), two small children in the garden, the little boy standing stock-still facing the camera, arms by his side. The girl, now leaner, mud-smudged, legs

11

spread in a triangle, arms akimbo, shouting. She took one of these. Once Milan learned his parentage, he would need to know that his nature came mostly from his Uncle Honza, the better to guard against that nature. Little Honza, who regarded her first with baby admiration, then with passionate and clinging devotion, now with distaste.

Hana at seven, crouched on all fours with one hand raised in imitation of a predatory clawed paw, her face grimacing in a growl. Opposite her, also on all fours in a similar stance, was her father. Were they playing at fighting tigers? Her mother would not have descended to such inelegance and would have tried to dissuade her husband from encouraging Hana's unfeminine and clumsy unruliness.

'That one should have been born the boy,' people said, commenting in a single aside on both children. But their mother did not regret that her son was not more boisterous. He came home from playing at the specified time and went uncomplaining to collect the sticky lime flowers from which their mother made the tea they had to drink. She recommended it as a natural purgative. Hana detested the floating bits in the hot water, poured hers away and was constipated. These days she did not force lime tea on her son but watched his bowel movements closely nevertheless.

The last picture of her mother, slim as a girl in a tight-waisted light summer frock, sunny and relaxed. Wearing gloves for some reason. Hana remembered her mother's gaiety increased after her weekly visit to the woman who gave her a massage. Her mother would smell of the scented oil the woman used, and she danced, whirling in the garden to demonstrate her youth, her health. And died six months later of a breast cancer that barely had time to announce itself before it consumed her small body entirely. She chewed coffee beans to sweeten her breath.

At night, in the room Hana shared with little Honza, there was a silence where before their mother's breathing had been. She had always slept in the room with her children, although sometimes Hana watched her slip from her bed to the strip of light at the door where their father stood, come to fetch his wife.

'Don't worry,' wept their father, inconsolable. 'I'll see to everything, I'll look after you both just as Mama did.' But he couldn't, was incapable. How had she done it? The house had been clean, meals had been prepared and eaten. Food had been bought, laid in, preserved, stored. She had danced. She had read with her children, listened to them while they recited their homework, stood over them at their prayers, sung them to sleep, flitted to her husband, instructed him when to wallop their daughter for bad marks or impudence. Hana read the fable of the ant and the grasshopper and thereafter saw her father as the helpless and hopeless grasshopper gambolling the summer months away. She had never had a playmate as willing and delighted as he and realised, suddenly, that now she had no parents at all. Squaring her shoulders in front of the mirror, she had taken over. Her slightly bossy streak had come into its own.

She marched about the house noting what needed to be done, but did not know how to do it. She chivvied her father off to the pharmacy and led Honza to his kindergarten. She went to school alone. In the evenings her father offered them, apologetically, bread and cheese and gherkins. It was not a state of affairs to last long.

Hana laid the tiger-fighting picture and the last snap of her mother with the others. It was getting late and there were still many photographs to sort through. She stretched, flexed her legs and looked round her room. On the mantelpiece was a small bottle of whisky, a duty-free present from the friend of a friend a year ago. She had intended to keep it in case she should need to bribe the doctor out to Milan at night but Alena had broken into it one day when Josef had gone missing with a lady friend. The bottle was still almost full. She didn't drink. The hell she didn't. She poured herself a sizeable measure and sucked in a small sip, gasped, swallowed air, swallowed more air and sipped again.

Merunkov, 1952. No longer the perfect handwriting of her mother but the ungainly scrawl of Peter's English mother, Nora. Thanks be to Nora! Hana bowed her head over the photograph. Without Nora, nothing. This time she did remember who had taken the picture and exactly how she had felt when it was taken. It was the Cernys' neighbour, summoned in by Nora. 'Mr Tvrdohlavy!' she had called out in her atrociously accented Czech. 'Photograph us, please. Like a family.' Dr Cerny had scowled at his wife. 'Nora, are you crazy or what?' The scowl had remained on his face while the astonished neighbour snapped evidence of the newcomers. At the back of the family scene, angry Dr Cerny presenting his profile to show he wanted no part of this. Next to him his loony wife with one arm round the shoulders of her plump son Peter and with the other trying to draw in the awkward and bony eight-year-old Hana. Hana looking down, her hands on little Honza's shoulders. Compliant as usual, he was staring fixedly at the camera and smiling. He was the only one who was smiling. Nora would have liked to smile but seemed too flustered. Peter was plainly bewildered.

Round the corner, at the Three Bears, the regulars had not been bewildered at all, foaming beer in tall glasses ready at their chins. 'There's this guy,' said one, 'comes in with a prescription for some antibiotic he's got from the doctor for an abscess. And the pharmacist looks at it, and shakes his head and says, "Oh I don't know about that. Haven't got any of that left. 'They've' had it all. Know what I mean?" And then he laughs and the guy laughs too and leaves without his medicine, and two days later, boom, he's in the nick.'

'Silly damn fool,' they chorused, raised their glasses and laughed quietly with callous sympathy. No heaving shoulders.

But the pub wags had been less well informed than they thought, for it was not the pharmacist's own careless quip that had landed him in trouble, but his daughter's. He had known well enough, with constant prompting from his wife, not to talk politics – he had none anyway – in front of his children. He did not mock the books they brought home from school, he did not demur when they clamoured to have their clothes perfect for the May Day parade. But he was not continually vigilant. As some of his customers would observe, he didn't concentrate. The remark that put him in jail had indeed been his own, offered to an old friend over a mug of tea, as an example of what he would have liked to have said to the disappointed official with the abscess, had he had the courage. Hana had been doing a silent headstand and, upside-down, overheard her father's joke. She did not understand it but knew it was funny because her father's friend had chuckled, and wheezed, 'Ssh! Ssh!', flapping his hand as if he was batting away a persistent wasp. She wanted the same success, and in a game of doctors with a schoolfriend she repeated what her father had said. That evening, the schoolfriend had, quite innocently, gone to her father and said, with a question in her voice, 'Daddy?' And Daddy, who was not too slow-witted to have a nose for the times, had raised the matter at the first party meeting he was privileged to attend.

When he was arrested, Hana's father would not swear that the quip had never crossed his lips, for it had, and he was bringing up his children not to lie. How 'they' had come to find out he would never know. Hana grew up with the story in the version they told in the Three Bears. The only person who probably had an inkling of what may have happened was that old friend who had sat in the window drinking tea with the pharmacist and chuckling. But of course it would have made no difference. Trying to explain would doubtless have made things worse. Why had he not told the authorities himself about the pharmacist's lack of faith in his country's economic arrangements, especially when the innocence of children was at stake? Conceivably, Hana's father could have suffered a sentence longer than the three years he got. It could have been doubled for turning the minds of the future generation against the state. So, all in all, the way they told it at the Three Bears turned out for the best, things being as they were.

Three

English Nora had spoken Czech with an atrocious accent, which troubled her not at all. She was not ashamed, she asserted with the vigour of one too well acquainted with unfounded criticism. She had already coiled her tongue round French and German, studied in class and polished at the Swiss finishing school her parents had relied on to provide her with a husband. But built big, and with an exceptionally healthy appetite, Nora had grown larger in Switzerland and flowed into a mould of rippling obesity which wartime rationing at home in Littlehampton barely affected.

She did not especially want a husband, yet nor was she a spinster by persuasion. She watched her upright brother Gerald marry Dilys, his wispy and whispering bride with a small square mouth like a letterbox. Dilys simpered inaudibly up at her new husband and bent her pliant little waist under his hand. Nora turned her head away. Then, at the Red Lion Hotel where they served oxtail soup, she carried small plates of canapés at her younger sister's wedding reception after a mumbled marriage to a ginger-haired young officer, so young he was uncouth – but by that time Nora was getting on, as they said. When the newly-weds departed for two days at Lyme Regis, everyone turned to look at Nora. So she left her parental home to spare them further embarrassment and prepared to run a boarding-house, although she had not yet learned to cook.

The furnishing of her lodgers' rooms was eclectic. Each item had been bought where she happened to find it most cheaply. Sturdy painted kitchen chairs, a Georgian bureau recognised for what it was neither by its vendor nor by Nora, a large stained-black refectory table for the kitchen, its stretcher worn yellow along the rims by the soles of many feet. She hung swathes of brightly flowered cloth, which she had intended to sew into tent-shaped dresses, across the windows in place of curtains because the statutory black-out blinds depressed her. She forgot to wash up.

Her boarders, who tended not to stay too long, were Czech and Polish servicemen. Dr Cerny, then not yet qualified, was seven years her junior, balding, laconic and a lover of order. In the evenings, when it was possible and his compatriots had gone out drinking, he stayed in the quiet of his room stolidly reading his way through a multi-volume political history borrowed from the lending library, methodically marking the margins by twirling on the paper the finely sharpened point of a pencil to produce a faint grey dot. When he had finished reading for the night he returned to his pencil dots and made notes in tiny writing in two columns on sheet after sheet of paper. Then he carefully rubbed out the pencil dots. He sat in his coat with the collar turned up against the draught that seemed to reach around every side of the closed sash-window. He marvelled at the English ignorance of double-glazing and was lonely.

In the next-door room, Nora leafed through old fashion magazines eating madeira cake and dropping the crumbs on her wide thighs. In the evenings then, apart from the two of them, the boarding house was empty. Even at the time, they were not an obvious match. But Nora had plentiful and glossy black hair and knew by heart a number of French poems which she declaimed with conviction.

When they married, her family gathered to watch. Dr Cerny was regarded with curious sympathy. The Czech and Polish servicemen seemed to them indistinguishable with their mousey hair and grey faces. They drank a lot of beer and shouted what were clearly encouraging commands at the groom, who appeared ill at ease. Nora's parents, wanting to be helpful to their son-in-law, advised him where to apply to complete his medical studies so that he could, perhaps, take a junior hospital post somewhere in the region.

'But we shall go back to my country when the war is finished,' he said precisely. The parents, amazed, looked at Nora. This put a different complexion on things.

'Oh yes,' said Nora firmly, her face grown a little pale. You could tell, they said to each other as they made their various ways home, that this was the first she had heard of it. But that would be unfair to Dr Cerny. He had quite often and quite categorically explained to Nora that, as soon as the situation allowed, he, or rather they, would be going back to Czechoslovakia where there was a great deal to be done. If she had not taken this in, it was because she could not imagine how someone would wish to live there when they could live here. Briefly, although she castigated herself for it, Nora wished the war to be prolonged so that her husband might become more accustomed and change his mind. Reports of the battle of Stalingrad, therefore, had to her an ominous rather than a hopeful tone. She set about conceiving a child – an English child. To her annoyance, that conception was elusive, and she had to make several efforts over a year and more.

Soon after Peter was born – an experience which convinced her it should not be repeated – the war came to an end and Dr Cerny immediately and efficiently packed all his belongings in his small brown suitcase and instructed his wife to pack hers. But he found this was a task she was incapable of fulfilling, and so he did it for her. Nora sat on a wooden chair in the middle of the floor, surrounded by her clothes, which lay in heaps like the colourful droppings of some passing bird of fantasy. Then the three of them were swallowed into the shuffling mass of European migration that had long been crisscrossing the continent. Grey and white newsreels showed families with battered suitcases, the men with their hats pulled down, the women in scarves, the children silent or crying, united in their bewilderment. Careful scrutiny of such pictures might have picked out a large disgruntled woman clutching a baby. Next to her, a smallish man as insignificant as any other, in homburg and worn coat. Only the look in his eyes suggested that he knew what he was doing and why. The clipped-toned triumph of the newsreader and the hectic music sat ill with the reality.

But Nora's resentment didn't last long, at least not in its first phase, for resentment needs time in which to brood and feed on itself, and to begin with Nora was short of time. She was hampered also by curiosity and found herself astonished that the country she had come to was less war-damaged than her own, that it was – pardon her ignorance – developed; that people were distressingly ordinary, could she but understand them. She resolved to learn just enough to understand but not enough to be taken for a native, and in this she was entirely successful. She would preserve herself as English Nora and this

18

would be an advantage. In that early resolution she had no idea just how much of an advantage it would indeed turn out to be – the more so since she found, again to her complete amazement, that her new countrymen were not particularly anglophile. Those who had any inclination to be at all interested in her informed her that her country had betrayed theirs. She doubted that but luckily had not the means to say so.

While her husband hastened to complete his medical qualifications at Olomouc, she made the acquaintance of her son in their tiny apartment and found him rather pleasant. She did not hold it against him that he had failed to keep his father in England. She too had failed, and she was considerably bigger.

'A great big mummy you've got,' she cried, and bounced him up and down on her spongy stomach, which he enjoyed. Then she said, slowly and emphatically, 'You and I are going to speak English together. The King's English.' Reminded of the King, Nora sniffed. She carried her son about the cobbled streets of the small provincial town of Merunkov to which her husband had brought her. She queued for bread and began very slowly to exchange glances of recognition with the women whom she encountered once in a while. For the sake of the baby they helped her. They too had children. When they learned that her husband was on the way to becoming Dr Cerny, a paediatrician, they helped even more. She understood that her husband was about to be much in demand and that this might be useful. She repainted all the furniture in the apartment in bright colours, yellow for the chairs, green for the chest of drawers, red legs for the table. And was told off. She tossed her head.

When Peter was two and the country slithered unprotesting into communist rule, she found her husband to be entirely enthusiastic and had no opinions about the matter herself. In England, the aim of politics was that politics should exist as little as possible. In this place it seemed there was nothing else and she could not comprehend the passion. The arguments that drove her to bed early and kept Dr Cerny up late at night with other men were beyond her. She could barely follow what was being said, word by word, although she was just able to distinguish between the strands of argument. She could feel for both sides – those who wanted to return to the pre-war liberalism and those who thought it had let them down. The liberal lot appealed to her marginally more, not because they were less prescriptive but because they had better manners. However, there was a preponderance of ex-partisans among the com-

19

munists, and that seemed to her more manly. She thought of her brother Gerald and could not imagine him sabotaging anything more dangerous than their childhood games, although – and she smiled – he had considered that to be risky enough. She had liked her servicemen but had been chosen by the least overtly virile of them all.

Two years later she had grown adept at circumventing Dr Cerny's unyielding moral code. When patients came with presents of eggs or coffee, which he firmly refused, she waylaid them on the stairs and took the gifts from their reluctant hands. He had his principles. Their son needed the eggs. She decided that the liberals had been right after all because the communists couldn't provide. So Peter grew big and healthy and she lost less weight than perhaps she ought. She gave parties at which she served the cakes she had mastered, using the donated food of gratitude, and called her parties her salons. Assembled round her, the local mothers observed her stretched languidly on the sofa and concluded that the doctor had married into nobility. She became exotic, a lady of great repute, taken to no one's heart but impossible to ignore. It was better than nothing.

She saw her husband sporadically. By day he seemed to be seeing more patients than the supply of gifts warranted. In the evenings he read Marxist tracts with a dogged concentration in inverse proportion to the success of the system he had espoused. He seemed contrite that he had brought his outsider wife into difficulties with which he had no right to expect her to identify, and determined to make up for it. This he did by taking upon himself as many of the household chores as he could, buying whatever he could obtain on his way to and from the hospital. It was a mistake. Committed to improving the lot of mankind, Dr Cerny was a poor judge of persons and had failed to observe that his large, increasingly irritable wife was bored. He had not realised that she thrived on crisis. She might, who knows, have proved a more adept shopper than he was. Instead, he ran constantly from home to clinic with his string bag, while Nora, bereft of Peter, who had started nursery and no longer wanted to speak English even at home, painted and repainted her furniture. Now at last she had time to work on her resentment.

In the memory that her imagination had dreamed up for her it was not a boarding-house she had run but a residential hotel. She endowed it with an elegance it had not had and her clientele with rank they had not possessed. She had been, so she chose

20

to recall, something like the equivalent of a duchess in a locality peopled largely with figures of taste and eminence. There had been no pervading odour of boiled parsnips, no ersatz eggs, no chicory in the coffee, no rowdy drunkenness, no rain. Against her will she had been transplanted into a state of permanent provincialism where people talked only of food, for the lack of it and for fear of talking of anything else. Even her husband seemed to have nothing to say to her but buried himself in his books which, when she enquired about their contents, she was told she would not understand. Fair enough. Nor did she much wish to.

When the pharmacist was arrested and placed in an already overcrowded jail, Nora learned that he was the sole parent of two small children. She waddled to the pharmacist's dwelling, arriving in time to find the children in the care of a policeman who was removing them to a state orphanage.

'Nonsense,' she boomed, allowing her untutored Czech full rein. 'They staying with me and my man the doctor. Is arranged. Is nowhere better place.' And that, as far as she was concerned, was that.

So her decision not to go native had been a wise one, her original motive notwithstanding. For in keeping herself linguistically aloof she had remained sufficiently isolated and, therefore, insulated from the seeping and servile terror in which others lived. Ignorance was her most powerful weapon and it was a genuine ignorance. The unfortunate policeman, who had heard tell of her as a foreign and almost definitely demented woman, found himself gaping, his protest lodged like a ball in his mouth. His last view of her and the nurslings of the state was their retreating backs: a mountainous, pear-shaped, flowered lady stumping away from him and dangling a jiggling skinny child from each arm like bags of shopping. It was then his duty to report to his senior officer that Dr Cerny's mad wife had removed the slanderer's offspring from under his very nose, and we do not know what happened to him after that.

One hundred yards from the apartment building where she lived with her husband and schoolboy son, Nora began calling out to them to come down and see what she'd brought home. Her voice, which could be shrill and penetrating when she chose, carried ahead of her like the siren of some emergency vehicle. It was a voice the vicinity had learned to recognise and, raised as it was that day, usually promised entertainment. Heads popped out of windows, took note of the children on either side of her swaying figure and popped back in again. On all sides, people were locking their windows firmly as if that simple action could shut out the awful reality and postpone the future.

It was an exceptionally fine day, the sort of day that invites picnicking; and there was nothing better, Nora thought, than a picnic to allow children to get to know one another. Her husband and son were waiting for her by the front entrance, impelled by her swooping summons. The street was completely deserted despite the perfect weather. Only their immediate neighbour, Engineer Tvrdohlavy (which translates as 'Hardhead' or, possibly, 'Toughnut'), had remained out of doors because he was flat on his back under the mayor's car, whether, on a Sunday, for money or something else no one could be sure. Nora halted by his protruding feet and, clinging more tightly than before to the children in order not to lose her balance, gave those feet a poke with one of her own.

'Mr Engineer,' she said. He surfaced – ankles, ragged and oily knees, belt, paunch, chins and grey crew-cut. He sat in the road looking up at the expanse of flowered material and seemed about to say something. But Nora spoke again. 'Mr Engineer. Get camera.' And, as practised in mime as she had not become in language, she bent slightly, mimicking the action of taking a photograph, all the while clasping the children's hands so that they were forced to stand on tiptoe as their arms were stretched over their heads. It was easier to do as she said and be rid of her than to argue. He fetched his camera and found, when he re-emerged, the group posed at the ready.

'Mr Tvrdohlavy!' she called out. 'Photograph us, please. Like a family.'

'Nora, are you crazy or what?' hissed her husband, and was snapped with his face in profile, lips framing the final infuriated syllable. Seeing through the viewfinder unorthodoxies that he had not taken in with his eyes alone, Engineer Tvrdohlavy thrust his camera into Peter's hand and remembered some urgent business.

Ten days later Dr Cerny was arrested for harbouring in his house the children of a man sentenced for spreading malicious rumours. Mrs Cerny was passed over, being English and possibly, therefore, unpredictable. It is worth noting that Hana and Honza were not removed from her care because no one could decide who should be the one to go down there and do the removing. Hence Nora was in her element: she had contrived to create, though not entirely without help, a state of crisis.

Peter had recognised his mother's lumbering gait from a great distance as she came trundling in pursuit of her voice. He also noticed that in each hand she held the hand of a child, but they were still so far off he could not gauge how old these children might be because his mother so dwarfed them. As they drew nearer, he saw that the girl was older than the boy, the boy was tidier than the girl, both were skinny and subdued. They seemed not to know what was going on. No more did he until late that night when he overheard his parents in dispute. His mother's voice seemed to whinny. His father, who didn't want the pharmacist's brats anywhere near his house, was nevertheless trying to hush her, concerned lest she wake the children.

'They've got relatives, haven't they?' his father said.

'Not so far as I know,' lied his mother.

'Yes they have. They've got an aunt.'

'She can't look after them.'

'Why not?'

'Because she's old. Incapacitated. And besides she lives miles away.'

'Miles away from where?'

'From here.'

'What's that got to do with it?'

'Everything. They're staying here.'

'Why, all of a sudden? You don't even like children.'

'Nor do you.'

'That's another reason for not having them here.'

'What's the first?'

'If you don't know that, you shouldn't be living here.'

'I shouldn't be living here anyway.'

'Don't shout. You'll wake the children.' And that was it. Dr Cerny, never quick on the uptake, had defeated himself. 'You'll wake the children,' he said, and instantly Nora assumed he had relented. He who does not want to wake the children can be presumed to be giving them board and lodging.

Hana remembered coming in from picking blueberries with Honza. Could not forget it. Mrs Novakova from next door was standing by the wall. She whispered to Hana that her father

23

had had to go away. Inside the house was a policeman who told her, overhearing Mrs Novakova, that her father was a criminal who had defamed the state and insulted the Czechoslovak people, that he was not fit to be in charge of children, that she and her brother would now be looked after and taught in a place where qualified people would finally introduce them to the correct and healthier understanding of their place in society. But a very large woman in a flowered dress smelling of some herb came in and grabbed her and then grabbed Honza, who shrank away, though the woman didn't notice. The woman shouted at the policeman in a funny voice so that Hana couldn't understand. Nor did the policeman because he didn't say anything back. Then she was dragged off down the road by the fat woman, who held Honza on the other side. The woman had immense soft hips that bumped Hana's hand. She looked up and saw the woman was muttering and twitching her head. She was suddenly scared that the woman was a witch, not yet able to know, as she would later, that Nora had relished her confrontation with the law. The woman started howling in a high-pitched voice, and Hana wondered whether Honza was as scared as she was and if he was going to cry. He could certainly cry when he wanted to. Outside a block of flats at the end of the road she could see a parked car with someone under it and a man and a boy standing. The boy was plumpish and the man was white and angry, chewing his lips.

Nora's crisis lasted eighteen months, which is on the long side for a crisis to be enjoyable. As the spouse of a criminal convicted for activities inimical to the state she lost her right to remain in the apartment of the jailed doctor. Within a few weeks she learned what she had earlier determined to ignore. Shrewdly, she took her two gaunt charges with her and barged into the office of the Secretary of the town's Party Organisation. Peter she had left at home: he was still plumper than was useful. She pushed the children forward, pressing them between her bulk and the rim of the man's desk.

'Comrade Leader,' she said. 'These children thin. Will be being ill. Will be in hospital. Will be expensive. State need them for socialism. Must have school. Must have food. Must have place to live.'

Comrade Leader pointed out, first, that he wished to be addressed as Comrade Secretary and, second, that one does not house the brats of outcasts outside the institutions that so generously offer to give them shelter, in spite of everything. Nora leant forward over the children, bending them under her weight, put one hand on the desk top and with the other pounded it a number of times with what she gauged to be deliberate menace. With each thump, the picture of President Gottwald on the wall above the Comrade Secretary's head clacked against the wall in slow applause.

'Please stop that,' requested the Comrade Secretary, fearing for the glass on the picture. Nora thumped again. 'Leave my office immediately,' suggested the Comrade Secretary.

Nora sat down and gathered the children on to her lap. Through the layers of clothing and fat, they could feel her heart beating. 'If necessary,' she was thinking, 'I shall go through the British Embassy and get us all out of here and back home; I'll write a letter to *The Times*.' 'Why isn't this abominable woman frightened?' he wondered, his stomach cold. She was right, of course, and he sympathised with the two thin little things she was smothering on her knee. It was not their fault what their father did. But it was not for him to flout the practice. You didn't house the children of outcasts. If people knew that they'd take greater care over what they did, they'd watch their big mouths. And what could he do about it? If he authorised the return of her tenure they'd want to know why. She didn't have to have the children. Everybody knew that she'd forced them on her husband and look where he was now! If she couldn't cope with what she'd done she shouldn't have done it, that was his opinion.

'It's not a decision I can make,' he said. 'I'll have to refer to my superiors.' He pulled out a sheet of paper from a drawer and scrawled a few marks on it to demonstrate that her case was already being looked into.

Nora sat on. 'When will I hear?'

'I can't say. These things take time. It's not as simple as you think.'

'Is absolutely simple. Children hungry and cold.' She was hungry too but it would be a long time before that would be visible. She ransacked her memory for further ammunition and located a long-forgotten image of success in the amateur dramatics society of the Swiss finishing school. She produced a low, quivering sob. 'Children will die,' she wailed.

The Comrade Secretary, who always went to the theatre with a large handkerchief, felt a responding sob rise in his chest. He straightened in his chair and examined a blister in the paintwork of the door behind her.

'I'll do what I can, Mrs Cerna. You have to be patient. And, if you take my advice, you should be a bit more . . . a bit more . . . peaceful.'

'Peaceful!' Nora stood up, forgetting the children, who slid on to the floor. 'You are all too peaceful.' She turned and marched out, the two children scampering mutely after her.

'Interfering, pig-headed, arrogant bitch,' thought the Comrade Secretary, and threw the piece of paper into the waste-paper basket. Nevertheless, Nora lived on in the apartment.

It would be ridiculous to suppose that Dr Cerny was in prison for harbouring the children of outcasts – he could not have been for there was no such crime on the statute. To imagine that there might have been is to impute to the state a degree of cynicism of which it would not have been capable, although there may have been one or two people who perhaps regretted that. The crime, therefore, that had been drawn to the attention of the authorities was one, they were reliably informed, that Dr Cerny had been committing systematically for the past four years: embezzlement and theft – taking from the mouths of the weak and the sick, who consulted him in their hour of pain and in all trust, items of food for which they had sweated in honest toil. What were people to think when they learned of such perversion, especially from a member of the medical profession? whispered the prosecutor into his microphone. The workers and peasants would be unable to escape the conclusion that the doctor and his family had waxed fat at their expense, that their suffering had been transmuted into his comfort. They might even be led to suppose that the doctor somehow imagined good food was scarce, which would be a calumny on the peasants, a slur on the socialist paradise, an infamous slander of the great Soviet Union to which everything was owed. Did not the doctor agree, said the prosecutor, whose wife had provided Nora with a handsome box of chocolates when their daughter came safely through measles, that all the bribes he must have accepted over a period of four years could have fed an entire collective? And since this was so, was he not deeply ashamed? He was. So deeply and sincerely ashamed, in fact, and not a little confused, that the court was quite taken aback, and on the basis of considerable experience assumed he must be dissembling. Out of consideration for the fact that he had a child to support and perhaps because the region didn't have

26

another paediatrician, he was sent down for no more than eighteen months and almost wept with gratitude.

Fellow feeling of a sort, pity for the children, admiration (at a distance) for Nora's blustering stance – or perhaps force of habit . . . Could these have been the reasons why, from time to time, she still found small packages of food outside her door? Three eggs. Half a loaf of bread. Sugar in a twist of paper, sometimes even a couple of carrots. They managed. They got by. Hana and Honza, who had been skinny by nature rather than from deprivation, remained as they were. Nora and her son suffered considerable pangs but looked immeasurably the better – as Nora, regarding her changing shape in the mirror, had to concede. She decided, however, that as a matter of principle she would see to it that things, including her size, would be returned to normal as soon as she could arrange it.

Four

Dr Cerny's jailors and his cellmates noted what might be called a dialectical development of attitude in the new prisoner. Very silent for the first few weeks, although not apparently cowed, he appeared perplexed. The crime for which he had been found guilty as charged was a serious one and deserved, if anything, harsher punishment. However, as he confided to a local farmer, who had miscalculated in his annual accounts to the tune of one and a half pigs and was therefore serving a similar term for embezzlement, he could not actually remember receiving any bribes. Yet, if they said he had, he must have. He would give it thought. 'I should, if I were you,' his cellmate recommended drily, then turned over on his shoulder and went to sleep.

As meticulous in thought as he was in daily practice, Dr Cerny sat on his bunk and reconstructed, moment by moment, the previous four years of his life. To his complete dismay, he found himself innocent of all charges but, as this plainly could not be, he began again from the beginning. The result was the same. He asked the farmer for assistance. 'Well,' said his cellmate, 'perhaps you're not looking at things from the right angle', and he turned over on to his other shoulder and went to sleep again.

But what other angle could there be? Dr Cerny's life had been blameless to the point of disaster. He had risen at exactly five in the morning every day of the week, Sundays included, cleaned the flat to save Nora any further trouble, gone to the clinic in the morning, returned briefly in the early afternoon with his string bag of shopping, gone out again to do home visits. Sometimes, by way of respite, he had lingered in the Moscow Coffee House for a game of chess with a new and eager young colleague Roztomil, who played without concentration, and lost. This gave Dr Cerny scant pleasure because his assiduity craved a more formidable adversary. In the evenings he had changed his outdoor shoes for slippers and seated himself immediately at the table to do the day's accounts. He wrote in one column exactly how much he had spent and on what, and pressed his wife to cast her mind back to every crown that had left her hands – and for what reason. Then he added up the numbers. It was not poverty that prompted this but a desire always to know how things stood. His wife said, 'You're mean, you're tight-fisted', which was not true, and hurt him. Then he had eaten his meal with his family and retreated into his room to practise scales on his small pale piano, later to read and mark the margins of his tome with the finely sharpened point of his pencil. After that he had gone to sleep. No matter which angle he adopted, he could not recall any occasion on which someone had put something irregular into his hands. He would most certainly have prevented them.

On Sundays he had gone for a quiet walk to the town square and then round it, raising his hat to the mothers of his patients as they passed. In the afternoon he tried – and it tested his patience sorely – to instil into his son some extra knowledge of the world in which they lived. But the more he instructed, the less the child paid attention, tending instead to interrupt with irrelevant observations of his own. 'Leave the poor little thing alone,' Nora always said, but he could not, for then his son would grow up ignorant. He had to learn, as soon as possible, how learning itself was done so that when he began at school in earnest he would do justice to himself and therefore, ultimately, to his country. Nora, after all, did not defend with any logical argument Peter's right to stand on one leg and suck his thumb, his eyes anywhere but where they should be. She was simply too lazy to undertake the boy's education herself. And it seemed to Dr Cerny that his son was equally idle. Peter's inclination to listen to his father's methodical explanations of the solar system, the digestive system and the national system waned as the doctor's own enthusiasm for the exposition grew.

What, after all, had Nora been doing all the time? She 'ran up' the flowered tents she wore; she gave tea in the English manner to the local wives, who no doubt laughed over it afterwards; and from time to time, when the mood was upon her, she cooked. He had always admitted, and quite without begrudging her the praise, an unqualified appreciation of the suddenness with which she had learned to conjure up some exquisite dishes out of almost nothing. And to think that she had developed that talent here in Merunkov where, with all the problems the country was facing, there was maybe not quite the choice of comestibles there had been even in wartime England.

Never a man to fuss about his food, but not lavishly provided for in jail, Dr Cerny found himself, like so many others, musing on good meals once had. He remembered particularly, could very nearly restore the taste on his tongue, a fine soufflé sprinkled with herbs that Nora had rushed on to the table from the oven. Pale cream, moist and light as foam, it had seemed at the time like a special reward for his tussle over the life of Mrs Mandlikova's three-year-old son. He could not say that he would not have struggled so hard over any child, but, knowing as he did that difficulties at birth meant this one was to be her only child, he had been very nearly as grateful for the successful outcome as she had been.

Nora had then, complaining bitterly as she did it, mastered the skills of the pastry cook – which touched him, for he had tried to keep to himself his weakness for sweet things, judging it to be an unmasculine taste. One Saturday evening he had lain exhausted in his chair, eyes closed behind his reading glasses, drained from an overnight duty at the hospital. It was the second epidemic of food poisoning in the town and rumour had it that the meat coming from the collective was contaminated. The matron in his wards had folded the last piece of offensively soiled linen and said wearily, 'They'd rather everyone was poisoned than admit it and withdraw the meat.' She was an elderly woman, nearing retirement: too old to be teachable. He had advised her curtly to keep her opinions to herself and himself said nothing to anyone. At home that evening, after a full twenty-four hours of work, he had crawled into his box of a study intending to read a while but dozed off almost immediately. It was a light sleep. He floated in a pleasing state of exhaustion and from time to time seemed to hear, at a distance, the muted voices of his wife and son. He seemed to smell something sweet and pungent; became aware of a presence in the room; foggily opened his eyes. Swaying in front of him, hands outstretched in front of her, stood Nora, offering something. He raised himself, forced himself, would rather have slept on. On a plate was a gâteau, with cream and chocolate shavings. She had made it. It was a miracle. He had eaten the miracle, shared it with his family but savoured it the most, savoured it still on his prison bunk. Dozing once more, this time in a cell rather than in a chair, Dr Cerny mused over this gâteau. Try as he might, he had never been able to procure cream.

In the middle of the night he awoke abruptly having finally understood it all.

No longer perplexed, he entered into the second developmental stage which lasted exactly one month, during which time he was racked with plain, unadulterated fury. He did not hold against his wife his eighteen-month incarceration, for it was quite plain that one of them had to be in jail under the circumstances, and that one might as well be him. What he could not forgive her was the crime itself. Now that he knew himself to be guilty by association, for he had eaten the soufflé, the gâteau and, once he began working it out, countless other dainties, he recalled the prosecutor's accusation. It was indeed likely, he calculated, that the collective could have enjoyed at least one excellent dinner from the cumulative gifts received over those four years in medical practice. He railed against Nora, bitterly in his mind, explosively in public.

'Damn that woman!' he concluded. His cellmate, Farmer Zlomil, recognised strong speech.

'Go easy! Easy, there!'

'Go easy, you say! And why should I? D'you know what that woman has done?'

'Fed her family, I'd say,' observed Farmer Zlomil with approval.

Dr Cerny wasn't listening. 'She's a thief!'

'Oh come on now, doctor. People bring you a dozen eggs because their baby has the runs and you make him better. That's not thievery. That's honest-to-goodness common sense. It's turning them down that don't make no sense.'

Dr Cerny still wasn't listening. 'She has stolen my rectitude!' he declared, and immediately wished he hadn't.

'Oh, that,' said Farmer Zlomil.

No one has an endless capacity for rage and Dr Cerny had less than most. As his anger burned itself out he began to see the whole affair from yet another point of view. Mentally he ticked off the issues on his fingers. 'One, Nora is a foreigner and I was wrong to expect her to grasp the full import of what it is we are trying to do here. Two, Nora is a woman and I was wrong to expect her to be able to place abstract ideals above the natural, womanly desire to feed her son on the very best she could lay her hands on.' Here, Dr Cerny paused briefly as if there were some doubt in his mind about whose stomach and palate his large wife had thought of when she broke the laws of the land. But having begun with the intention of exonerating her he proceeded, feeling it would be churlish to backtrack now. 'Three, Nora certainly became a very good cook and I was wrong not to have noticed at the time that she could not possibly have produced such results from the shopping I provided. Four, I was wrong to have eaten those meals. Five, I was wrong to let myself get so angry with her for accepting those gifts when in fact what I really cared about was the preservation of my own integrity.'

In sentencing Dr Cerny the court had advised him to devote the period of his incarceration to an analysis of his crimes, his shortcomings, the extent of his betrayal of the working class. And the doctor, who always inclined to be zealous, was not going to let the side down. He was only sorry that his confession was a mental one and was tempted to rehearse it all over again, aloud, for the benefit of Farmer Zlomil. But, sensing that Farmer Zlomil might not take it in the spirit in which it was intended, he bit it back and kept his contrition to himself.

Perplexity and rage, having resulted in an exhaustive self-analysis, merged to produce the final stage of the doctor's development: perfect contentment. Once he had grasped the extent of his wrong-doing – a full five unanswerable charges he had laid against himself – then the eighteen-month jail term, of which only fifteen months now remained, seemed to him a heaven-sent opportunity to purge his soul. The punishment had been designed to precipitate virtue; so he could not, he reflected, have been luckier if he had tried.

Five

The doctor's flat now contained one fat woman, three children but no fathers. Nineteen fifty-two was a year for fathers to be in jail.

Honza sat with his puny body folded at right angles, knees and feet pressed neatly together like a girl's. He was polite and offered to wash the potatoes and clear the table. He followed his sister wherever he could, with his eyes where he could not. He got on Nora's nerves. She packed him out into the open air, where he least wished to be, with her son and Hana. She did not, she said, want him under her feet all day.

Hana was a different creature altogether, quite rude and developing a pout. Detesting the female condition, Nora none the less insisted that Hana, as the only other woman, albeit an incomplete one, should undertake some womanly roles in the house – help her with the cleaning, with the shopping (now paid for with the proceeds of the sale of Nora's sideboard). She needed another pair of hands to perform the tasks that were once the prerogative of her husband, but Hana showed no sign of falling in with this arrangement. Prepared to be responsible for her brother and be his parent, she was not going to run around for the mad fat Englishwoman, as she had learned to refer to her, following local parlance. Resistance was simple. She would not understand Nora's strange speech.

'Help potatoes!' commanded Nora.

'What?'

'Help potatoes!'

'I don't know what you mean!' shouted Hana, as one does to foreigners. Reproducing her father's familiar gesture of resignation, she shrugged and spread her hands palms upwards. The temper rose in Nora and with it a seed of admiration. The child flounced out of the house pulling Honza behind her, his

33

eyebrows puckered in consternation. Nora cleaned one potato for herself, one for Peter, one for Honza, and left the fourth encrusted in dried earth. Thus she baked them. Thus they ate them, Hana with loud relish.

Peter joined his friends at the wood's edge to dam a rivulet. Nora instructed him to take the two newcomers with him, and he raised no objection. There was a silence when the three children arrived. Hana, Peter and Honza stood side by side in a line. Facing them were the friends who had not been consulted. Engineer Tvrdohlavy's eldest son was group chairman.

'Your father's a criminal,' he accused Hana.

'No, he isn't.'

'He's in prison, isn't he?'

'So's his.' She pointed at Peter.

'Your father was a criminal first.'

'No, he wasn't.'

'Oh yes, he was. He insulted Comrade Stalin.' The group whistled through their teeth. 'That's what my Dad said.' The group knew the engineer.

They set about building their dam. It was to be a long-term project that required co-operation and some planning. Somebody had found some sprays of cut willow in the next valley. They would stick these in the ground across the stream from bank to bank, digging them into the river bed. Then they would weave a matting of bark, mud and pebbles between the willow twigs and change the face of nature. Hana was adept and strong, Honza compliant, and Peter obscurely gratified that he was no longer alone.

In their classrooms, Hana, Peter, Honza and a handful of others were seated to one side, quarantined in recognition of their respective fathers' whereabouts. As the year progressed this side of the classroom collected more pupils. When half the class had had to move places, the system was abandoned.

With their arms folded behind their backs – to improve posture and discourage doodling – and therefore able to communicate only illicitly with their feet under the desks, the children learned that they were the guardians of a new age. The future was in their hands, they were the future, and if they only listened carefully they would learn how to avoid the errors of past eras.

They learned that these eras had been steeped in evil. The past had been concluded only the day before.

'Children,' instructed their teacher, 'open your books at page one hundred and sixty-one.' Along the rows books were opened. 'On the right-hand side you will see the photograph of Comrade Gottwald. On the left-hand page there is, alas, a picture of the man who plotted the death and downfall of each and every one of you. Tear him out.' Page one hundred and sixty, in forty copies, was removed in a careful and synchronised rip. Practised pupils know how to tear the pages from a book without leaving jagged edges. 'And now,' continued the teacher, who had gathered the forty discarded pages into a pile which she was trying to tear in half but could not because, united, forty single sheets of paper are stronger than the hands of any teacher, 'get out your thickest black pencils. And your rulers. Turn to page one hundred and sixty-four, paragraph two. When I say "Go!", cross this paragraph out. And let's see who can make the thickest, blackest lines of all. Are you ready?' They were. 'Go!' Heads down, pencils bolt upright for maximum pressure, down the paragraph with the rulers they went, line by line, from 'Thanks to the superhuman efforts of General Secretary Slansky . . .' to '. . . under the wisdom of his guiding hand.' The teacher walked along the rows and monitored their progress. 'That's very good,' she encouraged, and the children tittered with embarrassment at the unaccustomed praise.

They learned how to do cartwheels, first on two hands, then on only one. Hana excelled at this. Peter was fearful. They rehearsed jumping-jacks in the playground outside, in their rows, with such precision that an aerial picture would have portrayed each body as but a tiny element of a single, coherent whole, although it might not have made clear what that whole was. In the afternoons they continued damming the rivulet.

One morning, as they stood with their heads thrown back, singing a hymn for Stalin, faces alight, hearts pounding, the school principal burst into the room, gasping and overcome. He seemed unable to breathe, and clasped the edge of the class teacher's table with both hands, his head bent into his chest. The children fixed terrified eyes on their teacher but continued singing because they had not been told to stop. Some voices wavered. The class teacher, frozen with uncertainty, pulled herself together and tentatively put a hand on the principal's arm, fearing the man was dying. At that warm human touch the principal expelled a howl of agony, put his arms around the teacher like a child in distress and sobbed on to her proffered shoulder.

'He's gone! It's Comrade Stalin, he's gone! I can't bear it. What are we going to do?'

The singing ceased instantly and, standing exactly as they had stood a moment before, the children bowed their heads and wept with their principal.

Honza cried with confusion and conviction, shedding his tears for the father and mother he was told he had just lost. His classmates bawled with him, simultaneously orphaned. He wondered how so many people's parents could have died at the same moment. He wondered how they hadn't known his mother was already dead. He wanted to find Hana and ask her to take him home.

In the room next door, Hana stood next to Peter and rubbed her eyes with the backs of her hands to redden them and saw he was doing the same. Through the window she saw people motionless in the street, the men unhatted, eyes downcast. She couldn't see their faces.

Nora carried Dr Cerny's string bag with part of a cabbage in it. The loudspeakers had distorted the message but clearly something had happened.

'What it is?' she whispered.

'Sssh! Comrade Stalin. He is d . . .' but the man in the queue couldn't bring himself to finish. With his collar turned up against the cold, his expression was unfathomable.

'Oh, jolly good,' said Nora in English. 'And about time too.'

Six

Eventually the jails across the country began to discharge themselves of their petty subversives and embezzlers. The urge to keep the cells crowded was dissipated until only common criminals and those agents of foreign powers that remained alive were still behind bars. Hana's father did not return, having died, so the letter informed them, of a heart attack. Hana was to grow up with the conviction that he had been beaten to death on some cold morning while the other prisoners blocked their ears. The letter, however, was not lying. Unable to imagine how he would live out his days without his vivacious brown-haired wife, the pharmacist had allowed his heart to come to a stop from a purely personal despair. But his children, who had imagined themselves sufficient reason for him to live, were learning that official explanations must, by definition, be discounted.

Precisely eighteen months after he had been escorted into the Centre of Correction, Dr Cerny was escorted out again. He looked pallid as jailbirds do, mildly undernourished (in common with the population at large), but otherwise unchanged. The change in the outside world was not much greater.

Outside in the road stood the mayor's car with Engineer Tvrdohlavy prostrate beneath it. Although he had, in the intervening period, become the mayor and the car was now his, the vehicle was not co-operating with the change in his status so an uncertain portion of the working week had to be dedicated to the maintenance of its engine. Dr Cerny paused to gaze down on the familiar pair of shoes. He gave them a gentle nudge with his foot and said tentatively, 'Good day.'

'Day,' said the mayor. A moment's silence and he wriggled out from under the car, shoes, ankles, oiled trousers and

37

paunch. He lay in the road looking up at the doctor looking down at him. He got up and held out his hand but did not meet Dr Cerny's eyes. 'They're all at home, I expect,' he muttered, and lowered himself to the ground again.

The mayor may have had his private reasons to be embarrassed but Dr Cerny could not understand why his wife and son spoke in hushed voices in his presence, why they seemed to find it difficult to address him directly, why he felt a constant need to touch his face expecting to find there some sudden and hideous disfigurement. He tried to think of topics for conversation but could find none. Only the pharmacist's two children, about whom he had completely forgotten, treated him as naturally as one might treat a total stranger. Seeing them reminded him of the reasons, as he had once thought, for his arrest. Their presence kindled an ember of doubt in the guilt to which he had become wedded and from which he did not wish to be divorced. Besides, they made the house untidy.

'Time to pack those children off to their aunt,' he said.

'You do know their father died.'

'All the more reason. They should be with family. The aunt will have to see to it.'

'She's an old woman, she's never been married. How is she going to look after a couple of kids she's never set eyes on?'

'The sooner she does, the more time she'll have to get used to them.'

'Peter will miss them.'

'Will he? Why?'

'He doesn't like being alone.'

'He isn't alone. He's got you. And me.'

'It isn't the same.'

'He's got schoolfriends.'

'It isn't the same.'

'Well, let it be the same. It had better be the same. I don't want them here any more.'

'Why not? They haven't done you any harm.'

'Haven't they?'

'Well, have they? What harm have they done you?'

'You don't know?'

'No, I don't.'

'You can't guess?'

'No, I can't.'

Had Nora understood the process whereby Dr Cerny had managed to absolve everyone except himself of guilt, had she

38

been a wilier woman, she might have given in sooner – and then delayed the children's departure until Dr Cerny himself gave in. But impulsive and wont to speak her mind, irrespective of the wisdom of it, she made things worse.

'What can you possibly have against a pair of children?'

'Eighteen months.'

'Oh, so you think you went to prison because of them?'

'Certainly.'

'I thought you went because you took bribes.'

'What bribes?'

'Food. Presents of food.'

'*I* never took any.' Silence.

'Well, you ate it anyway.'

'I didn't know that . . . at the time. And you shouldn't have done it.'

'Why not? People brought things and we needed them.'

'Those people needed them more than we did.'

'I had a child to feed.'

'So did they.'

'I can't spend my time thinking about other people's children.'

'Then don't, and send these two off to their aunt.'

'If they go to that aunt I shall go back to England.'

'By all means.'

'And I shall take Peter with me.'

'You can't. He belongs here.'

'He's a British citizen.'

'Not any more. Not by my reckoning. Not by the state's. He belongs here, in this flat, in this town. Those two belong with their aunt. And don't make so much noise. You'll wake the children.'

On this occasion Dr Cerny prevailed. Hana and Honza were sent to their aunt. Nora stayed where she was.

Merunkov – February 1954: black ink for Nora's sprawling calligraphy. Hana couldn't remember who could have taken the picture. She looked at the grainy representation of her younger self on the station platform, still skinny in an over-long flowered skirt bunched at the waist, donated by Nora. Child Hana wore a fat school satchel on her shoulders and squinted into the spring sunlight. She held her brother by the left hand, or was it the right? – she was never sure how images were reversed by the camera. In his other hand Honza carried a bulging string bag. Nora towered triangular behind them, a hat like a cake pinned to her glossy hair, her favourite pendant a dark stain on her chest. She had nearly regained her lost weight. Dr Cerny, scowling again because, perhaps, it was his string bag, stood with both hands, fingers forwards, claiming ownership of Peter's shoulders as if drawing the boy apart, returning him to a more manageable past. Peter looked sullen or distressed – difficult to tell sometimes with Peter. She thought herself into the picture, turning as she did so as if to face the way the little girl was facing. Who took the snap? Not Mayor Tvrdohlavy. Dr Cerny wouldn't have tolerated that even if Nora still couldn't see why not. There had been no need to label the back of the photograph. Above their heads the station sign witnessed this departure as no more than one of many.

Of course, it was the stationmaster who took the photograph! Nora had gripped the man's elbow and forced the viewfinder up to his eye. Hustling her subjects into their valedictory poses, she had shouted instructions. The stationmaster had been too bemused to demur, but he'd complain about it afterwards. No wonder Dr Cerny had been so put out.

Hana sat by the window with Honza beside her and her back to the engine. Nora jerked backwards, jerked again and then slid away until she was no more than an agitated mound. Dr Cerny and Peter had disappeared.

It was a slow grinding journey westward from the small Moravian town where she had lived, and the only place she knew. There were many long and unexplained pauses. Hana felt empty but responsible, and touched by the memory of Peter's miserable face. She was in charge now again. She hoped Honza wouldn't pester her to amuse him or keep asking her whether they were nearly there yet. But he slept immediately, as always when he was afraid. When he woke up she unpacked the school satchel and the string bag. Across their laps she laid a large offcut of bright material on which, item by item, she displayed to their fellow passengers the picnic that Nora had provided. Sausages, two eggs, wedges of bread, half a cake, a bottle of fizzy lemonade each and even the box of Dr Cerny's Bassett's Allsorts (sent once a year by his father-in-law in England) which he thought he had kept hidden in the cupboard. Nora had credited them with appetites to match her own.

'Would you like some?' Hana ventured to the compartment at large. 'We can't eat all this.' But the compartment could, so the children arrived at Prague Main Station with their bags empty. The old woman who waited for them there noted this and said aloud, 'Too mean even to give them a crust of bread, poor little things.' Skin and bone. Well, they wouldn't do much better with her either, and that was the truth!

Aunt Veronika was a wizened version of Hana's mother, whose slenderness was here dried and shrunken. Her stockings looped on her legs.

'Well,' she said, looking down at them from no great height as they stood side by side to attention in front of her. 'So that's who you are.'

They acknowledged this observation, recognising, as someone else might not, that it implied a good deal. Of how many aunts, after all, can it be said (especially if they are single) that they have never laid eyes on the offspring of their only sibling? What could have prevented it? There was a reason: quite simply that Aunt Veronika, impressed by neither her country's democratic traditions nor the stated aspirations of its present government, believed her sister had married beneath her and had said as much. She did not, she had declared after a first meeting, think the pharmacist could be an adequate husband. 'You're just jealous,' retorted her sister, and the two women had broken off relations.

Aunt Veronika – she would have to get used to the title – had been many a man's lover but no man's wife, having lost her chosen one to another woman through sheer negligence. He had been a hungry sculptor and she had omitted to learn to cook. Since then, she had been much on her own with no pressing reason to grate potatoes or mix dumplings. In the mornings she drank two cups of coffee. At midday she queued for a pair of sausages from the stall across the way, and ate them where she bought them, served with a triangle of bread and yellow mustard on a square of cardboard. In the evenings she fed on fish, round the corner at Vanha's fish restaurant off Wenceslas Square.

'Wash your hands now, won't you?' she said. 'You never know what you pick up on a train.'

Germs terrorised her. In the tiny bathroom, painted mauve, a white towel hung on a hook. Next to it a small wire basket was screwed to the wall. In the basket a pile of face flannels, ironed and folded, rose to a point halfway up the mirror. Below the basket on the floor stood a wooden box without a lid. Aunt Veronika remembered too late.

'What did you dry your hands on?' she asked sharply when Honza emerged from the bathroom.

'The towel.' Honza, amazed at the obvious, still had much to learn.

'Never, never do that again.' Aunt Veronika hopped to the bathroom, plucked the towel between finger and thumb from its hook and dropped it into the wooden box. 'The towel is mine. No one else uses it, do you understand? Yes? Both of you? When you want to dry your hands, you take a face flannel and then you put it in the box. When you need to dry your hands again, you take another face flannel. I wash them every day. I shall clearly have to try and get some more. We all have to take care of our own health. If my dear, foolish sister, your mother, had only taken greater care . . . but then it's too late to be worrying over that now, isn't it?' She replaced her soiled towel with a fresh one from the cupboard.

Hana looked into the wooden box. Beneath the towel she saw the corners of two brightly coloured face flannels. 'Did you have two visitors today or one visitor who washed her hands twice?' Aunt Veronika inhaled deeply, opened her mouth to speak and exhaled instead.

Seven

Over the following ten years the children and their aunt learned to live, inconveniently, side by side. They took this task, like everything else, in turns. First she got up in the mornings, then they did. Now they had the upper hand, now she. Honza appeared to buy his aunt's package wholesale, for compliance was preferable to confrontation. He drank two cups of milk (instead of coffee) every morning and ate his sausages (though without the mustard). He even became skilled at picking out the bones from his fish before eating it, laying them in a row around the rim of his plate. He brought home his school books and recited his lessons for his aunt to hear, got straight As and observed the face flannel rule assiduously, convinced that only thus would he remain free of the parasites and bacteria that had seen his mother to her grave.

There had been a time when, so they were repeatedly told, the apartment had been spacious, after Aunt Veronika inherited it on her parents' death. In 1949 the authorities had sent a man who measured it, pacing the length and breadth of each room, without the basic courtesy of first removing his street-soiled shoes at the door. He left, saying nothing. A week later she received a letter from the local Citizens' Committee informing her that as five rooms were evidently too many for an ageing woman on her own she would be pleased to cede two rooms to a family in need. Another man came, who did take off his shoes, and hammered up some wooden partitions but left the sawdust on the floor and splinters in the wood. Mr Zastupnik, who moved in with his wife and bawling baby, made a brief visit looking truculent but shamefaced. He planed off the splinters and left her a pot of yellowing paint which she had never opened. Two years later 'they' came to whittle down her quar-

43

ters some more. The one room with its kitchen corner and the tiny bathroom were all that was left.

'Do you think if I told them there are three of us now they'd give me my old rooms back?' she cackled. Honza nodded solemnly and could not understand why she didn't go then and there to put her case.

Hana was more selective, being older maybe. She liked the two cups of coffee and forced herself to drink them without milk. She ate her sausages with the bright mustard. However, nothing would persuade her even to try the fish, so Aunt Veronika and Honza would set off without her every evening, leaving her to make her own arrangements with bread, cheese and gherkins. Aunt Veronika knew nothing about child-rearing, three square meals, bone development and bowel regularity – in all of which her younger sister, now passed on, had been something of an expert. But other expertise was at hand, just beyond the planed wooden partition. Mrs Zastupnikova, mother of the bawling baby, now a dimpled five-year-old girl, took her nutrition very seriously indeed. One thing she knew: the old woman next door never did any cooking because you'd have been able to smell it if she had.

Hana looked down into the street at the departing figures of her aunt and her brother. On the other side of the partition so did Mrs Zastupnikova, her folded forearms resting on the cushion she kept on the window-sill. Aunt Veronika tottered a little on her fine ankles as she walked, with perhaps a touch of enfeebled theatricality. Her nephew's hand was locked into the crook of her elbow, not as a child's might be but rather in the manner of a solicitous escort. Young Mr Honza Masnik was taking his elderly but coquettish aunt out to dine, even if his head did not yet reach her shoulder.

Mrs Z. tapped on the partition. Hana heard but ignored the signal, not recognising it for what it was. She already knew the Zastupniks as well as if they lived in the same flat – which, after all, they did. There was constipation in the family, suffered both by the little girl Zdenka and by her heavy-footed father. Mrs Z. made them sit together at the table and each drink a glass of prune juice which she had made herself from plums culled from somewhere in the countryside and dried on the boiler. They complained bitterly, for the plums were sour when Mrs Z. had picked them, probably in the dark, and the drying, soaking, stewing and straining had not improved them. Father and daughter rushed for the toilet and suffered differently but just as audibly there. Hana wondered at first why Mrs Z. did not stagger the ministering of her medicines, until further aural acquaintance with her neighbours taught her that Mrs Z. was a busy woman with a time for everything.

She bounced with her husband on their bed twice a week, on Wednesdays and Sundays at half past eight, and padded off to pee immediately afterwards. Aunt Veronika, touched by some quaint concern for the children's morals, had tried to drown the noise by playing Brahms's Second Symphony loudly on the gramophone, but the music was more disturbing to Honza's sleep than the Zastupniks' conjugal precision, and at eight twenty-five, when she rose from her chair to take the record from its worn sleeve, the boy would turn restlessly in his bed.

The Zastupniks got out of bed at five o'clock and left their flat for kindergarten, milkshop and factory. They returned at four in the afternoon. Mr Z. went to collect his beer. Mrs Z. began her cooking. Little Zdenka sang tunelessly to her mother, drumming her heels on the partition. Had there been a demand for it, Hana would have known exactly where to go for carrots in December and how much the butcher expected under the counter for the weekend's piece of pork. She learned the words, if not the melodies, of the ditties the children in the kindergarten were taught, and she knew exactly what her neighbours thought of her aunt. But like everybody else Aunt Veronika had become adept at not hearing what she did not wish to hear, and only very occasionally raised her voice when she wished to comment on the interlopers next door.

So Hana did not respond to Mrs Z.'s tapping on the partition until she heard the lady's low voice suggesting she might like to pop round for a spot of something to eat.

'Well, and I don't think much of fish either,' said Mrs Z., as she opened the door.

Mrs Zastupnikova, not yet thirty, wore her middle-aged body with resignation and was the third woman in Hana's life convinced that the child's natural thinness was the result of deliberate malnourishment. She instilled into her, with great success, the assertion that you can only get your man and then keep him if you feed him as his mother did – but better. And since Aunt Veronika was clearly the negative example of that maxim Hana was inclined to believe her. While Honza ate his evening fish at Vanha's, Hana supped with the Zastupniks, read stories to Zdenka and began her apprenticeship as assistant to Mrs Z.

in the kitchen – but grew no fatter. As the years passed, her forearms developed sinewy muscles from kneading the hard dough from which Mrs Z. made her own noodles, while the tips of her fingers became alert to the exact moment when the consistency of the crumbly paste for Mrs Z.'s Christmas cookies was just so. Mrs Z. wiped her hands on her apron after washing off the flour and to this Hana attributed the Zastupnik constipation. Aunt Veronika's face flannels were still in the ascendant.

Then, quite suddenly, Aunt Veronika began shrinking. It was Honza, aged thirteen, who noticed it first. He was standing in the room practising callisthenics for a national display for which he, exceptionally, had been selected. As he lunged to the left he shouted, 'Health!', to the right, 'Strength!', arms up, 'Beauty!', and, to accompanying jumping-jacks, 'Our salvation and our duty! Hooray! Hooray! Hooray!'

His rehearsal, by its very nature, banished his aunt and his sister to the outer fringes of their accommodation: Aunt Veronika was flattened against the partition, recently daubed by Honza (not wanting to be outshone by Hana's cooking) from the tin of yellowed paint. Hana sat with her feet inside the room and her bottom outside on the narrow balcony where Aunt Veronika, like everyone, stored her beer.

Six years had passed. Hana was wearying of her role as Honza's protector but saw no escape. Honza was beginning to perspire because of the exercises, and therefore to smell, but his face was as calm as a sleepwalker's. Watching her brother swing his left arm, his right arm, the two arms together with that military verve, Hana was overcome with an urge to put him down.

'God, you look silly,' she said. He had made it into the Spartakiada team. She had not, because anyone could tell she lacked commitment, in mind and body.

'You're just jealous because you weren't good enough to get in.'

This was an observation so accurate it prompted Hana to reach for the nearest object and throw it at him. At the very moment the beer bottle, flying wide of its mark, smashed against the newly decorated partition, Aunt Veronika decided the room was too small for domestic disagreements of this kind and intervened.

46

'Stop!' she said, and followed this up by placing herself between the warring sides.

There was a silence, and Honza, finding himself staring straight into his aunt's eyes, felt a lurch of panic in his stomach. She was no bigger than he was! And that meant that . . .

'Hana, come here a minute.' The tension in his voice caused her to obey and she came to stand next to him. He was right. His sister was bigger than his aunt.

Now there were a great many criticisms Honza might have had to make about his living arrangements ever since he had come to Prague. Lack of space would have been one, but as it was also everybody else's he would have lost his complaint in a generalised discontent. Having to eat fish every night with his aunt while his sister ate noodles next door would have been another, and it did not cross his mind that someone would ask him why he had gone on doing this, since an alternative was clearly possible. A third would have been the very personality of his aunt, who veered between moods of fluttering terror induced by the bacteria he brought in from the street to a shrill command, issued in the name of his deceased mother, which would not be brooked. Had he been consulted, he would not have chosen to live here with his dessicated relative in the single room that hygiene dictated had to be cleaned three times a day. He would rather have stayed with Nora, even if she were mad, and played with Peter down by the river; but he had not been consulted, and now he had been living with Aunt Veronika for nearly as long as he had ever lived anywhere. If Aunt Veronika, like all old people, were to shrink, shrivel and die, he would be required to move on again and all of a sudden he decided he could not stand it.

'She's shrinking. She's getting so old she's shrinking. What are we going to do? She's getting older and older.'

'Nonsense,' quibbled Aunt Veronika. 'I'm not getting older. You are. Let's go to the country.'

This would have been all very well but for the fact that Aunt Veronika detested the countryside. In all the years they had so far spent together she had not once ventured out of Prague. Now she was adamant, determined, filled with a purpose that made brother and sister nervous.

'Coats,' she said. 'Hats, scarves.'

'But it's sunny outside. It's nearly summer.'

'That's here. You never know what they might not arrange out there.'

So, coats on, with a hat stuffed in one pocket and a scarf in the other, they followed their aunt across the square to catch a tram to Smichov Station. She knew where she was going. She bought the three tickets, urged, 'Come along now, they won't wait while the pair of you are dawdling', fussed them up to the platform and on to a waiting train.

'Is it far?'

'Not far at all.'

'Will it take long?'

'No, Honza. About forty-five minutes.'

And indeed the train soon deposited them and two men on the small platform at Bytlice and departed. The two men, who had shared their carriage with so many others, now turned, nodded, bade them 'Good day' and set off with the knowledge-able nonchalance of people whose feet, even in their sleep, will bring them to their chosen destination.

'Now then,' said Aunt Veronika, 'it's this way.'

She walked along the road a short distance and suddenly plunged off on to a rough track leading away to the left. Her thin ankles wobbled as the stones skittered beneath her high heels. Honza caught up with her and offered her his arm as if he were escorting her over the treacherous cobbles of the city. The track climbed steeply and then forked.

'Ah,' observed Aunt Veronika. 'Yes. Now then. I wonder.' To the left and right the tracks rose and curved into the trees. Amongst the trees were houses, each in its garden, the country residences of the sometime wealthy. 'This way, I think.'

They climbed to the right, and again the track forked, and again each branch was all but indistinguishable from the other. A man was descending from the dark of the trees above them, walking stolidly, head down eyeing the terrain.

'Good day,' he said.

'Good day.'

They watched him until he was out of sight and then set off once more. Again the track forked. Aunt Veronika hesitated and chose the left fork, more by whim than wisdom, Hana thought, but she said nothing. The track curved, climbed fur-ther, levelled out, ran a little downhill and forked again.

'You'd think they could have a sign or something,' they heard her mutter. 'Probably can't read, these country types.'

A woman pushing a bicycle with a small child in the basket passed them.

'Good day.'

'Good day.'

Honza had been monitoring their progress. 'We could have gone wrong three times so far, and if we go back to the beginning and take the left fork first time, and if all the tracks have forks in them like they have so far, supposing we took only the right forks, and then went back and took only the left ones, altogether we'd have – '

'Got lost,' said Hana, piqued by her brother's mathematical curiosity. 'Perhaps we shouldn't have left the road at all.'

'Nonsense,' said Aunt Veronika. 'It has to be here somewhere and it wasn't on the road in the old days so it can't be now.'

'What wasn't?'

'My house.'

'Your house!' they said in unison.

Aunt Veronika looked about her. 'In the old days,' she whispered stridently, 'when they knew what they were doing, you had a fine flat in town and a fine house in the country. When my parents passed on they bequeathed to us, to my dear foolish sister, your mother, and to me, both these dwellings. Your father took your mother away to insignificance in Merunkov, where she had no use for the flat or the house, and therefore I own both. It must be said, however, that my house in the country was not in good repair when I last saw it. I have heard it has quite fallen down. I wish to verify this.'

A man in blue overalls with a long stout stick in one hand was picking his way directly downhill in between the trees.

'Good day.'

'Good day.'

'Actually,' added Hana, 'we're looking for her house. Do you know where it is?'

The man paused and looked at Aunt Veronika. 'A house, you say.'

'My house, yes, above the village.'

'Oh yes?'

'Oh yes.'

'Live in it, do you?'

'Well, no. No, not for a long time.'

'Empty, is it, then?'

'I sincerely hope so.'

'Up from town, are you?'

'Yes.'

'Not local, then.'

'Well, I suppose not.'

49

'And got another house in town?'

'Not a house. A room. These two live in it with me.' There was triumph in her tone at last.

The man clucked in sympathy. 'Dear, dear. Well, that's how it is these days, eh? So what number's this house of yours?'

Aunt Veronika pulled a large iron key from her bag. It was labelled.

'Number 64,' she pronounced in the ringing tones of the chatelaine.

'Oh, Number 64. Oh yes, Number 64. Oh, dear me, ha! ha! A house, you call it. Oh well, I dare say it takes all sorts . . . You go down to where the road forks, you take the other fork to the end, then you bear right and take the first fork to the left and the second to the right and you come to the shop. Remember a shop, do you?' Aunt Veronika nodded enthusiastically. Honza was writing down the instructions with a pencil in a notebook. 'You go past the shop and with your back to the rubbish bins you go straight up as far as you can, take no notice of any turns, just go on up to the top. That's where you'll find it. A house, eh? Well, well, well.' And he plodded off down the hill.

'Down,' commanded Honza. 'Right . . . left . . . right, no, not this one, next one . . .'

Eventually they came to the shop. A lorry stood in a clearing on packed earth under the trees. Two men and a boy were unloading crates of mineral water and beer. There were three women in the shop.

'I'm hungry,' said Honza.

They bought half a loaf of bread, all the assistant would sell them even though she plainly had more, a large piece of pale rindy cheese and some mineral water. The customers and the men working on the lorry gathered together to watch them leave, while they trudged up the hill as it became steeper. At last they came to a point where there were no more houses, among the trees. The track led away into the forest, skirting a nursery of finger-high young pines.

'That's it,' said Aunt Veronika.

At the pinnacle of a steep wilderness of spiny yellow grass and weeds stood the house. There was the tall rectangle for french windows looking out over the valley, but no frames, no glass anywhere. The terrace, on to which the french windows might open, was raised from the falling ground by a wall of small stones, many of which were missing. At the side, a small doorway down three steps led into a cellar, to which there was no door. The front door, in fact at the back, was firmly locked, setting its teeth against the open entrance the other walls afforded.

'This is the way we'll go in,' said Aunt Veronika, and thrust her giant key into the lock.

Chickens screeched and panicked, running in a fan of terror. Some of them, unable to find the way out immediately, ran into the walls of the main room. Others threw themselves through the french windows on to the terrace and flopped over the supporting wall into the long grass below. The floor was evidence of how long the chickens had been in residence. Aunt Veronika and Honza retreated.

'Ridiculous!' she said. 'If they were going to take the place over they should have put people inside, not chickens. Chickens, of course, will be easier to evict, when the time comes. And this, my dears, is the kitchen.' She pushed in front of them through a narrow door. 'Look!' – and disappeared. There was a large hole in the floor. Aunt Veronika was now in the cellar underneath.

'I'm hungry,' shouted Honza through the hole.

'So am I,' yelled his aunt. 'Get the cutlery, and we'll have our lunch outside.'

Hana reached across the hole to a small cupboard with two drawers in it. She found a single, rusted knife which she carried around to the missing cellar door to retrieve Aunt Veronika. The old lady was limping and smeared in coaldust.

'This would never happen in centres of civilisation,' she said angrily. 'If my dear foolish sister, your mother, had not left the capital with that nonentity, your father, who knows . . . ?'

She led them round the outside of the house to a flattened mound. They sat on their coats with their backs to a bank of azaleas coloured salmon and magenta and looked down over the trees to the thin white line of the river. Hana cut the bread with the rusted knife, jutting out her stomach like Mrs Z. and slicing towards herself. Honza opened the bottle of mineral water, levering one against another like men with beer but no bottle-opener. It was a trick he was proud of and he would not say where he had picked it up.

'So there we are,' said Aunt Veronika, and Honza led them downhill, reversing his written instructions, impeccably all the way to the road.

Aunt Veronika continued to shrink faster, if anything, than before. True, Hana and Honza were approaching adulthood, flexing their nearly complete bodies, but there was now no getting away from the fact that she was withering away. She lay on her bed, with an ache in her shoulder which had begun with the fall into the cellar at Number 64. Rheumatism had followed and, with it, despondency at the flight of time. Hana's hands, widened and muscular from kneading Mrs Z.'s noodles, kneaded Aunt Veronika's shoulder as well.

'Aooow!' An initial, ill-considered reaction. But then, 'You're very good at this, my dear. You should become a professional . . . ouch . . . physiotherapist.'

No profession awaited Hana, too impatient to study, easily bored by the requirement to concentrate. Besides, one brain in the family was enough and Honza had made it straight to grammar school at fourteen. He would go on to the university, no doubt about it, and that would have to do.

She took a job in a shop selling the pink nylon 'modes' that properly belonged to a former decade, and waited for the world to change. She was not yet in a hurry, having no conception of the nature of the change she expected. A room of her own, a little more money and something to spend it on were the sum of her ambitions. Aunt Veronika, swathed in blankets in her armchair, ate the nourishing soups her niece prepared and decided the time had come to widen the girl's horizons.

'You'll get married in time,' she said.

'Yes, I expect so.'

'Ah no, my dear. Don't expect, don't expect. You never get anything if all you do is sit around expecting. You ask me, I know all about it.'

'So what should I do?'

Aunt Veronika surveyed her own meagre experience of marriage and shook her head. 'Well,' she said tentatively, 'you can cook, I'll say that for you. But you need to . . . to know a bit more.'

'What about?'

'About men.'

'What about them?'

Aunt Veronika considered what she knew herself. 'You mustn't let them get away.'

'What do you mean, Auntie? Get away from what?'

'From you, my dear. If they get away from you, they'll get away with anything and we can't have that . . .'

52

'But how am I supposed to stop them?'

'It's very simple, dear. Marry them. Marry them as soon as they ask you.'

'All of them?'

'Every single one. As soon as they ask you. You can always change your mind afterwards. It's always better to start from a position of something to get rid of than nothing at all. Do you understand?'

'Yes.'

'Do you promise?'

'I promise.'

And Aunt Veronika, knowing her niece to be a girl of integrity for whom a promise made was a promise kept, smiled. What she herself had not achieved she now felt certain her niece would achieve in her name. Her life's work was complete. Some weeks later she fell out of her chair on to her side and curled up on the floor, crackling like a bunch of dried twigs.

Eight

After they had buried Aunt Veronika, Hana went back to her clothes shop to paint her nails and wait. It was 1964, and out on the streets, when the wind was right, you could smell the first faint aroma of change. Hana noticed neither this nor anything else. So preoccupied and vacant was her expression that her customers, seasoned shoppers though they were, shuffled their feet, commented aloud to one another in raised voices and finally demanded the book of wishes and complaints. Hana hunted for it absently, finding it, eventually, crammed and crumpled at the back of a drawer. On behalf of them all one stout matron wagged a finger at Hana, reminding her that the book was meant to be prominently displayed, and entered into it her displeasure at the lacklustre service of the shopgirl with the short hair. Hana hung her head, already resigned to the automatic docking of her wages that would follow. She would not explain to the manageress that she had shuttered her face because there was much on her mind, that if she had not served the impatiently waiting women it was because she had not noticed them.

Aunt Veronika had left a will in which she passed on to her niece and nephew both the room they lived in and the chicken house at Bytlice. She had also left for each of them a sealed envelope which, after a decent period of time, they opened. The contents were instructions. Hana's read 'Start practising!'

'What does that mean?' asked Honza.

'I don't know,' said Hana, and blushed for the untruth. 'What does yours say?'

Honza's note was just as terse. 'Always dry between your toes!' He was offended. 'She didn't have to say that. I do anyway.'

But Hana wasn't listening. She felt keenly her obligation to the aunt who had housed her, and, remembering her promise, set about keeping it. She was young, slim, with wide grey eyes and a wide mouth. It was not a problem.

Honza, however, was becoming a revolutionary. Hana's first inkling of this came one evening when she saw him furtively drying his fingertips on Aunt Veronika's towel, left hanging on its hook in deference to her memory. The old lady, of course, was as dead as the last Five-Year Plan so it was not, perhaps, an act of great bravado, but one has to begin somewhere.

For the third time Hana was in charge. She swept (only a little less rigorously than Aunt Veronika), she baked, she sent Honza to his studies in clothes clean and ironed. They both took up smoking, although Hana carefully emptied the ashtrays each night. They grew older. Without Aunt Veronika the flat seemed scarcely larger, for the old woman had occupied no discernible space. Only there was a darting bubble of silence where once her voice had been.

Year by year, Honza bent his head to his books in the university library, rehearsing what he was required to master, and appeared not to know that his sister daily obeyed their aunt's last instructions on the narrow sofa at home. She was growing skilled. On the other side of the partition Mrs Z. heard it, shook her head and clattered her saucepans. Young Zdenka was adolescent and headstrong.

Then one evening there was a knock on the door. Hana, aproned and dough-studded, opened it. There, a bulging rucksack on his back, tall in the shadows of the landing, stood someone bulky but familiar. Peter stepped in, wedging through the doorway, pulling off the rucksack as he came.

'Hi! It's me.'

Hana automatically cast an assessing glance over him and just as automatically reproved herself. Honza was on his feet in consternation. Peter beamed.

'Can you put me up? I've made it. I've finally made it. Got a transfer, and I'm joining you' – to Honza – 'at the university.'

Hana recalled a debt.

'Of course,' she said, 'why not?', but harbouring doubts. This was no longer Nora's plump, lonely son but an almost-man who would be making no offers. She was used to Honza's rank adolescent smell. This would be different.

Honza tried to cavil. 'We're very cramped.'

'Honza, be quiet.'

'No, but what about the student hostel?'

'Honza, be quiet.'

'Well, but Hana, I mean, there's no room.'

'Honza, shut up! We owe. We'll make room,' pronounced Hana with big-sister authority so that Honza was silenced.

Then began a routine of military ferocity under Hana's iron command: bedding laid out, bedding folded away; meals eaten at home at fixed hours; a bathroom rota – one-two, one-two. The young men chafed, joined forces, mimicked her behind her back but never to her face, and, thinking she did not notice, plotted rebellion. It was not needed.

A letter from Nora – crippled, it quavered, with back strain. 'And your father, Peter, has the flu.' Mother requests the return of her son from the big city, needing his kind care. But he had only just escaped, Peter wailed, reading the letter aloud. Besides, how could he nurse anyone? He didn't have what it took, didn't have the skills, couldn't cook, wouldn't cook – eyes on Hana, who packed a bag willingly enough, flattered but not fooled. And more than a little curious to dip into the past. Also, since not a single citizen of Prague had suggested marriage and the ranks were mutinous, she saw no immediate disadvantage in returning to Merunkov to play nurse.

Dr Cerny lay in bed coughing irritably. At the sight of her his mood instantly worsened.

'What is that girl doing here?' Hana heard him hissing as she made up her bed.

'She's come to pay us a little visit.'

'Visit? We can't have visitors in the state we're in.'

'Well, I'm sure she'll help out.'

'Don't you believe it. Young girls like that, with her hair cut like that. She's here on the scrounge. Just like last time.'

Nora lay on the floor like a beached whale, the hard surface recommended by the doctor for her aching back. Around her lay the objects that had been dropped over the preceding days and that she had been unable and anyway disinclined to pick up. Some potato peelings, a couple of dishcloths, a broken saucer, Dr Cerny's medicine bottle . . .

Come to nurse, Hana was going to do it seriously. So swiftly did she clean up the apartment, and so thoroughly, that Nora became alarmed. Dr Cerny, on the other hand, observing the boiling of the sheets, the beating of the carpets on the racks outside and the reorganisation of cupboards and shelves, nodded to himself and tapped his teeth with his pencil in appreciation. The girl made her own noodles – by contrast with Nora, who had long abandoned cooking altogether, for political reasons. You could never tell who might not say a flapjack was a piece of provocation.

Dr Cerny's flu retreated before the onslaught of hygiene and good food, and after only a short convalescence, which he felt uncharacteristically inclined to prolong, he went back to his juvenile patients and to the Moscow Coffee House and his game of chess with Roztomil – no longer such a junior colleague and rising fast. They sat at the same small marble-topped table on gilt-legged chairs, flimsy as props from an operetta. Behind them, on black plastic banquettes, the local youth stirred their ice-creams with long tin spoons. Roztomil wore check shirts, his hair was thick and parted on the side. His sandals were of plaited leather. Basically the man was sound.

'We've got a young visitor,' said Dr Cerny, and deprived Roztomil of a bishop. 'She works and cleans.'

'Keep her,' said Roztomil.

But things were changing. Dr Cerny saw it as he went on his rounds, he heard it in the tittle-tattle of the surgery, and the nightly news bulletin was becoming confusing. People who should have been behind bars were expressing, uncorrected, opinions informed by terrible heresy. Hana was running wild, her head filled with phrases he didn't doubt she barely under-stood.

She signed a great many petitions for and against things, although later she was not able to remember exactly for or against what, queuing at small tables on street corners to do it. She stood in the newly crowded square in the evenings to listen to the broadcasts on the public address system; she might have listened in greater comfort with Dr Cerny, huddled in his study, but the radio message was heightened by the company of strangers to whom she felt unaccountably related, all of them enthral-led and still not quite able to believe what they were hearing. The Prague spring was under way and a new, smiling Bolshevik had even managed to improve the weather.

Mayor Tvrdohlavy lost his job. Dr Cerny, more bewildered than ever, could not make up his mind whether to grieve or gloat. Meanwhile, Nora, growing aware that something out of the ordinary was happening out there in the sunshine, was torn between maintaining the demeanour of one who is very sick and in constant, immobilising pain and the desire to find out what all the fuss was about. Pleasant as it was to be so efficiently mollycoddled, she was bored. So she covered herself with a flowing blue and pink invention of her own making and went to celebrate her new-found health in the main square, where Hana was out strolling with a fulfilled and smug young man on either arm. There Hana saw her and, slipping her arms from the enclosing elbows of her escorts, she gave each of them a gentle shove.

'Clearly,' she said severely to Nora, who had turned with her hands to her mouth like a child caught with the sugar, 'you don't need me any more. I'm going home to pack.'

For the second time Hana stood on the platform at Merunkov waiting for the Prague train, not sent packing this time but departing of her own choice, a grown woman who had repaid her debt, at least in part, and seen the ghost of her childhood to bed. To nurse the Cernys in their weakness had been a pleasure. It had returned to them their health and to her a measure of dignity – Hana still thought things were that simple.

Dr Cerny held her right hand clasped in his and gripped her elbow with his left. He kissed her drily on either cheek but did not release her hand.

'I am so sorry, my dear girl. This is a sad day for me. It's all such a bad business.' He gave her a bottle of lemonade and a bread roll for the journey and retreated to blow his nose.

Hana turned to Nora, who stood, still sheepish, almost nervous, saying nothing. 'I knew you were all right all along, you know, Mrs Cerna.' Nora's eyebrows twisted. 'Yes, I did. Honestly. I used to hear you through the door after I'd gone out. You'd get up off the floor and dance.' To Strauss, ponderously, round the fringes of carpet. 'I haven't said anything to Dr Cerny.' Nora relaxed.

'You are good girl. I not forgetting.' And she didn't.

So Hana left Merunkov and the Cernys', where she had become welcome, to return to Prague, where she was not. She let herself into the tiny flat. It was midday. The windows were closed, the beds had not been put away, clothes lay on the floor, the ashtrays were full, no one had washed up. No one was in. She put down her suitcase very slowly and, with an enormous rage, stamped first one foot, then the other, lit a cigarette, stubbed it out and cleaned up.

'Christ! She's back!' A hiss of annoyance that she could not attribute woke her in the early hours.

Who knows what irritations might not have followed but for the telegram from England sent by Nora's brother, summoning Nora home to their father's deathbed. And bring Peter, it commanded.

With his rucksack on his shoulders once more Peter waved gleefully from the street below. In his pocket was the airline ticket paid for by his English Uncle Gerald.

'I'll be back,' he threatened. 'Don't let anyone take my place.'

Arms folded on her cushion on the window-sill, Mrs Z. watched him go. Good to see the back of him, she thought. Those young men had been up to no good while Hana was away. It had made her young Zdenka restless.

Peter's English grandfather dozed in his neatly made bed, the stiff sheets folded with hospital corners. His mottled hands poked motionless from the cuffs of his striped pyjamas. He was very old, fairly ill and concluded his time had come. He could see that his son, Gerald, and his daughter-in-law, Dilys, tended to agree. Their children appeared to have no opinion on the matter. Only his equally aged wife sat immovably on a high-backed chair at his head, wringing her hands. He felt vaguely sorry about this but his mind was already toying with the next world, the present one having run out of adequate entertainment. He had been grateful but humiliated when Gerald and Dilys had dutifully taken the two of them into the house – a well run establishment, nothing to complain about, but just a little dull. They told him they had sent for Nora and her boy. 'Just to cheer you up,' they had said. 'Nothing special in it.' Of course not. He knew what it implied.

Downstairs the front door banged. He heard voices, the stairs creaking. He opened his eyes to find his view of the room blocked by the figure of his daughter.

'Well, Nora,' he observed in dry delight, 'I see they don't starve you over there.' Whereupon Nora delivered herself of such a speech, in such furious and reproachful tones, that he decided his final moments might reasonably be delayed.

For her part Nora decided it was time to put down new roots; she would be in demand, returned from exotic parts. It was a condition she had looked forward to, one to which she felt herself entitled, for she had a wisdom gained from experiences

59

those around her could scarcely imagine. She saw in them, in her sister-in-law especially, evidence of frailty, of parochialism, of a naïvety that needed correcting. She set about putting this to rights. First of all, she did not think much of the way her nephew and niece had been brought up. 'Callow' was how she described them – to their mother. Wonderful to be able to use such language at last, wonderful, too, the bright colours people wore, although she found the younger generation insufficiently deferential. It was what she had meant by 'callow', but Dilys seemed wilfully to misunderstand. Dilys also appeared not to comprehend that it was necessary for Nora to stock up, in every sense of the word – making up for the lost years, lost tastes, lost sensations. This would take time.

Nora reached out and gathered to her, with both round arms and on Gerald's bank account, everything she realised she had been missing. Peter roared about the streets of Guildford riding pillion on his cousin's motorbike. Weeks passed.

One morning, when Dilys had finished clearing away after another substantial breakfast, Gerald exchanged a conspiratorial glance with his wife and cleared his throat.

'Um, Nora, we were wondering, Dilys and I, just wondering when you were thinking of leaving. That is . . . .'

'Leaving?' said Nora, amazed. 'Leaving? Why? And where to, may I ask?'

Her brother shifted from foot to foot. 'Dilys thinks . . . Dilys feels it would be better if you . . .'

'If I what? And where does Dilys feel I should go, at this time when our father, *our* father, Gerald, not hers, is at death's door?'

'Well, come now, Nora. He isn't any more is he? Not really. I mean, look at all the gardening he's been doing. He's repainting the front fence today and he's going to take Mother on a sea trip next week. Not a man at death's door, Nora, not really.'

'Is it that we're taking up too much space, Peter and I? I thought, in this great house of yours, you had enough room for the two of us for a while. Or is it that we're not paying our way? Because if that's it, well, I'm sorry, Gerald, but there's nothing I can do about it. I haven't any money. You know that. You know what those governments are like, or rather you don't, of course, but let me tell you, you and your Dilys wouldn't last a month, not a week. You have to have a bit more know-how, a little more knowledge of the world, Gerald, *savoir-faire*. You have to know how to handle people with delicacy, and they're quite different from the suburban sorts you're used to. Nothing so banal there. People are concerned with more . . . spiritual . . . issues. It's not a matter of repainting the garden fence, not at all.'

'So what is it then?' whispered brave Dilys.

Nora tried to recall. She made a *moue*. There was no point going into it; some things were beyond explaining to some people.

'Oh,' said Dilys, who fancied she detected a permanence in Nora's presence. She sensed she was expected to make up to Nora for privations suffered because she had not seen fit to suffer in the same way. She could not see why she should be held responsible, why Nora had to eat so much, why Peter had to pad around in his socks all the time. 'It certainly sounds very exciting. You must be longing to get back.'

'Oh I am, I am. As soon as Father is really, truly better, we'll be off like the wind. You'll see. As a matter of fact, I was just saying to Peter how well Father has been looking and what about getting ourselves together and going back. My husband will be wondering what's become of us, and Peter's term will be starting again soon. Anyway, I don't want to feel that I'm a burden on people, especially not on family. However.' It was time for her afternoon lie-down.

On the landing half-way up the stairs Nora lingered to watch, through the lattice window, her sister-in-law Dilys dead-heading the roses in the garden with secateurs, a rustic trug over her arm.

Gerald was at his most content in the early morning on a summer's day and knew he had much to be thankful for. He sat in his dark solicitor's suit on his patio at the table which was white and frilled as a doily, and faced his breakfast: a cup and saucer, matching jug and sugar bowl, tiny tongs in the sugar, triangular toast in the silver rack, tea in a pot and extra hot water in a thermos, frosted pats of butter, currant jam and a spoon to serve it with; and the newspaper. Before his eyes spread his perfect, rectangular garden.

This morning, particularly, Gerald knew the meaning of peace of mind. Nora had packed. Peter had been told to do likewise. A cab would drive them to the airport and Dilys would be able to relax. Next time his father sickened he would not be in such a hurry to telegraph his sister. He poured his first cup

61

of tea, raised the slender china cup to his lips and, over the rim, caught sight of something which froze his soul. There, at the far end of the garden, was a dark moist pimple on his lawn. Had he a more superstitious nature Gerald would have recognised it as an evil omen. All he saw was the molehill.

He hurried for a space and, ignoring the smear of earth on one of his polished shoes, shaved his lawn. When Dilys emerged on to the patio in her quilted primrose dressing-gown she saw instantly that something had happened. Her husband's vantage point on the patio was deserted, his breakfast still in place on the tray, the newspaper still folded as it had been pulled from the letterbox. She stood and clasped together the lapels of the dressing-gown over her breasts, warding off the unidentified menace. She drank the cup of cooling tea; buttered a leathery triangle of toast; stood with the toast in one hand, posting one of its three corners into her square postbox mouth; unfolded the newspaper. 21 August: SOVIET TANKS CRUSH PRAGUE SPRING. A shrill wail wafted from her throat and instantly her husband was at her side.

She tapped the newspaper with her forefinger. 'Do you realise what this means?'

Gerald took up his position behind her and massaged her shoulder-blades. Nora was not going to leave. 'Never mind, dear,' he consoled. 'Let's try and look on the bright side.'

And so they did, and there was one. For quite fortuitously Nora and Peter had acquired the value of celebrities. Dilys and Gerald decided to throw an 'invasion party' and invite all the neighbours.

The weather was perfect. Gerald had his fairy-lights up in the garden, Dilys had inserted mushrooms into a flotilla of tiny vol-au-vent cases and piped mayonnaise around the edges. Nora had inserted herself into a dark green caftan, which Dilys had ironed for her. Peter wore his suit. It was, Dilys realised with pleasure, an adequately foreign-looking product; ill-made and belted, the trousers gathered in ungainly pleats at the waist. It made him look just like a refugee, as did his clipped hair. The neighbours arrived at seven thirty for eight, fresh from tennis and badminton, to inspect.

Introduced to each in turn, Gerald holding him under the elbow, Peter shook hands with the friends of the people who were feeding him and enquired politely after their health. They found him charming, such good English, just a hint of an accent. Nora made her own introductions. She was resplendent

62

as a Christmas tree, baubles jangling at her ears, proffering her hand to the guests, who fanned out in a welcoming committee. One of them, who had once had a German wife, kissed her hand and clicked his heels.

Nora's parents sat proudly side by side on the patio bench. Everyone else stood and drank Gerald's fruit cup. Dilys moved amongst them with her vol-au-vents. They spoke of the unusually fine summer, of alterations to their houses, of their children's inconsiderate ways. But, just as people gathered after a funeral in the widow's house avoid mention of the deceased, so they did not speak about the reason behind the party they were attending. Indeed, they appeared embarrassed. With his third glass of fruit cup in his hand, Peter moved to the table Dilys had laid out on the patio; the guests swayed out of his path, ushering him forward with gentle hands and dropping their voices. He felt his presence was making these people uneasy and considered taking his mother by the arm and departing. Let them enjoy themselves, let them get on with it.

Nora was also disconcerted. Inexplicably, here among her own, where every inflection spoke to her, she found herself tongue-tied, a disappointment to herself, to her brother. There was nothing to be done but join her son at the table and eat. There the two of them stood and chomped in silence on Dilys's party food, watched by the stalwarts of the Home Counties who had all taken care to eat a light lunch.

The following day a reporter from the *Guildford North Gazette* telephoned and asked if she might come to the house to interview the exiles about their experiences. Dilys was enchanted. She gave the girl coffee and biscuits in the lounge because Gerald was cutting the grass. 'You know,' she confided, lowering her almost inaudible voice, 'I think they're finding it very hard to adapt. My sister-in-law has been out of the country for so long and she's had to get used to their primitive ways. She's never seen an iron and she didn't dare help me with the cooking or anything. I think she finds my equipment frightening. I expect she's had to cook on an open fire or something.'

A photographer arrived and sat Peter and Nora side by side on the settee. The paper put them under the headline SAD EXILES, and because they were both liverish from overeating they looked properly distressed.

'I haven't heard from my father,' says worried 23-year-old Peter, who has been staying with his aunt and uncle. His mother, Nora, married to a famous paediatrician, clasps her hands, too worried to speak. After 23 years in Communist Czechoslovakia she finds it hard to speak English.

'I only ever spoke in Czechoslovakian of course,' she explains. And modern-day England is awesome too. 'We had to cook in the open,' she told her sister-in-law, Dilys Short, wife of solicitor Gerald Short.

Stranded in Guildford, while the tanks tear through the narrow cobbled streets of their home town, Peter and Nora Cerny are at their wits' end.

'It may be impossible to get back,' sobs Nora, while Peter fears for the lives of his fellow students at the University in Prague where he hoped to graduate in two years. 'The Russians are barbarians,' he says. If Peter and Nora can't get home, he'll be looking for a job here. 'Now my priority is to look after my mother.' Who will help this devoted son?

Dilys rang her friends and they all bought a copy of the paper. The reporter telephoned again to say there were five offers of work for Peter. She invited him to lunch.

She wore her hair long and her flamingo skirt short. She drove him into the country in her blue and silver Sunbeam Alpine to a lovely little pub she knew where she bought him a ploughman's and half a Guinness. Peter was shaken by the colour and the thick head of foam, yet he said nothing, but dipped his lips into the heavy, tepid substance. There was more to being English than speaking the language. The reporter was called Marilyn. She was hoping to make the grade, she said, and move up to London into Fleet Street. Her knickers were white with thread-fine pink stripes matching the flamingo skirt. Because of them Peter made love to her on the tartan blanket he found neatly folded in the back of her car, and then again, repeatedly, in her bedroom at her parents' home, which had a garden front and back, smaller than Uncle Gerald's but not dissimilar.

The bedroom was decorated in matching two-tone apricot. Afterwards, her mother, nervous rather than liberated, served them tea and digestive biscuits and smiled silently at the young man on whom she looked in vain for signs of war wounds. She was distressed by his habit of removing his shoes as he came through the front door. His socks were not quite clean. Peter, too, was distressed, even between the impeccable sheets, by the thought that he was only welcome in this bed because he was an exile from Prague, where others were, where he should have been. He was failing them, said his head, but his sexual organs paid no attention.

Nine

In deference to the new situation Dr Cerny wrote to his son in English.

My dear Peter,

Everything is much calmer now than it was and must soon return to normal, so you should be thinking of making plans for your return. Don't forget that the new term begins in two weeks and you should be graduating next year. I accept, of course, that your mother may wish to remain where she is. That is understandable. She never belonged here and as you know made no effort to fit in or settle down. Let her stay with her family if they can look after her. If they cannot, I am sure some charitable organisation of the sort the English have so many of will take her in. But you, Peter, belong here. You have grown up here, you have been educated by our country and like all your generation you owe it a great deal. Dr Medlinek at the hospital sends you his regards and looks forward to a visit from you in the New Year. He has had some small problems with his knees, but, as I tell him, more exercise and less alcohol would benefit him.

Please be sure to give my best wishes to Nora's brother. How are his roses growing? I remember that at this time of year he was always concerned that they should be properly 'mulched'.

With best wishes,
Father

Peter replied in Czech.

Dear Father,

It was good to hear from you and everyone here is relieved that you are well. I passed on your message to Uncle Gerald who says that he mulches in July but anyway the roses are Aunt Dilys's responsibility. They aren't flowering any more but I'm sure they were splendid when they did. Mother has decided to stay in England and, as a matter of fact, so have I. It seems that if I want to continue my studies here, all sorts of universities would be prepared to give me a place and I am seriously thinking of taking a course in architecture or sociology, or whatever's going. In the meantime I am working as a clerk for a company here in Guildford. It is boring, but it will have to do for a while longer.

Have you had any news from Hana and Honza? Please try to understand my decision. I don't want to spend the rest of my life under Soviet domination, especially after those few months when we all saw how different things could be. Believe me, if I thought my return could be of any use, in the way I see it, then I would come back.

Love,
Peter

This time the reply was also in Czech.

Dear Peter,

I cannot pretend that I am not deeply disappointed in you. When I was a young man I had, I believe, a sense of idealism which I am afraid you do not seem to have inherited. I looked around me and saw here, as in so many other lands, poverty, dereliction, despair, prostitution. I asked myself what could be done about these things and it became clear to me that only Marxism held the answer. Since then, of course, I have learned that things were not so simple. Some mistakes were made. We should not, for example, have opened up the Party to non-communists who joined purely for opportunistic reasons in order to further their careers. But we were following Lenin's dictum that socialism should be built with all elements of society, the bad as well as the good, the uneducated and the stupid as well as good Marxists. We also did not realise at the time that among those people who applied the correct party line were some who were not as correct themselves as they might have been, and so the truth of what was done was occasionally sullied by the failings of certain

67

individuals. I also saw that only the Soviet Union was prepared to stand up against the fascists. The country you say you have chosen to live in, to use the English phrase, 'sold us down the river', as you ought to know. The French were no better. But the Soviet Union alone stood firm and we owe our freedom entirely to it, then as now.

You young Prague intellectuals may have found these recent months a great game, a students' party, but there is something you do not understand because you are too young and you lack the experience of history. The fascism from which we were delivered exists still, everywhere, like eels in a pot, only waiting for someone to remove the lid. Do not imagine that twenty years has been enough to dull their evil intentions. They are simply biding their time, waiting for the first release from the ignominy in which our system, alone, has kept them.

I accept that nobody likes to see the tanks of another nation in their streets. It was a shock to me as well. But *you* have to accept that we need the Soviet Union now as much as ever. What you do not seem to realise is that our country was recently in the grip of disruptive elements who were trying to bring an end to socialism and making common cause with the West Germans to help them. Did you know that there were West German tanks massing on our western borders, that West German units disguised as tourists and business-men were infiltrating our enterprises? You may think the sort of people you went around with in Prague, who were of course very young and easily influenced, were representative of the views and feelings of our people. I can assure you they were not. I know, and the people know, that their security depends on our socialism.

You will be impressed by the smart clothes and the big cars of Nora's family and friends in Guildford. I am not going to pretend that these things don't exist. But before you are completely taken in, ask yourself at what cost these material advantages, or apparent advantages, have been procured.

Also, Peter, you should consider that you are being used as a tool of Western propaganda. You say you have been offered the chance of a university place by a number of institutions. But I have lived in England, you must remember, and I happen to know something about the way the system works there. These universities have been told to offer you a place to tempt you away from the path you know you ought to follow, to win publicity for the generosity of English society towards someone who calls himself a refugee. But you are not a refugee because a refugee is someone who is fleeing for his life. We saw that under the fascist occupation and we knew only too well what it meant. You are lucky, you and your generation, that you did not have to live through those dark days, but now you are turning your back on the work we have done, still in the process of completion, to opt for the comfort you will no doubt find, while your duty lies elsewhere. I am telling you to reconsider and when you have given your full attention to the matter you will pack your bags and come home.

Tell your mother that I am unable to send on her things. I cannot afford the postage and there would anyway be certain difficulties. I notice anyway that she took her jewellery with her, which was naturally her right as it was given to her by her father before we were married. However, I am inclined to ask myself whether she hurried off to Guildford to see her sick father or whether she had already other aims in mind.

I have not heard from Hana or Honza. I expect that Honza is attending his lectures as a good student should and that Hana is working too hard to have time to be in contact with me.

Please send me a packet of Earl Grey tea and some Bassett's Allsorts. I should also be grateful for a packet of Gillette razor blades.

Your loving Father

Peter was young and lucky, also shrewd. He grew his hair longer and brushed it back from his temples; he was deferential and ironed the fronts of his shirts, with the result that he was offered employment even where he did not seek it. When the council provided them with a flat, Nora baulked at the humiliation of it so loudly that Peter covered his ears. Lines grew down from the corners of her mouth and sectioned her chin.

'She ought to be grateful,' whispered Dilys. 'I'm sure there are English people who'd be glad of a flat like that.'

'Yes, dear, but she *is* English, don't forget.'

'Well, you know what I mean.'

If pressed, Nora would have had to admit that the flat was adequate, apart from the metal window-frames and the rubber-gripped linoleum of the communal stairs that led up to it. But it was precisely these emblems of public provision that Nora so resented, as well as the name of the complex, 'The Orchards', where no trees grew. It was one thing to be so housed in Merunkov, where you could not be judged by your own four walls; in England, where it was surely not compulsory that the approach to one's front door should smell of cabbage, it was quite another. On the balconies, between small boxes of yellowing geraniums, stood the drying-racks on which her new neighbours draped the family linen. Nora did not wish to be demeaned by having to invite her friends to a salon in a council flat, but, having as yet no friends who could be invited to such a gathering, the problem remained theoretical. She had become just another fat council tenant, remarkable for nothing but her failure to be living elsewhere. No, grateful she was not.

Gerald felt for his sister and made over to her a small secret weekly allowance. With it Nora employed one of her neighbours as a cleaner, and sat with her feet up on the settee to keep them out of the way of Mrs Mason's carpet sweeper. While Mrs Mason swept, she reminisced with closed eyes about the whirl of life that had been wrested from her by the Russians, about the parties she had given graced by the best society of Merunkov, about the place of national importance her husband had occupied and her fears for his safety. And Mrs Mason, with a face red from bending as she tried to sweep out the cake crumbs from beneath the settee, said, 'You poor soul. Just you wait till I tell my Larry. He always did say them Bolsheviks was a lot of commies.'

Ten

It was getting late and Hana had still not finished her packing. She shifted her position on the floor. Her thighs ached from sitting so long cross-legged, the bones of her buttocks boring through the flesh. Her head was swimming from the whisky. Really, she couldn't take her drink any more, but she was damned well going to finish the bottle. In front of her there were the three piles of photographs: those she had so far selected to take with her, those she had rejected and the heap she had yet to examine.

There was her son Milan on his first day at school, solemn, standing in the front row, being among the smallest in his class; to the left and to the right of him other round-eyed children, also nervous. And at the back, on the far left, their teacher, the tenacious Mrs Hulkova, careless of the bouquet of flowers she held like an unwelcome baby. Behind them on the wall, the dark outline of the loudspeaker that had, only a moment before, carried the President's yearly message to every child across the country at the start of the new academic year. Early home on that first morning, Milan had been pompous with the responsibilities the President had laid on him. It was a picture Hana detested but she had to take it with her. Milan triumphant in a swimming pool somewhere, his eyes puffy from the chlorine, one thin fist raised in self-acclamation because he had just made it across the shallow end without water-wings in a flurry of frantic strokes. Milan in the pear tree. Milan grimacing and dwarfed by the Frantisek boys. Milan asleep on his stomach under the azaleas. Milan wan and pathetic after his tonsilectomy. Milan, Milan, Milan. She loved her son, of course. No one better. But these photographs seemed to her to be a dossier rather than evidence of a mother's delight, and, besides, in their stillness they did not remind her really of her son. Instead

71

they brought back memories of her brother, whom these days she did not acknowledge. Despicable Honza, on to whose narrow shoulders she had offloaded all the burden of her contempt.

It was a harsh judgement. The skinny child had grown into a tall, thin young man with an over-large nose, which could not have been foreseen. Honza's nose, long rather than wide, dominated his face because the surrounding structure was so narrow, the teeth slightly protruding, the mousey-brown hair upstanding. It was tempting to take his appearance at face value, even if he was exceptionally sensitive to the smell of change in the air, even if his desire was always to keep a sense of proportion. Circumstances had made him what he was. He would surely have rebuffed, had he been able, the oppressive vigilance of his sister, Nora's generous but unthinking interference, Aunt Veronika's fish. It was not his fault that Hana was the first-born, noisier and more wayward, nor that he folded his napkin after dinner, as his mother had taught him to do. He did not choose to be one of those whose nature dictates that he must at all times try to please.

It was out of trying to please that Honza had launched himself on to the streets to be among his comrades, to blend his voice in the jeering and whistling that greeted the Soviet tanks in that famous August; and joined a small company of saboteurs who raced about the countryside turning the road signs to confuse the invaders and switching the points on the railways to send Soviet trains into forsaken sidings. But it was also out of trying to please that, nearly one year later, Honza was among the first to put his name to a document – presented to him most politely and with visible regret on the face of the official concerned – which invited him to express his gratitude for the timely assistance rendered to the endangered republic by the neighbouring armies.

An experiment was under way.

'Gentlemen,' said the Head of Department, recently given back the job he had lost during the counter-revolution, 'we have an awesome task before us. We are being required' – here, he jutted his chin towards the ceiling – 'to collect signatures. We are expected to match last year's counter-revolutionary petitions name for name. But if we can't do that then they want the same number of names. It doesn't matter where you get them.'

He was standing on a small wooden platform of the type that normally supports a teacher's desk, speaking to the thirty-five men summoned that morning to attend, and now sitting in rows on wooden chairs. The meeting was in a cellar, quite unnecessarily, since there was adequate space and more comfortable accommodation in the conference room above. Someone, however, had decided that the delicacy of the mission dictated the surroundings.

No one could deny that he was a reasonable man who had to answer to his superiors, who in turn had to answer to theirs. Miracles were not expected. One hundred per cent success would be pleasant, although one had to be realistic; but an excess of realism might not go down too well and everyone's job was on the line. So perhaps, suggested the Head of Department, almost wheedling, a quota of 75 per cent might be acceptable for starters.

The men trooped up the stone stairs, each carrying a file, and without even pausing to wish one another good luck they went their separate ways.

It must have been about four in the afternoon when the official arrived at Aunt Veronika's flat with everything conspiring against him. Although it was early summer it had been raining most of the day, his shoes were sodden, and the papers in the file were beginning to disintegrate. He was, as yet, far from achieving his quota, had not yet managed to collect a single signature, he needed a crap, he had not had any lunch and had promised his wife he would be home in time for dinner. When the door was opened by a thin-faced student he was near to tears. Knowing that rumour moves more swiftly than even the most loyal official, he began his speech in the middle.

'Of course I understand your qualms completely,' he pleaded, 'but this will really make so little difference you'll hardly notice it. I only want you to sign your name here' – tapping the paper with his pen – 'and I'll go away. I won't trouble you again. No one will trouble you again. It's not a lot to ask, is it?'

Honza could see that the poor man was in a state of some distress. He said, 'Of course', and held out his hand for the file.

Why should Honza be censured? Somebody had to be the first to sign, for it is certainly true that in the end he could be said to have started a trend. Was it Honza's fault that he happened to be in when the official called and that he could not bear to send the poor bedraggled man away disappointed? Was there so much for his detractors to congratulate themselves on

73

when all that separated their final positions from his was a certain amount of stalling? At least he spared himself the self-disgust that was most troublesome to those who prevaricated the longest, and at least he made one dejected individual a little less unhappy. Besides, he had grown up learning to recognise the earliest signs of an unequal fight and could see little value in deliberately putting himself on the losing side.

It was perhaps unfortunate that on this particular occasion Honza's signature was the only one that this official was able to collect, indeed the only signature that was collected by all the thirty-five men together, thus making Honza a figure of some interest in the Department.

It was also unfortunate that Hana returned from shopping just in time to pass the official on the stairs as he was on his way out.

'Who was that?' she asked.

Honza picked a piece of fluff from the tablecloth. 'Oh, just some minor official.'

'You signed, didn't you?' Honza shrugged. 'Well, didn't you?' Honza shrugged again. He was sweating and reeked of shame.

'And so will you.' Which then and there, Hana swore, inelegantly, that she would not.

Her declaration of fortitude made her, in time, the loser. First, her integrity was observed by no other than Honza, who had already proved himself an unworthy witness. Second, there was her intemperate language while Honza was so cool. Then, within weeks he was offered the position of lecturer, second grade, at the Institute of Economics. Receiving the news as she stood behind the counter of the clothes shop, Hana marvelled sceptically. In her view his diligence at his studies had not been matched by talent, but who was she to judge?

Then he said, 'Incidentally' – airily, but with his back to her – 'I'm thinking of getting married.' There would not be room in the flat for a wife, a sister and the washing machine he planned to acquire. 'I'm not as free as you are,' he said pointedly, rubbing it in. 'I'll have a family to think about.'

She lost her temper a second time and gave out a volley of horrible wails because she could not control herself and because she could not, even later when she was already a little ashamed of the noise she had made, find words. Stiffly she asked where he thought she was supposed to go. Gallantly he reminded her of the chicken house at Number 64, Bytlice.

Hana went to sulk among the pink nylon modes. While she was rubbing the ball of her thumb over the rough edge of a broken fingernail, a friend brought her the rumour that Honza was considered by his colleagues to be a man of principle.

'Don't be silly,' she coughed venomously, but still too honourable to say why.

'No, but really,' insisted the friend.

As everyone knew but nobody said, commissions had been convened all over the country, in centres of administration, among professional bodies, at institutes of learning. Their purpose was to succeed where the Department's earlier experiment had failed. Names were wanted, signatures on dotted lines. Nobody was required to believe what he signed – only to commit his identity to a piece of paper which might afterwards be filed.

Some individuals were in defiant mood when they took their turn on the chair provided, entering the room with a jocular 'Good day', to depart later invisibly, slipping out by stealth as if they hoped to escape intact, yet leaving a part of themselves behind. Those who were unlucky enough to meet a colleague along the way turned their eyes inward, indicating that, deep in thought, they must on no account be distracted.

Summoned to attend by the sealed note in his pigeon-hole, Honza had announced aloud, said Hana's informant, that he for one would sign nothing. But bravado, as everyone knew, is easily donned before the event. 'Sure,' they said and clapped him, ironically, on the shoulder. 'Sure, you won't. Nobody ever does.'

Perched perkily on the chair, Honza now waited, paying scant attention to the commission chairman's preamble.

'. . . and sign in the space marked by the dotted line, if you wouldn't mind.'

Honza did not stretch his hand out for the paper but leaned back, crossed his thin legs at the ankle and shook his head. 'Sorry. No.'

'I beg your pardon?'

'No. I don't want it. I'm not signing.'

Now here was a surprise. Newly appointed, nearly married, put in a request for a two-room flat and not signing?

'No.'

Even though he knew, he must know, they all knew how word got around, that everyone at the Institute and so on?

'Yes, but no.'

75

But what did he think he was trying to prove? The time for martyrdom was over, burnt offerings and all that. No publicity to be had, a small fish like him with unsavoury antecedents, sins of the fathers, one mustn't forget. Still no? But why on earth not?

'Because I already have.'

The commission chairman looked down his list. 'Comrade, I'm afraid you are mistaken. You have not appeared before us until today. Look, I can show you.' He walked around the end of the long table and, observing the proprieties of the moment, covered the names above with his hand as he held the list out to Honza's face. 'You see?'

Honza took out his diary. 'I signed on the twelfth of May this year, 1969.'

'But that's quite impossible. We were not convened in May. We didn't even know that we would be convening.'

'I think,' said Honza, 'that things have to be kept in order. I should not, for example, be expected nor, perhaps, even be encouraged to vote twice. It would be most irregular if I were to be registered as having signed twice. Would you please be so good as to consult your records.' With which bold challenge he stood up, bowed ever so slightly and left the room, closing the door with enough noise for it to be heard down the corridor. Education is a wonderful thing and Honza had paid attention to its most important lessons.

The three members of the commission stared at the vacated chair in dumbfounded silence. The chairman picked up the phone.

'He's right. He did. On the twelfth of May.'

'How could he?'

'There was some earlier experiment apparently. I didn't fully understand what they said.'

'So what do we do now?'

'Nothing. What can we do?'

'But we won't have 100 per cent. There'll be a gap.'

'Yes, but if he's already signed we can put him down as having signed.'

'But he didn't sign our document. He signed somebody else's. He wasn't even working here on the twelfth of May. He'll go down on somebody else's quota and we'll have a gap.'

'Yes, you're right. Calm down. We have to think about this coolly.'

76

'We could point out our position to him. You know, prevail on him.'

'Not as long as he's already signed. They've got his signature over there. At the Department.'

'Couldn't we ask the Department to give us that document, and get him back in here, then tear it up in front of him and get him to sign ours?'

The chairman picked up the phone again, his colleagues pressing against him trying to hear the distant voice of the man from the Department. The chairman's face fell.

'They won't let us have it. Some character there got a promotion because of him and, if they give up their paper, that chap's got no reason to hang on to his new post.'

'But who'd need to know that they'd passed it on to us? Their fellow can keep his job: it won't matter to him so long as he doesn't get demoted, and what's the odds to them if they pass on one measly document? It would give us our 100 per cent.'

'It seems it would lose them theirs. He *is* their 100 per cent.'

Thus it was that Honza gained himself that reputation of singleminded integrity and the three members of the commission lost their right to that year's spree on the Black Sea. When the chairman was informed of his loss he recalled the thin, obdurate and entirely correct young man, and snarled, 'Why did he have to be so damned zealous, for God's sake?'

So Hana had two reasons for moving to Bytlice. It depended upon her state of mind, self-pity or self-acclaim, which of these she cited. Sometimes she would say that Honza threw her out, without gratitude, because there wasn't room for her, his wife and the washing machine. Or she insisted that she had gone of her own volition, in disgust. She was leaving behind, she averred, an unease she felt in the presence of her brother, in the presence of the citizens with whom she had thought childhood could be prolonged. Where the city had been most euphoric so it was now most tainted by compromise; where it had been most enthusiastic it was most apathetic. But in the countryside the rhythm of the seasons, the unsullied snow, the depths of the sky at midnight and its proximity in the dusk of summer would breed a different people. It was not to be so simple.

'All right,' she said to her brother, 'I will move out. But not yet. And I shall take Aunt Veronika's inlaid table because you don't know how to polish it; I shall take her decanters and the crystal glasses and I shall take her bird prints because your wife won't like them. When I come for them you won't be able to stop me.'

Honza smiled and inclined his head magnanimously, for he remembered more clearly than Hana the condition of the chicken house at Number 64.

Next morning Hana took the train to Bytlice and hunted down her house among the trees and forking tracks. A new generation of chickens had made their home in it in the years since her last visit. The floor was slimy with their excrement and discarded feathers pocked the walls.

'Get out!' she shrieked, clapping her hands. 'Get out! Get out!' One of the chickens, which had been nesting in an upstairs room, made its escape through a hole in the roof. Hana spoke aloud as if only the sound of her own voice would make her promise binding. 'If it kills me, I'll do it. I'll show that shit of an arse-licking toady and all his friends. One day he'll see this place and what I'll have built here and he'll find out what life's all about.'

That day, all day long until it was time for her to run for the last train, Hana dragged branches and pieces of wood from the forest behind the plantation of young pines and blocked off the entrances to the house. Then she went back to Prague and bought a shovel.

Every weekend for six months she dug towards the floor-boards leaving great ill-smelling mounds on the grass outside. After which she would return to the city, the shop and her increasingly impatient brother. When Saturday came again and she resumed her digging, the mounds of excrement would be gone, spread on the vegetable plots of her new neighbours, whose acquaintance she had not yet made. From a distance they watched her, this diligent interloper who did not introduce herself, and a group of them went down to the local authority to check the records. They found that, indeed, the chicken house was registered in the name of one Veronika Kucerova of Prague, deceased. They waited to see what would happen next.

It was partly because she wished to avoid the company of her brother and partly in order to find new allies that Hana began frequenting the bar, and occasionally the auditorium, of a small theatre whose devotees, she could be almost sure, had signed nothing. And there, on a dusty blue chaise-longue tucked under a flight of stairs, she continued to do as Aunt

Veronika had asked, winning by this single but repeated act many new allies, a few friends but no serious suitors.

'Why are you never here at weekends?' asked dark-haired Karel, lying dishevelled next to her and leaning on his elbow. Hearing her story he pledged his help, desiring, in return, the promise of more love-making and a taste of her legendary cooking.

'You'll get that', said Hana curtly, 'when I've got a kitchen to cook in.'

Karel told his friend Tomas, and Tomas, finding the terms very acceptable, joined the team. Food and fucking, thought Hana wearily as she sat in the clothes shop. Wasn't there ever to be anything else?

Sometimes she wavered. There was too much to be done in Bytlice, more than she could manage. But when she saw, through the windows of the shop, the citizens of Prague going silently about their business, heads hung low, eyes downcast, her resolve was strengthened. In the country it would all be different.

She paid a carpenter and a glazier to put in windows and doors, wincing at the price of their illicit labour. She rolled blanketing and threadbare sheets into sausages which she laid along the walls to stop the draughts. Karel found a piece of lino that he laid over the hole in the kitchen floor. Tomas sat astride the ridge of the roof and hammered some metal sheeting over the hole in that, but eventually Honza could wait no longer.

'I've fixed it. It's all arranged. Next weekend and don't moan. You've kept me waiting three years. Surely you've knocked the place into shape by now?'

Hana did not attend her brother's wedding and by missing it deprived herself of a sighting of his wife, whom she was never to meet. She was busy at weekends, she told him acidly; she was sorry. But where was she to go? The house was not yet habitable. She had not found the money for a boiler to heat the coal and the water, she had not been able to find a cooker that no one else needed. The wet weather she could keep at bay; not so the biting frosts. She needed a little more time.

The following Sunday, arriving back at Aunt Veronika's flat expecting to find her furniture piled on the landing outside, she found instead a note from Honza. 'Dear Hana,' she read, 'you may stay on here after all. We have decided to move in with my in-laws. Zuzana, my wife, assures me they are not long for this world and they've got three rooms. I wish you every success with your flat in town and your house in the country. It's what Aunt Veronika would have wanted.'

Hana tore up the letter into very small pieces and then glued it together again, to be on the safe side. Now more than ever she wanted to be away from this flat, which seemed to be impregnated with her brother's spirit. She hoarded her earnings to complete her house, grew gaunt from eating too little, and when she finally packed her belongings she realised it had taken her five years. She was thirty years old, single, but for the time being well satisfied.

Karel and Tomas helped her move in. Then they sat together playing cards on Aunt Veronika's inlaid table while Hana cooked the second part of their bargain. When they had eaten their fill she shook their hands but dodged their embraces.

'I'm starting a new life and a new existence,' she told them, pushing them out of her door. 'Now I'm going to keep myself to myself and look after my house.'

They protested in unison. 'But Hani, after all the help we've given you.'

'I know. I'm very grateful. But your help didn't come free of charge, did it?'

Eleven

Hana hesitated before reaching out for the photograph clipped to a handbill with a clothes-peg, the photograph she had so often scrutinised with such attention and which she knew, even now, would make her guts lurch. That sensation had, in its time, been too painful to endure. Today she welcomed its bite, the upheaval. She put her hand in the shoebox and took out the photograph. Lukas leaned on her axe, gesturing towards the heap of logs he had chopped. 'Here, let me,' he had said, taking the axe from her to begin chopping. 'Got a beer? For afterwards? This is thirsty work.'

He had been brought out by friends who had said, on a summer weekend afternoon in the city, 'Let's look Hana up', anticipating a laze in the garden and a good meal, and getting both. But Hana, already mindful of the season to come, like the ant in the fable, was chopping firewood, not yet expert, tiring of it. And the young man who arrived with her hallooing friends took the axe and then posed with the results of his work like a hunter displaying a dead lion. The others lay in the grass, drinking and cheering. He was hot and stripped off his shirt. The light was behind him and there was light behind his eyes, Hana thought, bright light eyes. She dabbed at him with a towel to wipe off the sweat and the others cheered again. He was slender with a broad bony face. His fair hair curled to his shoulders like a picture of Our Lord. He raised his glass to her, downed it and drank another. Then he kissed her cheek. The friends chorused, 'Yeah! Get in there, man!' Hana hated them and flushed.

Lukas was a singer. 'You should come down and hear him, Hana.' But these days she was keeping herself away from the city as much as she could. She worked there, she shopped there; that was all. 'Oh, come on, girl. You can't cut yourself

81

off for ever.' She did not intend to, but wished, for the present, to listen to the foxes barking in the night and to learn to live alone. She would become a country-dweller. But there was light in the young man's eyes and he had held her eyes when he raised his glass. Someone would come by and give her a lift, they said. She allowed herself to be persuaded just this once, only to please her friends.

It had not been in the city itself but in the suburb of Branik – this small, smoke-filled pub, with its doors and windows open, and the smoke recoiling as it met the air. They had set out the wooden chairs in rows, as one might for a meeting, in the functions room at the back. Lukas sat on a similar chair on the wooden platform, one long leg bent so that the foot was twisted on to its side, its instep providing a support for the other foot. He nestled his guitar between his thighs, one under its waist, the other blocking its retreat. Already the room had filled with people who did not belong to that outer fringe of the city: one could tell from the face of the barman who had no fondness for strangers, but whose wiser back pocket prevailed.

Hana stood at the back and remembered Karel. 'Tell ten Russians to sing,' he had said, 'and you get a ten-part choir. Ten Poles, and you've got them bawling in unison. Ten Czechs and you need a hearing aid.' Lukas was wheedling a response from his audience, pleading with them to sing along with him. Their lips moved imperceptibly and from the corners of their mouths came a faint cheeping. Hana was incensed. She knew the words – it was an old folk song. They knew the words, they *must* know the words. Why would they not sing? They would spoil this performance and leave Lukas disappointed. She wanted someone to shout out the chorus but would not do it herself, for then heads would turn. She did not want Lukas to see she was there, standing at the back close to the door.

He stopped strumming his guitar, closed his eyes and, smiling, strained his head forward and to one side, cupped a hand behind one ear. 'Do you know,' he said, 'I had a dream once that I was giving a concert and the audience was singing with me. But they got quieter and quieter and then they stopped altogether except for two characters at opposite sides of the hall who were both wearing overcoats. And I thought, I bet you came in the same car. I wonder where you parked it?'

The tentative voices petered out completely; everyone looked askance at his neighbour. In the silence, Lukas giggled, like someone with a mouthful of water suppressing a choke. The incongruity of that laugh and the skill with which he had ambushed his audience startled Hana, who suddenly hooted. Too late she put a hand over her mouth, crimson before the questing faces that searched her out. Lukas acknowledged her with a single stab of his fist in the air, and began another song.

As if in some pain and with great deliberation, the cheeping recommenced, slowly at first like an old tape recorder. Lukas rotated an arm, cranking them up, looking into one face after another as if the briefest personal challenge would not be ignored. It seemed to Hana that he offered his eyes in particular to the women. She followed the progress of those eyes, trying to gauge whether anywhere there would be a signal of preference, and was ashamed. She would leave early, before the end, she would be noticed by her absence, she would not linger, she would go after the next song or perhaps in the middle of the one after that – and she only just made it out in time.

Wherever Lukas Vratka performed, there one might find Hana, skulking – it is true – in a corner, at the back of the crowd, behind a pillar. She was not, of course, as invisible as she supposed. Those who had first inveigled her to the pub in Branik rolled their eyes in her direction for one another's benefit. Ribald comments followed. But Hana opted not to notice. She was obsessed.

Lukas increased his repertoire. He began to sing ancient and disconcerting ballads from the distant past with the melodies and rhythms of medieval times. They required the extra accompaniment of an unresonant tambour. Lukas acquired it – a blond boy barely out of his teens, who sat cross-legged and almost immobile in the wings, the tambour wedged between his thighs, waiting. Hana was always touched by the dismal clacking from this boy's wooden drum. The boy himself (Pavel Dostalek, electrician) tapped away with his head thrown back, eyes closed as if he were weaving a spell to whose magic he would be the first to succumb. These were not the cosy songs of summer camp but dark and murderous, steeped in blood. Religious martyrs, hacked apart inch by inch for their faith, turn their eyes to heaven in anticipation of the final beatitude; a cruel king, rebuffed by the virginal maid he covets, has her locked in a dungeon to be whittled away by the executioner, so that at least no one else shall have her; a wandering minstrel, bringing Truth to implacable savages like a pedlar with ribbons, is pelted with filth, maligned and hounded to the wilderness where he dies, still carrying the Truth that no one was interested in sharing.

Lukas appeared not to mind whether people sang with these songs. He wanted them only to listen, and perhaps to remember. But the eerie melodies were so repetitive, the refrains so frequent, that they were easily learned. A musical *coup d'état* overthrew the national ditties. The audiences paid homage to the tunes of medieval wickedness, and Lukas's moments of dejection became rare. He no longer needed to depart hangdog and stricken as a child chastised without cause. Sometimes, Hana realised, when she left the auditorium but remained outside, unsafely concealed, to watch him go, he did not emerge until long after the last of the audience had gone in search of a drink. So the day came, as it was bound to do, when Hana stayed behind. What followed was what had to, and what Hana had presumably hoped would follow.

Lukas sat on the stage still cradling his guitar. It was very dark – the stage manager, the lights man, the audience all departed. No one was left but the singer on his wooden chair. Hana sniffed at the vacated space around her and was depressed. What an awful thing to do, to stay alone in the gloom, the evening's jubilation sucked out along with the people who had created it. For the second time she produced an inadvertent noise. And Lukas said, 'Hana! Hi!'

'How did you know it was me?'

'You're always here. Very loyal. I'm touched.'

'Do you see me?'

'Sometimes. Sometimes they tell me you've been. Why do you always gallop away like that? I thought we might have a drink.'

The evening was hot, and Lukas had a dry throat from singing, as did Hana from waiting. They drank a great deal too much. Lukas held it better than Hana, who might otherwise not have lost her head. Now at last she understood why Aunt Veronika had commanded her to start practising, for what she had been so desolately and intensely rehearsing. It had been a prolonged lesson to teach her to recognise the only man to whom, in future, she could devote herself entirely. From now on, she thought as she held him to her, smiling as she had never smiled before, it would be clear, it would be simple. It was final.

His eyes were closed and he, too, was smiling in sweet relaxation. 'We must do this again,' he said. And for a week they did, as if God had created the seven days for no other purpose. Then Lukas took her hands, kissed her fingertips lightly, said, 'See you around.' And departed.

Later, when she was sure she was pregnant, she wrote to him to tell him, offering him, she said, the most complete of gifts. In return she received a letter, a letter she kept implacably, despite the pain it caused. 'I have no need of a child. I do not want a child. What in the world did you think you were doing? Hana, I'm sorry, but please abort this child because I am hoping to get married.'

Twelve

When Milan was born and brought to Hana to be fed, wrapped as tight as a dry white slug and lifted from where he had been lying wedged in a row of similar slugs on a trolley, she sat up, oozing between her legs, and pulled back the blanketing from his face. She expected to see in his creased features some mark of his paternity, but he reminded her only of her younger brother. She all but threw the bundle on the floor, reprimanded herself, and set to the matter in hand. Later, she persuaded a nurse to take a photograph, and held out her son towards the lens, so that Lukas would see the puckered baby and relent. But when the film was developed the pictures emerged overexposed and Milan was no more than a dry white slug.

She wrote, she did not know why, to inform Nora in England and Dr Cerny in Merunkov. When a baby is born you send out cards. Nora responded with an ill-wrapped package out of which slithered a long white christening gown of old silk and a money order, the first of many, in pounds sterling. (Hana, like everybody, knew whom to go to get the best deal with that. She worked it out. At four times the official rate she could almost live on Nora's money.) On a scrap of lined paper torn from an exercise book was the single question: 'And who is the father?' Dr Cerny sent a closely written letter which asked no questions but offered detailed instructions on hygiene and nutrition.

She brought the baby home to her house, which she would not now be leaving each day for the city. They had said he was small. All babies were small, but, God, he was small. Suddenly she felt that she, not the baby, was weak and vulnerable. She would do for him whatever was needed to keep him safe, keep him fed, make him happy. Anything. No matter what it was. She laid Milan in the centre of her bed and rolled her feather-bed and pillows round him, went down to make herself coffee but left it standing cold on the table as she ran upstairs again. He was mummified in his shawl. Motionless and dead. She gasped, knelt by the bed and fingered the woollen shawl away from his face, its features so tiny, the skin so fine. The child was unreal. She stared into her son's face, her brother's face, and it contorted with a momentary inner spasm. Around the base of the nose were faint white bumps. His upper lips and its surround were blue. She feared disease. He was dying.

Milk spots and wind. Later, when she had learned enough, she was to laugh at that moment of panic.

She had lost hours uncountable gazing into that face while he coiled his fingers, their sharp nails so tiny she dared not trim them, around one of hers.

During the hours of daylight Milan was a sleeper, mewling at night. With her wiry forearms deep in the fetid soapy water, rubbing the strips of cloth she wrapped round her son's bottom, Hana had moments of bitter reflection. Had she not followed Mrs Z.'s advice and learned to cook to keep her man? Had she not obeyed Aunt Veronika's command and learned to fuck to get him in the first place? And how had she ended up? With neither Mrs Z.'s dozy husband nor Aunt Veronika's memories. Only a baby son who resembled her own toady of a brother, a baby who had not had the grace to look like its father for whom she hungered, whom she had not been allowed to know. Poor baby. It was not his fault. He had a bad mother. She rubbed the strips of cloth more vigorously, an extra effort towards cleanliness to make amends. She had not been truthful in her bitterness, not even truthful with herself. For did she not have Aunt Veronika's memories?

But Aunt Veronika's memories had been of men – a minor manager from Bata's with slicked-back hair and a strange rolling walk who presented her with a pair of shoes three times a year, sometimes shoes with buckles; an insurance man called Mikulik who was bald but held her wrist at the opera while he whispered an alternative and dirty libretto in her ear; Thierry (French), who didn't stay (but then, my dear, none of them did), who held her on his lap, repeatedly running over the contours of her face with the tip of his middle finger, and humming. (Charming at first, but you get irritated with that sort of thing.) He had proposed. She had failed to accept, had not really regretted it but subsequently counselled her niece always to say yes. And so Hana had promised, and what had it got her? Memories not of whole men but of penises, each of which fixed itself in her mind as a vegetable, often celery, and of mutterings which she could never catch because the words were absorbed into the pillow, or the grass, or the sacking above her head. Only Lukas remained with the light bright eyes, wielding his axe, sitting on the stage with his guitar upright on the floor between his knees like a shrunken cello, talking into the empty auditorium. Lukas clasped in her arms, between her legs, his breath on her shoulder, the scent of freshly chopped wood in her nostrils.

Hana would not fool herself. These were always the same images repeated and enhanced by repetition because there were no others. She had not known him long enough, well enough, had not known him at all. But he was Milan's father, where others could just as easily have been Milan's father but were not. Reason enough to keep the baby in bed with her and deny that bed henceforth to all outsiders.

Maybe, as he grew older, Milan would take on his father's features. They said children do change.

Children change; mothers don't. Coming upon Hana when she was alone and unprepared, motherhood had injected her with a singular capacity for worry. Her small son refused to thrive, would not grow, seemed not to grasp the principles of digestion. What did people do? What would her mother have done? And suddenly she knew.

With the proceeds of the very first of Nora's money orders distributed about her person, she went in search of carrots. It was early summer, but Milan, still undersized and wrapped in the woollen shawl, needed carrots. She was persuaded that his strength depended upon them, and recalled a soft orange mound of sieved carrots that her mother had once prepared for Honza. Why he was given them she could not remember, but her mother's remedies could not have been flawed. The carrots had been boiled until the colour ran out of them and pressed with a spoon through the fine mesh of the sieve. Hana had sat at the table and watched her mother, who had seemed, even at the time, to press some part of herself, some sort of conviction, through that sieve with the vegetable. Hana wanted to do the same for her son as a tribute to her mother, whose very stance she would repeat in the doing of it, bending her head as her mother had done, pressing with the spoon first this way then that. So she wound the still surprising body in the woollen shawl and set out to buy, if she could not beg, carrots from her neighbours. All of them claimed to have none, and regarded her curiously, some even with suspicion. This slim woman with her fatherless baby had held aloof but now came knocking, proffering too much money. It made you wonder. It made you opt, after some hesitation, for the safer path and you closed the door.

Hana proceeded down the hill, from one house to another, afraid, as she had never been before, that she might slip on the loose stones of the steep path and fall, in her inexperience, dropping the child. So she minced, flat-footed with tensed calves, leaning back.

In his garden at the bottom of the hill, Josef Frantisek straightened his back and observed her descent. Here she came, the young woman from up the hill who gave you good day and not a lot else. He knew what they said. They said she kept her figure by exercising in the nude to her record of Brahms's Second Symphony, which she played so loud you could hear it from the middle of the river. So loud, so they said, people knocking on the door couldn't make themselves heard. So what could they do but walk in and get an eyeful? And she squealed and ran for a shawl. Not as fast as she should, he'd heard them say. So Josef watched her coming his way with interest.

Frantisek the forester was large and bearded and played in goal for the football club of his favourite hostelry. His wife was pretty, his toddlers strapping, made in his image, and watching their father's every move. They heaved themselves from side to side in imitation of his wide-gaited walk; they tumbled on the concrete veranda he was building for their mother to sunbathe on; collected the eggs from his chickens; pulled the ears of his rabbits; lived just that little bit better than others but were too young to know it.

Their father knew what was expected of him. He passed precisely the required hours sitting among the trees and livestock of the forests in his care, conserving his energy for the improvement of his house; the cultivation of his vegetable garden; the most frequent copulation with his wife she would concede, topping up elsewhere when he had to; and a twice-weekly bout of drinking that ought to have incapacitated him. A genial if sometimes loud-mouthed father, he was, it was generally agreed, an exemplary citizen, party membership notwithstanding.

But Hana, who had held aloof, knew none of this. What she immediately recognised was the sensation of being looked over. Carrying a baby in this situation made her feel awkward. It crossed her mind to put the bundle down somewhere. Josef Frantisek looked at her frank face and her arse like a boy's. He saw her awkwardness and did not move, but waited for her to say something. To his astonishment she thrust out a fistful of notes.

'I've come to ask if you've got any carrots. I can pay.'

'If you need carrots, I'd give you carrots, but sorry. Haven't got any.'

Hana seemed to slump with disappointment. There were no houses left to call on. 'Why hasn't anybody got any? Not anybody? I can't believe it!'

'It's not so surprising. You wouldn't expect any at this time of year. They've not grown yet. Look.'

He took her by the elbow and led her across the garden to the vegetable plot. The rows of vegetables were as straight as if the drills had been drawn along a taut string. Josef bent and fondled the feathered leaves.

'See? Still babies. You're welcome to some, but you'll have to wait a while.'

Hana, ashamed of her ignorance and suddenly convinced that without an immediate injection of sieved carrots Milan would die, sprouted tears of panic and desperation.

'Hey, what's the matter? The world doesn't end without a few carrots, does it?' Josef peered into Hana's contorted face; and understood. 'They're for your little one, aren't they? Let me have a look.' In his arms Milan looked puny, a fragile runt. 'Boy?' Hana nodded. 'Could do with a bit of feeding up. Doesn't he eat?'

'Everything seems to make him sick.'

'Give him apples. Grate them with the skin on. That's what my old woman did with our lads when they had the runs. Got any apples? Well, I've still got a whole heap from last year. Come on in.' Here Hana was introduced to Alena threading lard into a chicken, and the sturdy toddlers each with a wedge of bread.

'Come and see me again – why don't you,' Alena had said on the doorstep, long after they should all have been in bed, Hana swaying from Josef's rum. You come seeking carrots and receive instead last year's apples. Thus are friendships made.

To be on the safe side Josef taught her how to dig and sow

seeds. Poor townie, who didn't know when you could expect to pull your first carrots. He covered the hole in her kitchen floor properly, renewed the entire floor, dammit, with the spare floorboards he had in the shed. He didn't like it, women on their own. It made them nervy. She needed someone in bed with her and he knew she knew he was thinking so. That was something she was used to, wherever it was she'd come from, men looking her over.

He secured for Hana a part-time job at the collective, an unproductive enterprise whose director, enjoying a spot of venison when it came his way, squeezed her hand and said, 'Josef's friend.' She was to be book-keeper, counting in the deliveries of fertiliser, cement and piping that arrived on the first of every month. If she should happen to notice that, by the third of the month, some of these commodities had moved beyond the confines of the collective, she need not feel obliged to point it out.

She lazed away her afternoons with Alena on the concrete veranda, watching Josef's fertile vegetables grow and listening to the whooping of the boys as they played under the trees beyond the cage where Josef's rabbits crouched, cowed by mortality. Pale as raw dough despite the sun, Milan struggled behind the Frantisek brothers, his legs thinned by his nappy.

Alena lay on her deckchair, ankles crossed, a beer at her side. Her midriff displayed a trio of faint creases and she tanned smoothly; but the two creases between her eyes were deeper and her hair was thin. Josef and his women.

As Milan grew he was sometimes convulsed by nightmares, screaming and unwakable. Then Alena would race up the hill to Hana's summons. After the screams subsided the two women paraded the boy up and down as he stared, dead eyes wide open, and shaking. Together, in a ritual, they talked him back into his waking world.

'Who is it, Milan? Who's here?'

'Auntie Alena.'

'And who am I?'

'Mummy.'

They grew to be, each of them, the closest friend either had ever had. They would tell one another everything, they promised, but held much back. Alena did not reveal her dislike of love-making, fearful lest Josef's philandering could be blamed on that, thinking also that this was something Hana might not understand, instantly ashamed for so thinking. For that reason she did not ask Hana who was poor little Twiglet's father – about whom Hana longed to speak.

Sometimes, when Alena sat by Hana's fire late at night, there was one of those amicable silences and Hana thought, now I'll tell her. God, what will her face do? Too many times she had rehearsed Alena's reaction, the lips freezing on the cigarette, the glass held motionless in the air, incredulity and envy in her stare. But to tell is to give away, and once given cannot be taken back to rehearse again. At the last moment, always, Hana resisted the urge to blab and crossed her legs. Upstairs her son coughed up mucus in his sleep.

Only the changing seasons gave distinguishable character to the passing days. Yesterday had been like today; tomorrow would be identical.

Winter, for Milan, began in November when, turning the page of the calendar, he embarked on the annual surveillance of his health, monitoring the first wheeze of his chest and scratch of his throat. He would clap his palm to his forehead suspecting fever, and run to fetch the thermometer, arriving there even ahead of his mother. It meant being wrapped in his mother's feather-bed, leaning over her elbow to see how far the silver line had progressed. It meant curling on his side while she read him fairy stories that were intended for younger children and so were comforting.

Hana read him in an admonitory tone the letters sent by the man she said was a children's doctor who was telling her what to do. She did not tell her son that she had begun the correspondence, terrorised by his fevers and the crowing cough she could not bear to hear. Dr Cerny's handwriting was meticulous, all the characters the same size, and his tone was cool. The advice never changed: keep the boy in bed, and at home for three days after the fever subsides. He recommended a hot poultice for his chest and suggested she make less fuss. Hana felt both reprimanded by these letters and reassured.

When summer came again Milan was still there, a little grown; and immediately he was off down the hill with his friends. Hana would follow and resume her posture on the concrete veranda. But alone at night she lay in her bed and masturbated sadly, trying but failing to feel the weight of Lukas's body on hers. From beyond the grave she heard the voice of Aunt Veronika grumbling, 'That's not what I meant at all, dear. How could you have been so stupid?' Then Hana felt doubly alone because she could not answer.

At the end of the Milan's seventh summer, therefore, when the postmistress brought her a letter from Dr Cerny inviting her to visit and bring the child, she turned to him and said, 'I know an old man who needs a bit of company. It wouldn't do you any harm to learn to be polite to someone like that, would it?' Milan, who had never been anything else, concurred.

But on the overnight train, returning to Merunkov, Hana remembered not the doctor's medical guidance nor his nose in his handkerchief and his hand on her elbow as they parted the last time; she saw instead, from many years ago, the scowl on his face as he turned away from the camera. 'Photograph us as a family,' Nora had commanded, but Dr Cerny had seen the threat to his family in the pharmacist's children and snarled, 'Are you crazy, Nora, or what?'

PART II

Thirteen

The train would be late. Nevertheless, Dr Cerny rose even earlier than usual to anticipate his guests, wrapped in his winter coat against the chill of approaching autumn. He carried a small bunch of flowers to welcome Hana and a Hungarian language primer to while away the time. However, his mind was not on the impossible conjugations he had determined to commit to memory. He closed the primer over his thumb, optimistically marking the place, and paced the platform. He was not alone, for here and there were other early risers hunched in their overcoats waiting for the train to carry them further down the line.

'Good day, doctor.' It was Mayor Tvrdohlavy, restored to office, his coat stretched tight over his wide belly. 'Going somewhere for the weekend?' With a bunch of flowers, a book and no luggage? Really! But the Mayor, always needing to know, could not be left unanswered.

'Good day, Comrade Mayor. No.'

'Waiting for someone, then?'

'Yes.'

'A visitor?'

'Yes.'

'Anyone we know?'

'I doubt if you'd remember her. Hana Masnikova.'

'Who? Oh yes, of course. The pharmacist's daughter.'

Damn the man's memory. 'That's right.'

'We haven't seen her down these parts since she was a girl.'

'No.'

'Will she be staying long?'

'I shouldn't have thought so. Just a visit with her boy.'

'With her boy? I didn't know she'd married.'

'She hasn't.'

'Really? So who's the little bastard's father?' This was a question Dr Cerny longed to have answered himself but he did not like to hear it coming from the Mayor's ill-shaven lips.

'I have no idea. It's none of my business.'

'Oh, come now, doctor. The girl lived with you when you were in . . . with your good wife. She was part of your family. It must be your business. It's everyone's business.'

Although he was inclined to agree, Dr Cerny shivered with dislike of the man, but quickly controlled himself. 'If you'll excuse me, I'll go and warm up for a moment in the waiting-room.'

'Yes, go on in. No point catching your death out here waiting for the damned train. It'll be late, you can bet. Nice flowers.'

'Yes. Thank you.'

The waiting-room was barely warmer than the platform but at least the Mayor had not followed him in. Dr Cerny sat on the narrow bench, leaned back against the cold of the concrete wall and wished he'd brought his hat. It had been a mistake to invite Hana on impulse, especially for a man who prided himself on his deliberation. Just because a moment of sentimentality had swept over him, remembering when she had last been in Merunkov, banging the dust out of the carpets. All those years and he had not resented his solitude, Nora gone, Peter gone. He had not minded. He had preferred it. You could get more done. And she had a child and no husband. Too much of that around and he didn't care for it.

What would they do, the two of them, in one another's company, alone together with that fatherless child of hers? Dr Cerny's uneasiness deepened. He had never been at his best in the company of children, finding them unpredictable and liable to make impromptu noises, and had therefore been much mocked by Nora for his choice of profession. She could never be made to understand that you did not need to like children to be an effective paediatrician. A good doctor needed only to be able to diagnose the ailment and then treat it in accordance with the recommendations of medical science and the remedies available. A workaday sort of doctor, as he proclaimed himself to be, was all the community expected, and all it got.

Maybe the boy would be ill again and he could at least exercise his profession with Hana fussing at his side, grateful and compliant. Dr Cerny shook his head, distressed that such a thought should enter his mind, but immediately acknowledged that one cannot at all times be on one's guard against rogue thoughts. What it proved without question, however, was the supreme importance of so organising one's time that the opportunity for unintended reflection was restricted to the unavoidable minimum.

It was day by now, and the sun, though still low on the horizon, sent an uninterrupted beam along the straight railway line and down the platform. Dr Cerny stepped outside and glanced surreptitiously about to assure himself that the gross figure of the Mayor was engaged in pestering someone else. Then he stationed himself in the sunlight where it was already noticeably warmer than inside. The public address system informed him that the expected train would be twenty minutes late. Not bad at all. He had imagined worse. Even so, twenty minutes was time enough to return to his Hungarian paradigms. He extracted his bruised thumb, turned his back to the sun to gather its warmth on his shoulders and once more set to whispering aloud the previous day's dispersed conjugations. Nearby, the waiting public recognised the paediatrician but respected his solitude. The doctor was at it again, always studying something.

'May I play on your piano?'

'Of course,' said Dr Cerny, just as Hana said loudly, 'No!'

Milan looked at his mother, in whom was all authority. Grey with lack of sleep, she was holding her coffee-cup in both hands. The grooves that sometimes appeared between her nose and the corners of her mouth were always deeper when she hadn't slept.

'But why shouldn't he?'

Hana, unable to explain that she was restricting her son for fear of annoying their host, offered Milan's inability as an excuse.

'Well, but that doesn't matter,' said Dr Cerny heartily. 'I can teach him. You'd like that, wouldn't you?'

'Yes.' Milan was not at all sure that he wanted to learn. He had hoped only to be allowed to experiment with the unfamiliar notes while his mother and the old man sat opposite one another in the window, drinking their coffee.

Hana thought: Oh God, no! Memories rushed upon her of Peter, plump and fidgeting, of Dr Cerny, insistently, 'Peter, *are* you listening, *are* you paying attention?', of Nora, 'Oh, leave the child alone, can't you see he's not interested?' And Dr

Cerny exhaling with impatience at his son's wavering concentration and his wife's indolence, always taking the easiest path. Hana and Honza had not been subjected to the doctor's urge to instruct and educate. They had been interlopers, Nora's creatures, no responsibility of his, and he had packed them off. Now, however, alone with his piano and an old cat he had got from somewhere, he was offering to make amends, proposing to Hana what he felt best suited to give: lessons for her son. There was nothing she wanted to do more than to protect Milan from that.

'I couldn't let you do even more work, doctor. And you know how tiring children are.' She shouldn't have said that, putting the blame on the child. Maybe one day he would understand. 'Still, as the doctor says you can, go along and play. But not too loud, mind.' Milan trailed out, puzzled.

Dr Cerny sipped his coffee and looked at Hana. Hana sipped her coffee but with her eyes closed. Thread lines gathered her top lip. She's ageing too, he thought; she was a child yesterday and now she's getting old. They heard the muffled and tentative sounds of Milan's musical experimentation. He was playing with one finger and he had closed the door.

In the first bright light of morning on the railway platform Dr Cerny had taken Hana's suitcase from her, thrust the flowers into her hands, grasped her elbow and kissed her drily on both cheeks. He had laid a hand on the child's head. Only then, when Milan looked up at him, had the old man taken a look at his face and gasped. Here was Hana, holding, it seemed, her own young brother by the hand. Honza must have been the same age when Nora came whooping up the road, an orphan dangling on either side. It was the same narrow, serious face, the same uncertain eyes and mousey upstanding hair. How had Hana produced this replica from the past who bore no signature of paternity? Had her desire for a child been so great that she had willed a conception in which no second party had been involved? A child without a father, unfathered, carried by his mother with the imprint of his uncle. Or perhaps the boy had been got by accident and the father had denied responsibility, the way so many did, and managed even to leave no trace of himself, consigning the mother and her son to re-create together an old childhood, to live together in isolation, belonging to no one. It must have been hard for her and unnecessary. Involuntarily he spoke his thoughts aloud.

'Surely an abortion could have been arranged.'

Hana opened her eyes, shocked. 'What?'

Too late. It had been said. Dr Cerny tried to retrieve his blunder.

'I mean, it can't be easy. Managing alone.'

'How can you say that? How can a paediatrician recommend an abortion? You've seen my son, you invited us. How can you say that?'

Dr Cerny looked down into his cup but retorted, 'How can a paediatrician recommend a fatherless childhood?'

'*I* had a fatherless childhood.'

'That was different. It was . . . it was . . . You didn't choose it. It was forced on you.'

'And I have forced it on Milan?'

'No, no. I'm sorry. I didn't mean that. I was clumsy. I'm sorry.' Dr Cerny turned to the window, avoiding Hana's outraged stare. 'How *do* you manage?'

'I've got a job.' Such a cold reply.

'Good one?'

'It's all right. Part-time book-keeper at the collective.'

'Oh, that's good. A responsible position and a valuable contribution.'

'Is it?'

'Yes, of course. There must be so much to keep an eye on.'

'Like what?'

'The finances. What comes in, what goes out.' Through the closed door Milan's finger was laboriously picking out a nursery rhyme. Dr Cerny stiffened, tensed against a wrong note.

Hana laughed, provoking. 'Oh no. I only have to write down what comes in. It's not my business what goes out.'

Dr Cerny sighed deeply and turned his face away. She thought it was funny, cheating the state. They all thought it was funny and clever. She was probably pilfering, the way they all did. He looked out of the window again. Across the courtyard he saw the faces of his neighbours pressed against their window-panes: Mrs Hulkova, Mrs Kocourkova, Mrs Seitlova, all looking down intently into the street. He checked his watch. Down on the flat roof of the supermarket below, steam was dispersing from the low chimney, sucked away by the late-morning warmth. A lorry drew into the back of the supermarket and Dr Cerny leapt from his reverie.

'Oh my goodness! Excuse me a moment. I won't be a minute. Oh, hurry!' Urging himself on, and he was running from the room.

'Dr Cerny, what is it? What's wrong?'

But the doctor was already taking himself down the tiled steps as fast as he dared. Slow, always too slow. Damn his old legs.

'Milan, stay where you are,' Hana called out to her son. 'I'll be back in a minute.' She bounded after the old man, catching up with him in the street.

'It's the meat. I must get to the head of the queue. I wanted to get something special for you, a piece of pork or even beef if there is some. But I'm too slow these days and those harridans are always on the lookout. I saw them. Did you see them, all in their windows, waiting, with their bags already in their hands?' He was right. The nimbler women relegated him to a position midway down the queue and he came away sullenly with a small piece of streaky ham.

'One day,' he vowed, 'I'll get there first. You see if I don't.'

'Never mind,' Hana consoled him. 'I'll make noodles to go with this. You like noodles.'

Dr Cerny beamed. 'Will you really? But it's too hot to be making noodles.'

'No, it isn't.'

It was. Her forehead glistened as she kneaded the stiff unyielding dough and the doctor, recognising woman's work, went in search of Milan.

'Look at my hands. See how I'm holding them? Now you do the same. No. Hold your elbows out a little and round your hands more. You have to touch the keys with your fingertips. That's better. Now try one note at a time, one for each finger starting with your thumb. One. Two. Three. Four. Five. And back again, come on. Five. Four. Three. Two. One. Very good. You see? Do it again and then we'll try the left hand.'

Sitting so close, the old man smelt strange leaning over him and he had hair growing from his ears. He smelt sour, fusty, like his mangy cat. Milan held his breath and watched his own fingers walking stiffly up and down the keys. His wrists were aching with tension.

'Can I stop now?'

'One more go with each hand, then I'll play you something. Come on. One. Two. Three . . .'

Soon Milan was in the armchair and the old man was saying, 'What will it be? What will it be?', leafing through sheets of

music. 'Something fast or something slow? What do boys like?'
Milan wondered where his mother was and what she was
doing. The old man had said to leave her alone – she was busy
and didn't need men under her feet. Strange. That was the sort
of thing Uncle Josef said, but he was different. Big and noisy,
banging into the furniture and putting his arms round Aunt
Alena from behind, making her jump.

'Mendelssohn, I think. Have you ever heard of Mendelssohn?
No? Hasn't your mother taught you anything? Well, perhaps
not. No time I expect. Never mind, it's never too late to start.
Well, Mendelssohn lived more than a hundred years ago, in
Germany, and he lived in the capital city called Berlin. His first
name was Felix, which is the Latin for happy or lucky. And his
parents liked music so much they had a piano in every room
of their house. Are you listening?'

'Yes.'

'Can you remember what I said?'

'His name was lucky and he had lots of pianos.'

'That's right. So he was lucky, wasn't he? Now listen again.'
The doctor spread a double sheet of music on the piano,
dense clusters of black dots like bees on a trellis. Milan drew
up his knees, curling them into the armchair. It smelt of the
old man, and the material on the arms was threadbare. Milan
laid his head on a worn patch, cupping his cheek in his hand.

'This is called a Song Without Words.' Why a song without
words? How could a song be without words? Why not call it
just a tune? Milan knew lots of songs, but they all had words.
This song was using all the old man's fingers, more fingers
than he had. There was a tune high up, loping slowly forwards
and back, like a swing, and underneath all the other fingers
tumbled like an ants' nest that has been disturbed. Milan had
once put the toe of his boot in an ants' nest, without meaning
to, without knowing it was there, and the ants had poured out
in all directions. He thought he could hear them screaming in
panic, running up the mountain of his boot. He thought of
being on a swing, way out of reach so that even at its lowest
point no one would be able to touch him, and he was swinging
over the tops of the trees, backwards and forwards, on and on,
carried by the tune so that he didn't have to pump his legs in
and out, and far below him hundreds of children, diminished
by the distance, ran underneath, chasing and reaching
upwards, wanting to get on the swing only they were too small,
too far away, and his hands were giant's hands on the bars of

the swing, the bars were straws, and he swooped and swooped and the tune that was pushing him mingled with the rushing of the wind and handed him over to the rushing of the wind in the treetops, and the uppermost branches, bending this way and that, propelled the swing like a machine, keeping pace with the music, steady.

Dr Cerny's mottled hands cupped the final chord. What a difference it made playing to an audience. He had not played as well for as long as he could remember and that was good, for it would make a suitable introduction for a young boy's first encounter with serious music. Two, three, four and lift. He raised both hands from the keyboard, arching his wrists, leaving the fingertips still dabbling on the surface of the keys.

'Well?' He turned to Milan for an opinion on the music and its rendition, but the child was asleep, wormed on his side in the armchair, his mouth slightly open. Dr Cerny was slack with disappointment. Had it all been wasted? Couldn't the boy have kept his mind on the music for those few minutes? Then he remembered Hana's strained and exhausted face, remembered that they had not slept on the train, told himself that the particular sweetness of the music he had selected and the flowing roundness of his tone, unappreciated, had been the lullaby without which the boy would not be sleeping in such abandoned relaxation in an armchair that was not his. Tomorrow would be time enough. Tomorrow, perhaps, if Milan had slept out his sleep, he would take him to the forest and teach him the names of the trees so that the boy might fix them. Maybe, living in Bytlice, he knew them already, if Hana had done her proper work.

In the middle of the night Hana woke and tossed. Dr Cerny had enjoyed his noodles. He had kept his bald head down so that she saw the age spots on the crown, and chewed methodically and noisily, perhaps counting to thirty for each forkful as an aid to proper digestion. He had hummed tunelessly, eating as if he were alone, like one who has grown used to solitude. Had she also grown boorish for being so much alone, breakfasting alone after Milan had left for school, dining alone when he slept, but less and less, with less and less appetite? Was this why the doctor had sent for her, not to salve his loneliness but to offer a balm to hers? Well, she had accepted.

She wouldn't have it, and could not sleep. She eased herself from the bed, unbreathing, thinking she would arrange something in the kitchen, do something mechanical until she was bored back to bed. She tiptoed with stiff and exaggerated steps into the kitchen where, by the light of a small table-lamp, she saw Dr Cerny hunched over a piece of newspaper spread upon his yellow plastic cloth, silently cleaning her shoes.

Hana froze in the doorway, watching the old man rubbing at the seams of leather with a damp cloth. His face was bent low but she fancied she saw a determination, an intensity in his expression as if he were explaining to her shoes, by his attentiveness to them, what he could not say to her. She thought she would make some slight sound to attract his attention, so that he should know she was there, that she had seen him, but desisted, realising that he would be covered in confusion and might regret this small service. Holding her breath again, she crept back to bed.

Fourteen

Dr Cerny, up with the dawn as ever, had laid out slices of cheese and sausage on a plate, buttered bread and pronged gherkins from their jar of brine. He beckoned Milan from his bed where he lay wondering, beckoned with one forefinger, the other laid on his lips. Hana must get her rest. He settled Milan at the table and urged the boy to eat, reminding him that a good breakfast was the only way to start the day.

'That's what Mum says.'

'Does she?' Dr Cerny nodded with approval. 'Well, she's quite right. And does she eat a good breakfast too?'

'I don't know.'

The old man bent down, puffing to lace his walking boots, glanced at Milan's trainers, shook his head just enough for Milan to register that something was not as it should be, and shouldered a bag into which he had packed an austere picnic of bread, eggs and mineral water. He wore his hat, for the morning was still sharp, and wrapped a scarf round the boy's neck, crossing the ends over his chest and tucking them in place with the boy's coat. You took no chances with weak chests in morning air.

Later, walking along the path that he took every Sunday through the woods, Dr Cerny was brought to notice much that he had missed before, for he was not by nature observant; it was not the eager eyes of the child bringing things to his attention but his own desire to point out the phenomena he understood. He stood beneath the trees, earnestly seeking out what might be explained. He selected a spider's web straddling two bushes, a symmetrical plane of rigging with its maker in the middle, poised for the faintest trembling on the outskirts of its universe. There was symmetry, too, in the spirals of the pine cones, whose horny kernels were stretched and bursting; in the arrangement of the seeds on the long grasses by the side of the path; in the fins on the undersides of the toadstool he upended with the tip of his boot. 'Now be sure not to put your fingers in your mouth. Here, wipe them on my handkerchief.' There was symmetry even in the holes of his walking boots through which the laces crissed and crossed. Patterns, he explained, in nature and in the things man made in imitation of nature, and in man himself.

Dr Cerny, by choice a brisk walker who walked for his health, to pass the time and to set his blood racing, now slowed his pace out of respect for the shortness of his companion's legs. He talked incessantly, as if releasing observations that had been stored over years pending the arriving of a worthy receptacle. Milan, who did not understand much of what was being said, none the less felt himself special in the old man's attention. No one had ever told him so much before. He hoped he would not be expected to remember it all, although he was trying.

'Why do all those things have patterns?'

'Because it makes them work better.'

'But how does it?'

Dr Cerny had to date only observed that wherever he looked patterns were repeated. He had not asked himself why. 'I don't know. But when we get home we'll find out. My books will say.'

'Will they say how they got to be like that?'

'I'm sure they will.'

'Mum says it's God.'

Dr Cerny stopped, the pine cone that had a moment before been his demonstration model for the order and structure of nature still in his hand. He believed profoundly that there was no God. He also believed that one should not undermine the authority of parents in the eyes of their children. He did not understand where Hana might have picked up a religious streak. Perhaps it was the influence of that aunt in Prague Nora had sent the children to? Turning the rough pine cone this way and that, Dr Cerny did not know what to do. Perhaps it would not hurt to let the boy believe the stories his mother told him, perhaps she simply used God as a shorthand for the science that eluded her. Yet a boy who asked questions ought to be answered, and there should be an answer for every question. If there were not, then one should look instead to the question, for that was where the flaw would lie.

Dr Cerny's prolonged silence, the fumbling of his thumb and

107

forefinger on the rough spines of the pine cone, the working of his eyebrows, all made Milan fear he had said something to make the old man angry. He certainly looked angry and distant, as if they had not been walking all morning through the woods, as if the old man had not been teaching him all those things about spiders and feathers and roots. What was more, Milan was hungry. He wanted to sit down in the warm sunshine and eat his sandwiches and put his ear to the ground to try and hear the marching of the ants in their subterranean tunnels. What if the old man had forgotten about lunch? Would he get angrier if Milan asked, and his mother so far away in the flat and maybe still asleep? Milan's hunger overcame his caution.

'I'm hungry. Can we have lunch now?'

Dr Cerny dropped the pine cone with relief. 'Of course. What a good idea. Where shall we sit? Over there in the sun? All right.'

Hana woke abruptly in the late morning to find herself alone in the bed and sensed, from the stillness of the air, that there was no one else in the flat. All the same, she sat up and called out, 'Milan?'

She felt heavy-headed and breathed deeply through her nose. The fetid smell of the doctor's old cat nauseated her and she ran to the kitchen for a glass of water. Perhaps they had just popped out for something. Perhaps Dr Cerny was taking Milan round the town square, poor kid. She could go out and meet them. But what if they were not there and came back while she was out? Milan wouldn't know where she was. He might panic and think she had disappeared. Of course, she could always leave them a note to say . . . Maybe it would be better to think about making them all some lunch instead. It would have to be soup. She could use the noodles left over from last night.

The morning passed, then the afternoon, and Hana moved restlessly about the flat drinking coffee, smoking, eyeing the clock. Her stomach tightened as the shadows outside grew longer. There was no one in this town she remembered any more, no one who would remember her if she went out asking. They would all know the doctor, of course, but they would think her hysterical.

The saucer she had been using as an ashtray filled steadily and the room stank. She opened the window. The doctor disapproved of smoking.

Hand in hand they came into view as she stood in the window looking down the road, arms akimbo, her face sour. *They* hadn't left a note to say where they were going, to say they were going at all. They had disappeared, the doctor and her son, into the countryside where an old man might stumble and twist his ankle, and where the boy, in his anxiety to help, would be lost. Now she saw them coming, Dr Cerny with his purposeful gait, bending forward slightly from the waist, Milan's bony knees pushing out the knees of his jeans, hand in hand like two people for whom the contact is new, trying it out. They would be hungry, they would be expecting. She hurried to the kitchen to switch on the gas under the soup, and then to the front door, placing herself in the communal hall at the top of the stairwell as if her mood might be improved, or maybe provoked to further bitterness, if she could snatch from the stairwell the words they shared as they came up. She saw her outline dimly reflected in the glass panel on the door opposite – her hands on her hips, feet rooted.

Dr Cerny's measured voice was giving advice. 'Don't hold them so tight. You'll spoil your arrangement.'

Milan's response came in a voice cracked with dust and walking. 'Like this? Is that all right?'

As if they could feel the accusation in her eyes bearing down on them from above, they looked up together, and their upturned faces, flushed with triumph, changed, together, to uncertainty. The doctor had an expression of timidity that Hana had never seen and she was suddenly suffused with jealousy and the knowledge that these two had passed a day in which she had not been included; the knowledge too that the lines of her face, the corners of her mouth were about to sour their day, that she had no right to do it. Abruptly she swept back into the flat trying to pretend that she had only momentarily and fortuitously been on the landing, had not noticed them, so that when they slunk in she was laying the table unnaturally slowly with all the time in the world to spare.

She heard the doctor: 'Now take your shoes off outside and give me your coat. I'll hang it up. Go in and tell your mother what we've been doing. My goodness, something smells good.'

She must iron out her face. She took a deep breath, stretched a smile. 'Hallo!' In tones of pleasure and surprise. 'Well, and where have the two of you been all day?'

She had not managed quite to wipe away the traces of recrimination but Milan was presenting her with a scrunched bouquet of wild flowers, the doctor was holding out his hat piled with a jumble of mushrooms moist as the forest. She was not hungry but ate with them, her appetite growing with the appetites they had brought back. At the end of the meal Dr Cerny put his hands together.

'Thank you, my dear. That was delicious. Wasn't it?' He turned to her son.

'Yes. Thank you, Mummy.'

Again that stab of jealousy that Milan was following Dr Cerny's lead, as if he had no manners of his own. The doctor stood up and began clearing away the plates. Instantly Milan helped him.

'And now,' the doctor was saying, 'it's our turn to do some work. Your mother has been busy all day. We'll wash up. You can dry.'

Hana sat back and closed her eyes, her limbs sagging with exhaustion, from not sleeping before, from sleeping too long after. They were talking in the kitchen.

'Shall we do piano again?'

'Not tonight. Tonight we're all going to bed early.'

'But I'm not tired.'

'Yes, you are.'

'I'm not. Really I'm not.'

'Well, I am. I'm an old man. I can't stay awake as long as you children.'

She couldn't understand it. He had not been like this with Peter, he had been – she was sure – gruff or offhand or, quite simply, absent. She should be pleased, and in a way she was gratified that her own son had seemed to reach something in the doctor she had not known was there. But she was also anxious, fearful that Milan was being seduced, although by what and for what reason she couldn't tell. Again they stood before her, side by side, complacent with virtue for having washed up and expecting thanks. These two men, waiting and watching. Milan looked as if he could do with a bath but if she said so it might sound reproachful. Yet the child was so grimy.

'You need a bath.'

'Yes,' Dr Cerny reinforced. 'You do. I'll run it for you.'

'He can do it himself. He does at home.'

'Oh!' The old man whistled through his teeth to show how impressed he was. The whistle was feeble – which made Milan laugh. He shouldn't laugh, she thought, it was rude; but she wanted to laugh herself.

She closed her eyes again, aware that the doctor had sat down opposite her. No doubt he was examining her face and thinking what an awful sour mother she was. She peered at him through her lashes. He was asleep, short snoring breaths puffing out the flabby corner of his mouth where his head lolled against the side of the chair. It was true what he had said. He was old. It had been too much for him, this outing with an unfamiliar child.

'Will you and Grandad come and say goodnight?'

Grandad? Hana sat up suddenly, releasing from her armpits the sweat of the cooped-up kitchen. Is that what he asked Milan to call him, having driven his own son away and now supposing he could purloin hers? Just look at him, slumped in his chair, feigning innocence, removing himself from her rightful challenge by going to sleep. You could no more wake an old man than you could wake a baby.

Bolt upright on her chair, Hana felt an urge to shake the doctor awake, shake his flabby unconscious body and beard him with his treachery there and then, in front of Milan, who stood in his pyjamas, still pink from his bath, probably insufficiently dried under the arms, in the groin, between the toes. Where had he left his towel? He couldn't reach the hook. It must be lying on the floor in the bathroom. They were guests, after all. She got stiffly to her feet and went to tidy the bathroom.

Dr Cerny, with his closed eyes and his snoring, was not sleeping. But they had slept, he and the boy, in the patch of sunshine Milan had selected and been woken by the high-pitched calls of two very small girls. The bigger one was chasing the smaller, the smaller one shrieking but laughing and calling out, 'Help! Grandad! Help!' A man in his fifties had emerged from the woods, assured himself that there was no real emergency and returned to the shadows, walking with the characteristic stoop of the mushroom-picker. Milan had raised himself on his elbows and looked after the girls.

'I'm too old to play chase,' the doctor had said, thinking the boy missed his playmates. But Milan had turned his wistful gaze towards the man in the woods, shaping his lips round the word.

'Can we pick mushrooms too, Grandad?'

'Do you like mushrooms?'

'No, but I like picking them. Mum loves them.'

'And what are we to put them in?'

111

'In your hat.'

His hat would smell of moss and mushrooms for weeks and he didn't have another. He let the boy search, running from tree to tree, with the promise that he would touch nothing until the doctor had verified its wholesomeness.

'Over here, Grandad, quick!' – as if his find might disappear under the leaf mould.

'Yes, that one's all right. It's a good one. It's called boletus. Will you remember that?'

'Yes. It's called boletus. Look, Grandad. There's another one. Is that all right too?' Grandad. Every time he said the word he glanced up waiting for the old man to acknowledge the name or rebuff it. And because Dr Cerny did neither Milan concluded that a tacit acceptance had gained him a relative.

Hana picked up Milan's towel, shook it out with a bellicose crack and hung it on its hook. She gathered his small items of clothing, filled the basin and put them in to soak; bent over the bathtub and scrubbed it round. She thought, as she was made to think so often when she washed out Milan's clothes, about Lukas, who had never seen the succession of underpants, T-shirts and trousers that his son had been sent and subsequently outgrown. She thought of Lukas more often when she handled Milan's clothes than she did when she handled the boy himself. There seemed to her to be something especially poignant about small empty garments, the faint brown smear in the under-pants, the socks rolled into balls on the floor where he had sat down to pull them off. Had she known where Lukas lived she would have sent him one of these socks in the post – she had never brought herself to send a communication in words – as if to say, 'Look, this is the size of your son's foot. Soon it will be bigger.' Such a package would cause dissent. His wife, whom she had never seen, who had so coolly snaffled Lukas at the eleventh hour, would look at the small grey sock, stretch it, smooth it out, measure it against her hand and ask her hus-band, 'Lukas, what does this mean?'

Dr Cerny was right. The older Milan grew, the more she felt he needed a father. She needed a father for him, preferably his own; but not for the reasons people supposed. She was strong. He was featherlight. She could lift him and swing him on to her shoulders the way Josef hoisted his lads. But Milan's father would not be as bluff and heavy-elbowed as Josef, who coun-

112

tered arguments with the barrel of his chest and liked his sons best when their voices were raucous with shouting, when they fell out of the neighbour's apple tree and had to be chastised to satisfy neighbourly relations. He would not be a father like her own, carving puppets when he should have been stacking logs and weeping because he found his children too beautiful. Nor would he be the father Dr Cerny had been, with his cross-referenced library, his facts and his certainties. With these three men, Hana had run out of fathers whom Lukas would not resemble; but she could not construct a better model. In her imagination, such as it was, Lukas sat perpetually cross-legged with the light behind his eyes and the sun in his hair, with their child cross-legged opposite him, and only played his guitar. It would not do. It would have to.

She rubbed the sweat-matted toes of Milan's socks and wrinkled her nose at the rank smell of wet wool. All very well, these hand-knitted best-quality gifts Nora bestowed on her, but they were the devil to wash. What she would have liked most at that moment was to be with Alena on the concrete veranda with a cup of coffee, Alena with her beer, to tell her finally about the secret of Milan's conception.

All the more reason, then, to wonder, as Hana herself wondered later, why she should have chosen to unburden herself to Dr Cerny, who had not even asked, who would not have dared to be so blunt a second time. It was not the single tiny glass of slivovitz they drank as a nightcap, for though no great drinker she would surely not be rendered so light-headed and careless by a thimbleful of spirits, nor by the wave of sentimentality brought on by the size of Milan's socks. Perhaps the years of self-restraint were beginning to tell. You can keep a secret only so long.

She came into the sitting-room drying her hands on her skirt, rubbing the chafed skin of too much washing, plumped herself down heavily and sighed, 'Hooo!', like the descending arm of an arc, a sound that called for someone else's appreciation of her labours.

Dr Cerny made an offer. 'I think, maybe, a small drink would do us no harm. What do you say? It's been a long day.'

That last he immediately regretted. It sounded as if he considered his outing with Milan had been a chore to be endured when the very opposite was the case; but Hana appeared not to have noticed. She sat back on the settee, her muscled legs splayed, shamelessly, he thought, then bit back the thought. Her eyes were closed but she held out her hand for the glass as if she were accustomed to alcohol before bedtime. Her fingers closed clumsily on the tiny glass, expecting something more substantial. Dr Cerny pecked a sip and was alarmed when Hana downed her drink in one.

'Another?' He unscrewed the top, hoping she would refuse, and was rewarded.

'No thanks.' She pulled her legs together and sat up. 'I have to tell you about Milan's father.' This was not the way she had planned it, but she had anyway determined that she would not visit Merunkov again. 'It was no accident. Milan was the child I wanted by the father I wanted.'

Dr Cerny did not mean to sound dry. 'And the father was less enthusiastic?' He'd come across a few like that in his time.

Hana blushed. 'There were . . . He had other commitments. As a matter of fact, it probably wouldn't have worked out. He had so much to do. He was so famous. You see' – she leaned forward, twirling her empty glass between the pads of her palms, realising defiantly that her lover's name would be anathema to the old man – 'he was the singer, Lukas Vratka.' There, Grandad, what do you think of that?

The doctor sipped again and took a deep breath. 'I'm sorry,' he said, 'I've never heard of him.'

But what a mistake, what ignorance not to know what he most wanted to understand. The voice or the face? The face or the voice? The one would lead to the other and both to the man. Dr Cerny carried this question with him as he tapped the unseasonally clogged chest of a strawberry-haired five-year-old girl, Marie, youngest daughter of the Mlynar family who had wanted sons.

'Don't say it's antibiotics again, please, doctor. I couldn't stand it.'

'I wonder,' said Dr Cerny, listening instead to the alternatives pulsing in his head. The face, presumably, would explain Hana's foolish passion. And the voice?

Mrs Mlynarova was totting up the cost of another fourteen days of penicillin if the pharmacy had run short again and she had to bribe it out of them. Perhaps, just this once, the doctor would give her the medicine direct. Everybody knew he was on the level, correct as the Pope on Good Friday. But of course that was why he sent them all with their prescriptions to the pharmacy. Probably didn't keep any medicine himself. If you don't hold what people want they can't keep you sweet, or twist your arm. He hadn't answered her question. Didn't he know? The doctor was supposed to know. He always knew, and told you straight out, and gave you a lecture to go with it – 'Three days in bed to deal with the fever, three days at home after that and see she wears a hat outdoors from the first of October. And stop your smoking.'

Dr Cerny looked up from the little girl's heaving chest, taut as a drum of water, and met the perplexed but uncomplaining gaze of the mother. The face. Mrs Mlynarova's face was wide at the cheekbones and wide again at the jaw, the bones fudged by motherhood, lines of disgruntlement in the twin pouches sagging at the corners of her lips like a tiny set of scales. Her large thighs threatened to force her knees apart but she willed them to remain together and won the day. Doctors were as may be, but a man was a man. She was looking at him with a face puckered in anxiety. And well she might.

'No,' he said firmly. 'No antibiotics. I'm afraid Marie has asthma. But don't you worry. We'll see to all that.' If only the woman wouldn't smoke so much. No wonder the child was wheezy. You could hear thirty a day on her mother's larynx, the dry hoarse huskiness that cabaret singers used to affect, like sand sliding off a tin roof. He remembered his father-in-law in England offering him a cheroot, wartime contraband, patting him on the shoulder, enjoying his English height and advising him, 'That voice in a man is brandy and cigars. In a woman, it's trouble. Stay away.' His father-in-law had chuckled, thinking the earnest, balding medical student hadn't understood. But Dr Cerny had understood and he had flinched. Could a voice be dangerous, not for what it represented but in itself? Might Hana have been so woefully entrapped by the sound of a voice? Unmindful of Mrs Mlynarova, who sat on waiting to be told to leave, Dr Cerny closed his eyes, hoping to retrieve in the caverns of his head the resonance of such a voice, but could not recall ever having been so entranced.

Faces are photographed, and this one had, apparently, been famous. Perhaps it still was. Therefore it would be found in a magazine, which would be held in the library. He opened his eyes to find Mrs Mlynarova still sitting patiently with her small, wheezing daughter on her knee. The child, who had not said a word, was staring at him fixedly with round, unblinking eyes. He felt uncomfortable.

'Yes, yes,' he said testily, as if in answer to a foolish question. 'As I said, Monday's the day. Bring her to the clinic on Monday. They'll see to everything. My colleague, Dr Roztomil, will be informed. You'll be in the best of hands. He's the consultant.'

Dr Cerny packed his bag and looked at his watch. Roztomil was likely to be at the Moscow Coffee House at this very moment, expecting him, without a doubt. The chess set would be laid out, all prepared, with the previous week's closing positions restored, ready for them to continue their game. It was tempting. Roztomil might already have downed his first cup of well-sugared coffee, and the doctor, imagining the taste, sucked his tongue. He felt inclined to delay his visit to the library, almost; he reproved himself, as if he were afraid of what he might discover there. Would it not be easier to forget the whole business and go home to Hana's soup and an evening stroll with the boy, stopping off on the way for a swift game of chess? He pictured himself efficiently manipulating Roztomil into defeat, and paused, surprised by a spasm of uneasiness. Roztomil was his junior by some twenty years, an indifferent doctor, to be honest, but at the top of the ladder. He was on every committee, almost a decision-maker at this local level, a jovial man who was enjoying every minute of his life. He was well connected. They said no one had better lines of communication to the upper echelons; Roztomil made a point of saying so himself. Dr Cerny smiled inwardly. No. For some reason that was not clear to him he would do without the game of chess this week. Roztomil would be disappointed but he would understand.

His bag tucked under his arm, Dr Cerny made his way, with deliberate steps, to the town square and the library. The librarian, who was absorbed in sucking her cuticles, acknowledged his arrival with the edge of one eyebrow. But when he dallied at her table, gauche as a schoolboy, instead of going to his usual seat, she sensed she might be required to exert herself and huffily removed her fingers from her mouth.

'Doctor?'

He bent low over the table, stiff-backed, like a Pole over a lady's hand, and whispered. The doctor always obeyed the rules.

'Sorry? What do you need?'

'Magazines. Music magazines.'

116

'What music magazines?'

'What the young people read.'

What the young people read! Perhaps he was preparing one of those lectures of his on hygiene – but of the spirit this time. 'You'll be wanting *Melody*. Bottom shelf over there.' She indicated the direction with her long nose and reinserted her fingers.

Dr Cerny tiptoed across, lowered himself to the floor one knee at a time and found himself in an attitude of prayer in front of a twelve-volume encyclopaedia of national agricultural practice. He restrained the impulse to take out the first volume, 1945–1948, subtitled 'An Analysis of Primitive Praxis and Paths to Modern Reconstruction'.

'Lower,' mumbled the librarian. 'Bottom shelf, I said. Should I help you?' She was manifestly reluctant. The doctor shook his head, finger on his lips, and bent lower.

In a cardboard box were the most recent editions of the youth magazines, *Young Front*, *Young World* and *Melody*, which was closely printed in three columns, with many photographs. A long-haired sultry girl looked back over her shoulder. A quartet of young men, two standing, two kneeling, all with their arms spread wide in a gesture of triumph, invited applause like circus acrobats who have just leapt to safety from one another's shoulders. Peeping over forearms folded across the back of a chair and smiling winsomely was the portrait of that dark-haired young man whose baritone vibrato was the radio stations' favourite. There he was again on the adjacent page, pressing his right cheek against the dimpled left cheek of a curly-haired toddler in ribbons; and again overleaf, down on one knee as if proposing, holding the paws of a small and astonished dog. But no Vratka

Carefully Dr Cerny restored *Melody* to its place and hauled himself up. His knees were aching. He returned to the librarian's table, embarrassed and therefore truculent.

'Haven't you any other editions?'

'They're filed in the back.' The long nose jerked over her shoulder. 'Was there anything particular you wanted?'

'No, no. I just wanted to look through. I'm not sure.'

'They go back three or four years, doctor. I can't get them all out. I mean, can you imagine!'

'No, of course not, you're quite right. I shouldn't have troubled you.'

'No trouble, doctor. Aren't you stopping today?' For Dr Cerny was already making his way out, knees clicking, a thwarted man.

Out on the pavement again he looked across the square, with its red and white benches and its flagpole, to the Moscow Coffee House and the record shop opposite. He had failed so far to find the face but the voice remained. He would try the record shop.

'Brahms, doctor? Bizet?' The assistant smiled to see him, colourful in her wide skirt.

'No, thank you. I was wondering what you have of Lukas Vratka.'

The assistant shrank back, her hands to her mouth. Then she stepped sharply forward and leaned across the counter to hiss that she had never heard of any such singer and therefore he could not have any records to his name. And was the doctor trying to lose her her job?

Dr Cerny stood quite still. What sort of man was this to whom Hana had given herself, who had fathered her son? Some sort of criminal, some sort of social parasite, an outcast whom it had been deemed necessary to remove from memory? He did not doubt it. The shop assistant's pinched nostrils, her hands over her mouth, told him so. His own mouth was dry. There was a rod of icy emptiness in his chest, sensations he thought he had consigned to the past, when you never knew and anyone any time . . . But not these days. These days the only people who should be afraid of being put away were the ones who deserved it. They had transgressed. Common thieves, embezzlers, murderers, slanderers. His heart sank. Hana had taken a slanderer to bed knowing him for what he was, approving of him for what he was. The slanderer's daughter come full circle, seeking out her own kind. And between them, the slanderer's daughter and her slanderer lover, they had made that sweet, timid, earnest boy who called him Grandad. But Milan looked like Honza, Hana's younger brother and the old slanderer's son. Dr Cerny frowned. He did not know what to think. He did not know what to do.

'Doctor?' He looked up. The shop assistant was leaning across the counter again. The shop was empty but she whispered.

'Yes?'

'Lukas Vratka.'

'What about him?'

'He isn't here any more.'

'What do you mean, "here"?'

118

'He ran away to the West. London, they said.'

'Who said?'

The shop assistant flushed. 'Oh, I just heard it . . . Someone told me.'

The doctor scowled. 'You shouldn't get involved with people like that.'

'Me?' The shop assistant was indignant at the injustice. 'I'm not involved. I'm not the one who's asking.'

'Nevertheless,' said Dr Cerny firmly, 'be sure you take my advice. Have nothing to do with that gentleman at all. Do as I do.' And he made his way with measured and dignified steps from the shop.

So what now? Clearly Hana was not aware that her lover had run out on her a second time. Was he to tell her? Should he take her to one side and advise her to put her relations with Vratka behind her, for her own sake, for reasons of prudence and, with both those in mind, above all for the sake of the poor child? Thank all the powers that arrange these things that Milan resembled only his uncle, whose standing in Prague made him a man well worth resembling. Better that Milan should never learn who his father was. He must at all costs be protected from that. And Dr Cerny was suffused with a longing for the strength and the skill, neither of which he had, to keep the boy safe and pure, uncontaminated by his father. You must not blame the boy. All that belonged to the past.

But how could she? A man like that. The sneering generation who laughed between their fingers at their parents' work. Feet on the table. Cigarette ash on the floor, trousers on the floor. Dr Cerny shuddered.

'So that's where you are!' A loud voice battered his ear, an energetic arm pressed on his shoulder. Roztomil.

'Yes, good day. I do apologise. I was on my way home. I'm expected there.'

'I know. The young lady. The Mayor told me. I realised you wouldn't be coming by this week. Been buying records, have you?'

'No, no. Not today. I was just asking . . . looking.'

'I envy you your musical understanding, you know that, Cerny? I've never been able to understand classical music. I prefer the "pops", if I'm honest. But I daresay that's not your taste, is it?'

'Not really.' Dr Cerny smiled self-deprecatingly. 'Well, look, I must get back, it's getting late.'

'Of course. You mustn't spoil a good dinner, eh? I'll see you next week, won't I?'

'Without fail.'

As he set off up the square Dr Cerny imagined he saw, from the corner of his eye, Roztomil entering the record shop.

Hana's evening soup and dumplings were not able to remove from the doctor's face an expression of perplexity and disquiet. She concluded that he had had an especially trying day with patients, about whose parents he never ceased to complain. He had quite lost his manners, stared at Milan, mumbled to himself, had shaken his head so that she thought senility was not far away. Her own mood was scarcely better, for it had been as she had feared. Lukas's name had been given into the ears least deserving to hear it. She felt she had thrown it away. In between them sat Milan, looking at his mother, looking at 'Grandad' and wondering what had gone wrong.

'Are we going out this evening?'

Dr Cerny breathed once in and once out and patted the boy's hand. 'No,' he said, 'I'm afraid I still have work to do. Doctors are always busy, you know. But tomorrow, maybe tomorrow.'

Fifteen

Serve her right for thinking the old man had changed, for offering up her son as a balm for the old man's loneliness like a maggot on a fishing line, to be nibbled at and spat out again. She should have known better. She should have realised that the doctor could no more warm to another human being than he could bear to be deflected from his routine. He had been very polite, but manifestly on edge. He had not sat down. He had followed her about, touching his books. He had picked up an empty vase, run his hands round its base and set it down again, leaned in the doorway, rubbed his elbows and pretended he did not hear Milan asking to go out to the woods, asking for a piano lesson. Pretended. There was no other word for it. The message was unmistakable: they were no longer welcome. They were being requested to pack themselves off, go home, get out of his hair.

Hana was so enraged on Milan's account that she took it out on Milan. He must have been burdensome, pestering the old doctor, who would have wanted to rest in peace and quiet; children have to learn not to get on people's nerves. What made Milan think Dr Cerny wanted a small boy under his feet all day long asking questions and banging on the piano? Perhaps he had damaged it. Had he been hitting the keys too hard? He should have been more careful. A fine musician like the doctor couldn't be expected to tolerate all that thumping.

Milan, who never thought his mother was wrong, could not believe she was right. He hadn't thumped the piano. He had played so quietly that Grandad kept saying, 'What's that? A little mouse running up and down? I can hardly hear you.' And he hadn't been asking questions all the time. Grandad had come looking for him to tell him things, finger on his lips at dawn. How could his mother have known? She had been asleep. Yet her face was so angry, with the little lines growing out of her top lip, that he did not dare disagree but retreated, in confusion, into sleep, his thin face rigid in her lap, a slender hand shielding his eyes from the wall of sunlight that would dog the train all the way home.

Hana looked down on her son, racked with remorse. Poor kid. She should have said straight out that the doctor obviously didn't care to have them in his house any more. All she had done was to make the boy's hurt worse. She should have known. They ought to have stayed in Bytlice. The old man had tried to be friendly but it was beyond him, so let him stew in his grammar books and his reading lists and when the time came he would die alone and she wouldn't give a damn. It would be no more than he deserved for violating the innocent trust of a child.

But Hana was not a grudge-bearer, and the rocking of the train with its plangent rhythm dissolved the nub of her bitterness. Each landmark – the spa at Teplice where the railtrack ran beside the river, the chemical works at Prerov in its ochre smog, the strange formation of trees on the horizon which looked like men marching with haversacks and which she had pointed out to Honza when, first ejected by Dr Cerny, they had travelled this route to the care of Aunt Veronika – proclaimed that she was getting nearer home, her house on the hill, *her* house on the hill, where no one would bother them. They would do as they pleased. Milan would run down to collect the eggs and shout out the day's count to her even though she could not hear. He would not have to be quiet, and when it was dusk she would let him start the night in her bed so that he could doze off to the distant plunking of the tennis balls on the courts at the bottom of the garden.

She was not disappointed. Stooped like one of those trees under the weight of her haversack, and trailing Milan still tousled and heavy-headed from his prolonged sleep of refuge, Hana allowed her feet to lead her home. As the rutted path began its steepest ascent she stopped automatically to let Milan catch his breath. They always paused here, had done ever since, aged four, he had baulked at the climb and burst out crying. 'It's not fair,' he had wailed. 'Why do we have to live so high up?' 'Because we're special. We're mountaineers.' 'But I don't want to be a mountaineer. I want to live down there' – turning and pointing back down the path towards the village. 'But think. It's all grey and ugly down there and all green and lovely up at the top.' Which, once he had been cajoled to the summit, Milan acknowledged. Ever since then, therefore, they would pause at the threshold of the most arduous section of the hill to glance back at the dreary complex below, before setting their noses to the task of completing their climb.

Milan's legs, grown, strengthened and accustomed, no longer complained. Hana's were beginning to. But the pause, sanctioned by time rather than need, was automatic, and this time Hana did not look down to the village but threw back her head and gazed between the arch of leaves to the fretwork of sky. Her sky. Even the air smelt different. Then they lugged their way to the top, greeted here and there by the elderly men and women tending their vegetables in the benevolent warmth of early evening. 'That cockerel of yours. Done you proud. Been looking after the place for you. Little lad looks well. Had a good time, have you?' In her garden, Hana was immediately surrounded by her chickens, which came racing with frenzied, extended steps, screeching from under the trees, expecting a handful of something good to eat.

Milan scampered off to find the Frantiseks – had found them, as she could hear from the high-pitched whooping that rose from the valley. She threw open the windows to let in the smell of the drying hay the Novaks had cut for their goat. There was laughter and sardonic applause from the tennis courts, and nowhere in the world that she would rather be. Never a loner by choice, Hana left her luggage on the floor and ran down the hill to share her exhilaration with Alena, who should be, if all was to be according to plan, sunning herself on Josef's concrete veranda.

Alena was indeed stretched out in the last light of evening, a loose white T-shirt over her bikini, beer glass to hand. She laughed with pleasure as Hana appeared round the corner of the veranda, already sharing the joke.

'I've heard all about it. Grandad says this and Grandad says that and this is how you hold your hands to play the piano' – she held her fingers out like claws – 'and you fry boletus like steak and pine cones grow in spirals. Did you enjoy yourself too?'

Hana pulled a face. 'Kids don't know anything. They only see what they want to. Yeah, it was all right.' From which Alena concluded that the visit had not been without its difficulties and that her friend's mood was fragile.

'I'll make you a coffee.'

'Thanks. Where's Josef?'

Now the grimace was reproduced on Alena's features, the familiar fleeting scowl of humiliation and contempt. So Josef was out on the razzle, boozing with his mates, or humping with some curvy girl who would like him for his curling beard, for the booming resonance of his voice. So there was to be no family gossip.

The women sat and sipped, looked out across Josef's immaculate garden, the vegetables heavy with the season, the northern wall of the outhouse stacked to the roof with logs all chopped to a single size, the chickens crooning as they minced fastidiously in the long grass. One of those silences that had tempted Hana to revelation in the past.

'Tell you what, though,' said Alena, sitting up excited, holding her glass under her bottom lip. 'You'll never guess who's run off to the West. Well?'

'Who has?'

'Lukas Vratka!'

'Don't be stupid.' Hana was snapping, shrewish. Alena stared at her friend's twisted face. 'Who told you?'

'I heard it on the Voice of America. And the BBC.'

Damn. Hana cursed inwardly. She had never been bothered with all that; it hadn't seemed worth it. 'What did they say? Where has he gone?'

'London.'

'What about his wife?'

'No. Not her. They didn't get on.'

Glory be to God. Hana, finding she had clasped her hands together against her breasts, released them. Out of the corner of her eye she espied Milan running behind the aviary.

'For God's sake, child, have you any idea what the time is? You should be in bed.'

She gathered him up, protesting and baffled for the second time that day, and fled. Behind her, she knew, stood Alena on the veranda, a sturdy son on either side, a trio with their mouths ajar.

Never had Milan been pitched into bed with such speed and so little attention to the cleanliness of his teeth, no flannel passed between his buttocks, everything allowed, everything overlooked. But he was thirsty. Yes, yes. Take a drink up to bed. Your bed? Yes, if he wanted, but quickly. So try a little more. Can I play Lego? Yes, why not. Go on. Play with it upstairs.

And then such a frantic pressing of buttons, twisting of the dial, the heavy transistor held against her stomach at an angle of 45 degrees. She span on her heels facing this way and that, extended the aerial as far as it would go, and all the world's chatter spat and crackled gobs of sport and music and ministerial meetings. Oh God, help me. Where is London? Her hands were sweating. Pull yourself together. Method. She needed method. One metre band at a time. Then she had it, a woman's voice calling her in Czech through cotton wool, so far away. England was so far away. 'This is London. And we'll be on the air again tomorrow morning at five and six, and again at five thirty and eight in the evening, on the 25, 31 and 49 metre bands. Until then, we wish you goodnight.'

Since then Hana had become expert. She knew that in the early morning she had to place the transistor on the stool by the window in the bathroom, at a right angle to the window, best of all if she stood just south-west of it. In the afternoon the signal was stronger but she had to take her radio to the entrance that led down to the boiler. At night, the hour of most convenient listening when Milan was asleep, the voices wavered, at times sucked away altogether, overlaid with a competing clamour that sounded Italian, sometimes Dutch. She had come to admire the British Prime Minister and the American President, for they were steadfast in their distrust where others prevaricated. She had discovered that the English had unemployment after all, even though she had tossed aside her daily newspaper for saying so. There had been only four mentions of Lukas's name. Twice she heard him speak, twice she heard him sing. All four appearances were in the very early days, just after his defection. Concerts were planned. A visit to the Netherlands and to America: someone was arranging the money. She had strained so hard to hear his voice she had not understood what he was saying, but was not distressed. She needed only to hear him. And so she kept listening, a new and exceptionally loyal listener whose avid attention had been unrewarded. She had been trying to learn English from the daily lessons for foreigners, as if the few embarrassed words she essayed in the empty room might bring her closer; as if Lukas might sense her effort, and be touched by it.

Milan started school without enjoying it, but he was no complainer. He sat perfectly still and upright, chanting the numbers and letters written on the board. He copied out pictures, covered the pages of his exercise book with pinnacled waves and figures of eight. Still he made no complaint. Milan had a goal. He must learn to write. He did not know which he longed for more, the ability to write or to read. It was not the picture books with their ponderous and sentimental little rhymes that spurred him on, nor the promise of being able to read for himself the stories that Hana read him at bedtime. Milan's determination stemmed from a suspicion (of which he was ashamed) that his mother was not on the level with him.

When the first letter arrived from Merunkov she had called out to him, 'Milan, guess what? You've got a letter.' She had looked at the postmark and frowned but by then it had been too late. 'Read it to me, read it now,' he had insisted. And listlessly, crossing and uncrossing her legs to show her boredom, she had obeyed. The letter said he was missed. It said: 'Do you remember our walk in the woods when you filled my hat with mushrooms? The hat still smells of them and whenever I put it on I think of you holding my hand, both of us slipping in the mud, me because I am old and clumsy and you because you were wearing those silly shoes you like so much.' The cat was no company, the letter complained. All she did was sleep all day. The letter requested a reply and it was signed 'Grandad'. 'Jesus Christ!' said Hana. She folded the paper smartly in four and shoved it back into its envelope.

Milan had taken it from her and gone upstairs to pick out the letters he knew. The last word he could read because he knew what it said. He copied it out. How could he possibly reply? In the end he had drawn a picture, his best, of a house on a hill. It was so good that he wanted to show it off to his mother. In one corner he had written 'Grandad'. When he brought the picture down he put his thumb over that corner. He felt she did not want him to send things to the old man but he did not know why and thought she would not tell him. But she had removed his thumb and said, 'And how would you post it? You can't write the address by yourself yet, can you?' She had addressed the envelope. He had put in the picture, and that

126

evening, using the little torch sent by the lady in England, he had traced the address on to a separate piece of paper and hidden it under the Lego windmill. That had made him feel bad because he realised he was doing something that would upset his mother, and what would upset her would not be the tracing but the secrecy.

There had been an answer to his picture. Grandad had said he liked it although he was afraid the house might slide off down the hill it was leaning over so much. When she read that bit, his mother had stopped and said, 'Silly pompous old fool!', and put the letter down. Milan had had to plead with her to finish. Grandad asked for more pictures and wanted to know if he was doing all his homework properly so that they could all be proud of him. His mother had said, 'Who the hell does he think he is?' Grandad told him to practise his finger exercises on the table so that next time he came to Merunkov he would play the piano even better. And Hana had said, 'What next time?' It was this that prompted Milan to struggle so hard to learn to read. He knew that his mother read him every letter that came. But how could he be certain that she read him every word? What if Grandad had actually invited them again? If his mother didn't want to go, she could stay at home. He wouldn't be afraid to be by himself on the bus. His Uncle Honza had been only seven and his mother ten when they had travelled from Merunkov to Prague to live with their old Aunt Veronika. Anyway, Grandad would meet him at the bus station.

But Hana, who had scrupulously read every single word – parodying the doctor's fastidious tone – dreaded the arrival of a letter that might contain such an invitation. As the weeks went by she helped him write out his replies and when he made a mistake told him to copy out his letters all over again, in spite of herself, not wanting anyone to be able to find fault with her son. But sometimes, when she watched Milan, fingers clamped tight around his pencil, scratching out his infantile message, she was speared by that old jealousy and hated herself that she could not bear to see so much effort go into an expression of love for someone else.

It was a strange winter – dark and somnolent without snow, sending Milan to his bed. Hana dipped into Nora's allowance and laid in a stock of antibiotics. She closed her doors and felt, within the bounds of this small world that was all hers, almost perfectly in control. Dr Cerny wrote. Why had he not heard from the boy? Was he ill? And wrote again, a full page of instructions that annoyed her for the implication that she might not do the right thing but for the unsought advice, and astonished her by its tone. How often had she heard the doctor scoff at what he called 'those panicking mothers' who fancied they saw an incipient pneumonia in the first runny nose? But here he was, sounding nearly frantic through the closely written page. Cold compresses. Warm soups. Could she possibly procure an orange or two from someone? She must surely try. An even temperature. No draughts. Keep him in bed for at least three days after the fever dropped. Did she, perhaps, need an expert opinion from a paediatrician? He could, for example, take the night bus, leaving at three in the morning. That could be the answer – some of the doctors nowadays were lacking in experience and, though he should not say so, commitment. The sort of thing that comes with age, he dared say. 'Thank you, no,' she wrote back, a little more tartly than she intended. She was coping quite adequately. She was perfectly in control.

Hard on the heels of Dr Cerny's letter came a packet from Nora, as if vying for her attention, Hana thought wryly. She took the parcel up to Milan, who lay damp and sweating under the soft mound of his feather-bed. Milan squeezed the parcel. It was soft – clothes. But what clothes? Nora's gifts were sometimes peculiar. Two summers before she had sent him a pair of football boots three sizes too large, the studs grey with dried English mud. Hana had sniffed the mud curiously and put the boots by. 'You'll grow into them.' But Milan was no footballer and the Frantiseks had been the lucky ones. Once she had sent an 'outfit' for Hana, deep mauve and glossy as a cat in the sun. It had tassels hanging around the hem like a lampshade and a hip-hugging low-slung waist. Hana had modelled it in front of Alena, then Alena had modelled it for Hana, and both women had hooted with laughter, jutting out their hips and running their fingers through their hair and along their pouting lips. Alena wondered where it might have been bought. Hana, the wiser, suspected Nora had made it from the swathes of one of her nightdresses.

The present parcel contained a diminutive pair of swimming trunks with 'Speedo' sewn into the side and a white Adidas T-shirt with a faint pink stain on the front where some small child had once dribbled strawberry ice-cream. Hana held the garments up, looked out of the window at the oozing grey light of winter and burst out laughing. Milan, disappointed at first, laughed because she laughed, and laughed so much that he began coughing so that Hana had to run down for a wet face flannel to lay across his forehead. 'When you're better,' she said, 'you'll wear them in the summer and everybody will be jealous.' Later she found a torn fragment of paper on the floor fastened to a five-pound note with a safety-pin. 'For the child' was scrawled in Nora's looping hand. Hana pocketed the note in silence, amazed at Nora's foolishness and at the safe arrival of the money.

The evening moments were Milan's favourite, when he was drowsy and there was no longer any reason why his mother should leave the house. He lay in her bed with only the little light on while she sat next to him propped up on her pillows and held his hand. They didn't talk and Milan sometimes wondered what she thought about. Tonight, with the regular rubbing back and forth of her thumb on his wrist, he hovered near sleep, aware at moments of the pressure of her thumb, of his warmth, of how strange his feet felt, light and enormous as if they did not belong to him. Sometimes he heard the distant cough of a fox in the plantation behind the house and, as always, felt a pang of pity for any creature that called with such desperation. He would write to Grandad tomorrow, all by himself, and address the envelope too. Only he would have to ask his mother to post it because he knew, the fever having abated only the day before, that it would be another six days before she would allow him out. He had protested, and with a strange smile on her face she had replied, 'Grandad said you were to stay in bed', so he had had to give in.

Stroking the boy's wrist hypnotised Hana too, so that she forgot it was her thumb moving so rhythmically and methodically on the boy's soft, damp skin. She thought of the doctor bolt upright, with his stinking cat on his lap, writing his letters on the table where they ate, sitting as he must with his back to the door and facing his glass-fronted bookshelves. She remembered, because she could not forget it, the two deep lines of anger like the downturned wings of a swallow, etched on either side of his mouth; anger when Nora had come hallooing along the road in triumph, trailing the pharmacist's outcast children; anger again when he returned from prison and found the children still there, living not camping, making every pretence of being permanent. But Hana had known what it had somehow been possible for Honza to ignore – that from the day of her

129

mother's death there would be no more permanence until she was in a position to create it for herself. Now she had done it. It was in this room with her, in this fuggy silence as she held the slender wrist of her sleeping son, lying on her bed, with her pillows, her furniture around her. Milan's illness was even a part of that permanence, as solid and expected as the snows that had failed to arrive. She relied on no one any more. But, as she shifted her weight warily, Nora's five-pound note crackled in her pocket, rebuking her for that brief arrogant supposition. Where would you be without the pull of foreign currency? How would you get the medicines for your son without that? 'I would manage,' Hana retorted, and immediately doubted it. Without Josef and the job he had arranged for her, without Nora and her allowance, how much independence would she have, how much permanence? She would manage. Everyone did. No one disappeared for want of food or shelter. It wasn't allowed.

Hana opened her eyes and asked herself why she was even thinking along these lines. There was no reason to suppose that she could lose her job or that Nora would withdraw her support. Nora was solid. She rested on Nora, Nora who had made strange flat English biscuits from oats stuck together with something sticky, so hard that you could not bite them. 'They is so in England,' she had maintained in her faltering Czech, gingerly grinding at one of them with her front teeth like a horse scraping at the bark of a tree, and no one had believed her. Hana remembered Nora appearing without warning at the Town Hall on the day of a neighbour's wedding party, festooned like a Turkish tent, whooping like a Red Indian and flinging handfuls of rice over the heads of the newly-weds, who shrank from her. A crowd had gathered, drawn by the outlandish noises, and it was Hana, aged nine and crimson with embarrassment, who had had to restrain her and lead her away. Later Hana had gone back and tried to pick up the precious grains from the pavement, but someone had got there before her. She had burst into tears of fury and frustration at the waste; how could any adult be so stupid? But now, thirty years on with a full bag of rice in her kitchen and more besides, she thought, for the first time, that there had been something necessary in that foolhardy and flamboyant gesture, as if Nora, with her husband in prison and burdened by the two extra children, had been protesting against the humiliation of mere survival.

In her childish rage, out there on the town square feeling

about among the cobbles, Hana had recognised her dependence on a woman who was surely demented. This woman had just sent some extra money, in cash, pinned to a scrap of paper, in the post for anyone to find. Did she have so much money that she didn't care if some of it went missing, or so little that, like the rice, she threw it to the winds to ward off despair? And with a sudden flash of remorse Hana realised she had never before questioned Nora's ability to provide for her, never once asked herself how Nora was living in London. London! Hana looked at her watch and slithered away from Milan, down the stairs to her radio. Superstition persuaded her that the day she failed to listen would be the one occasion they would again broadcast Lukas's voice.

It was a perfectly still night. Maybe the wilful soundwaves would remain steady for once and she would be able to hear. She took up her position with the radio wedged against her hip-bone, the aerial extended, and rotated on her heels. She had it! The distant voice was saying, '. . . since the deletion of all his records by Supraphon any remaining records are bound to become collectors' items. Among them, of course, songs like this one.'

Hana clasped her radio more tightly, bending her head to its tinny loudspeaker. A muted opening phrase on his guitar, a murmur in the background and applause like a crackle of interference: some recording of a live performance and the audience saluting a favourite song. She couldn't hear well enough, the chords were so quiet.

She bent her head lower still and heard that distant audience laughing in shame and recognition, as if they were enjoying a punishment they themselves had solicited: that song they always applauded in anticipation, knowing what they would get, not a folk-song but one of Lukas's own. It told the tale of an unnamed people somewhere far away who had traded their good king for a bad one because the bad one promised them gold, silver, wine and merry weddings – but only so long as they would for ever cry the king's name aloud on his birthday, ask no questions and give to him their wise men, who had rent their hair and shouted desperate prophecies.

It seemed so strange that this faraway song, whose words she could hear only because she knew them by heart anyway, was crackling and spluttering through the box she clutched against her midriff. That quite possibly, lost in the indistinguishable drone of that sometime audience, was her own voice,

131

her own embarrassed laughter and applause, that she too had exchanged those knowing glances with the people on either side of her, people whom she had never met before but who shared an experience and an understanding of it, and therefore needed no introduction.

Then the radio voice came back. 'Lukas Vratka there, with a song that we all know only too well, "The People's Pact". Now, according to our correspondent in Prague, samizdat versions of all Vratka's songs are being circulated, words and music, following the deletion of his records and the removal from the shops of any that were left. Well, Lukas Vratka is in the studio with me now. Tell me, what do you make of what's going on? It doesn't seem much of a surprise, does it?'

And then it came, that low, almost mumbling voice, his tongue in her mouth, an arm round her shoulders, an arm round her hips.

'No, of course not. I'm rather flattered actually. It would have been a bit worrying if they'd left the records on the shelves. I'd have thought I'd got it wrong. It's good to know I've still got them jumping. And if my songs get around well enough, there'll be all sorts of kids singing them – probably better than I did.' Then suddenly there was that incongruous, inward giggle.

'And what are you working on now?'

'Well, I'm hoping . . .' But the sound faded, swept away in a roar like the cracking of branches in a storm. Hana shook the radio, twisted her body this way and that. Oh Jesus! She tried to retune but the station had gone, overlaid in the nightly clamour of the world's peoples gabbling at one another.

Hana sat down, her arms wrapped around the transistor, troubled by the distance and insubstantiality of Lukas's voice, troubled that it could, even so, set her genitals twitching, bring a tightness to the bridge of her nose, swell her throat. She was also disquieted by a sudden sensation of outrage which she tried to bat off but which kept returning like a mosquito to its chosen victim. The song she knew so well, the one they always cheered, that same song – artfully selected like a silver bullet and fired from London, with her in its sights, with everyone she knew, the Frantiseks, the Novaks, the postmistress, the delivery drivers, Milan, his teacher, each of them and all of them its intended target – no longer spoke of self-knowledge, regretted but confessed. Instead it seemed barbed with mockery, as if the singer no longer considered himself a participant. Yet when the song was written, sung, recorded, he had most certainly been one of them. She felt frightened that all over the country people were thinking as she was, and would be angered by Lukas and his success, doing so well over there, telling his people how to behave. She wanted to reach out to him, to warn him. Be careful, my love, it doesn't sound the same; can't you tell?

But what Lukas said, and how it sounded when he said it, began suddenly to matter rather less. A young man by the name of Ondrei Sedlak, aged only nineteen and with stars in his eyes for the departed Vratka, had been put in jail. Sedlak had appointed himself custodian and propagator of the forbidden canon by circulating the texts of the songs. Until then known only to those who knew him, he had been swept to the attention of the circle of people interested in such things, and therefore to prominence. Barely had he embarked on his covert enterprise than the authorities had done what they could to help him publicise his cause – and arrested him. Charged with disseminating material defamatory to the state, he was sentenced to an unusually lenient eighteen months' imprisonment which so upset the state prosecutor (that day embarrassed at having to attend court with an incomplete set of teeth because the laboratory assistant making his new ones had failed to show up for work) that he insisted on going to appeal to have the sentence increased. The foreign radio stations had not bothered to inform themselves about the state of the prosecutor's dentures and were unanimously hostile.

This further offended the prosecutor and he pressed his case with energy and a certain amount of involuntary whistling and spitting. His reward was notional. Ondrei Sedlak was given no more than an extra two months, but to the prosecutor, whose naked and sensitive stumps suffered most when he was forced to speak audibly, it was some consolation. The foreign radio stations buzzed in vociferous complaint, Lukas Vratka was much interviewed and, in repeated tones of contrition, expressed his dismay that his young and hitherto obscure admirer should be martyred on his account, and in his place. He urged whomsoever might be listening to do nothing foolish; but his appeal for restraint was the impetus for a petition for the release of Ondrei Sedlak.

Sixteen

Hana covered her hair in a scarf drawn tight over her cheek-bones and scattered flour with practised abandon over a large wooden board. Ranged around its edges were finely chopped hazelnuts, icing sugar, eggs from her excellent chickens and a bottle of vanilla essence. From the depths of her cupboard she had retrieved the box of biscuit-cutters. Christmas was approaching and, with a concentration greater than anyone's, Hana was baking for it. With her fingers tickling at the sugary dough she realised that her bottle of vanilla essence was almost empty. If she ran down to Alena's for more, her dough would spoil. This dilemma filled her mind so that she was unprepared when later that evening Tomas and Karel, neither of whom she had seen since the days of Lukas's concerts, tapped on her door and stepped straight into her kitchen.

She had cried out, 'Hallo!' and 'What brings you here?', before she noticed behind them a young man, almost still a child. Hana glanced at him and was disturbed by a sense of recognition, as if there were something about that face she had seen, and seen often. She put the thought aside.

'Come on in.' She stepped back and waved them through. 'I'll just make us some coffee. Go on, go on in.'

The young man, wiping his boots rigorously on the mat before stooping to unlace them, held out his hand; but his grey eyes were cool, almost unfriendly.

'Ivan Meloun.' He introduced himself stiffly. 'But this isn't a social visit.'

Karel laid a hand on the boy's arm. 'Ssh,' he soothed, 'We're not in a hurry. Don't be so impatient. Let's have some of Hana's coffee. I want some, and I bet Tomas does too.'

She didn't immediately understand what it was they wanted of her because she was preoccupied with a nagging distress that this year, for the first time, her Christmas biscuits would be less than perfect. Also, seeing what the passing years had done to the faces of her friends, she had glanced briefly into Aunt Veronika's antique mirror and glimpsed there hillocks and valleys which she had not noticed before. Tomas and Karel had come to the point too quickly, ignoring the niceties of catching up on old times, assuming too much. It had not crossed her mind that the people with the petition might be people she knew. It had not crossed her mind that the people called upon to sign it might be as ordinary as herself.

She grew flustered. She sat them side by side on Aunt Veronika's chaise-longue and fled back to the kitchen to prepare coffee, hospitality her pretext, her fingernails still ringed with dried dough. The biscuits, cooling on sheets of greaseproof paper, looked flawless: row upon row of identical crescents, flowers, circles, white, beige and cinnamon brown. She picked out one whose edge had crumbled and put it in her mouth. There was that initial crispness and then it melted, exactly as it should. Perhaps the slight lack of vanilla didn't really matter; with luck no one would notice because the texture was so good. She could not keep her eyes away from what she had produced, the immaculate result of her skill. She had begun the day's baking with enormous pleasure, certain of the outcome, suffused with a sense of well-being because of that certainty. Now her biscuits suddenly seemed all that was certain.

She selected three of each type, arranged them on a plate and dusted them with icing sugar. Next she put the plate on a tray, the cups of coffee on either side of the plate, then carried the tray out to those old friends. She laid three small crocheted mats on the inlaid table and placed the cups on the mats, careful of the polished surface.

'Please,' she said, gesturing towards the Christmas biscuits. 'I made them only today.' Pre-empting polite restraint, she added, 'There's masses more out there. You should see. I don't know why I made so many.'

Only Tomas and Karel sipped at their coffee, sitting side by side on the chaise-longue, each taking a fragile biscuit, eating it, hand cupped under chin, to protect Hana's fastidious housekeeping from crumbs. For a moment the exquisite little pastries absorbed them entirely. Scrupulously, recognising the intention in the selection of biscuits, they each ate precisely their share, and Hana thought how incongruous the diminutive biscuits looked, pincered by those large male fingers. Their companion stood impatiently by the window looking out.

'We only thought,' said Karel, licking his fingertips and wiping them on his chest, 'that you were once such a buddy of Lukas's.'

'But this hasn't got anything to do with Lukas any more. I mean, he didn't ask Sedlak to distribute the songs. And anyway I don't know him.' She did not like the sound of her voice, and saw from their faces that neither did they. 'I haven't heard from Lukas in years. Haven't seen him for years. I don't even know where he is or what he's doing.'

'Come off it, Hana. You've got a radio.'

'So?'

Ivan Meloun suddenly leapt up and out to the kitchen and returned with the radio in his hand. 'Tuned to London.'

She tried again. 'I still don't see what it's got to do with him.'

'It's got everything to do with him. It's all connected. Everything is.'

Hana got up and took a small framed photograph from Aunt Veronika's walnut desk. She held it out. 'This is my son Milan. He's asleep upstairs.'

Tomas and Karel examined it. Meloun stood once more looking out of the window into the night, his hands in his pockets.

'Very nice. He doesn't look like you. How old is he?'

'He's seven, and he looks like my brother.'

Meloun glanced at the photograph over Karel's shoulder. 'What you're saying is, "I don't want to be involved." ' He glared at Hana with belligerent arrogance.

'I'm not a political type, you know.' Hana felt herself reddening, as if she ought to be apologising for some crass mistake. 'I've had problems enough, with my son and so on. I don't really know what's going on. I don't even go up to town much. Hardly at all any more.'

'Oh! So hiding away in this pretty little house is all there is to it, is that right? No one can touch you and that's fine by you. Leave me out of it, I'm not political.'

The cruel falsetto mockery in his voice touched something in Hana and she shivered with dislike for this bumptious young man who presumed to judge her.

'That's right, I'm not. And I'll be the one to decide when I want to be. And who you think you are to tell me what to do I really don't know. A child like you, and no manners.'

'Isn't that just like you, all you old sixty-eighters. "We've done our bit, you don't know what it was like, we had to stand up to the tanks, we had to make so many sacrifices for you children, we always had your interests at heart." Well, if you don't mind, we've had it up to here' – his hand slashed across his throat – 'we're not about to wait for you "grown-ups" to decide what it's all right and not all right to do. How you lot can look yourselves in the mirror . . .'

He was spitting, his nose was running, he was on the verge of tears. Angry, angry child. Hana put her hands to her ears and immediately lowered them again, seeing herself through the eyes of her friends. She said, 'Haven't I seen you before? Haven't I met you before? You look somehow familiar.'

The young man was now lacing up his boots, head down, face hidden. 'No, we've never met. These two here always said I reminded them of you, the way you were once. Well, I've seen you and they were right. But I hope the resemblance is only superficial. Goodbye.' And the boy slammed the door behind him.

Hana turned to her two friends, who had listened in silence, and implored them. 'Are you married, Tomas?'

'As a matter of fact I'm not. But he is.' He jerked his head.

Hana turned to Karel. 'And everything *is* connected, isn't it?'

'I think,' said Karel, 'we're wasting our time. Let's go, Tommie. I'm sure we can find someone else to pester. Hani, we didn't mean to scare you. People only sign who want to. We know what signing might mean.' He leaned across the table and wiped the ball of his thumb on Hana's cheek. 'Flour. See?' He held out his thumb, dusted in white, then repeated, 'You only sign if you want to. But, in case you change your mind, I'm in the phone book, still in the same place.'

The two men moved towards the door, then looked back at Hana, who had stayed where she was.

'The Christmas cookies were quite superb,' said Tomas sarcastically. 'Keep baking.'

Hana knew she would not be able to sleep. And could not. She felt herself blushing repeatedly, her stomach was hollow, and she had to keep swallowing like someone fighting nausea. She told herself that signing the petition would do nothing for Lukas, who needed no one's help; that Ondrei Sedlak in his prison cell could not be comforted because he would not be aware that such a petition existed; that the petition had no hope of success no matter how many signatures Tomas and Karel managed to collect; that they would not collect any; that maybe they would and hers would not be among them; that as the mother of Lukas's son, even if no one knew, and because Lukas was Milan's father, she of all people should be the first to sign or she would never be able to face him again; that she probably would never see him again; that she could see no purpose to her life if that were true; that the sarcasm in Tomas's voice when he left might have implied that the Christmas cookies really weren't any good because she had run out of vanilla; that they had no right to turn up like that, out of the blue after all those years and launch a surprise attack on her; that if they went everywhere with that young Ivan Meloun with his accusations and his bullying, they'd never get anyone to sign; that it would serve them right; that she ought to have expected it, or at least thought what she'd do; that she ought to have signed without a second thought; that she still could; that she dared not but hated feeling as she did and would never feel better if she did not sign; that they would come and take Milan away and put him in a home; that she did not know how to decide; that it was too much to have to decide alone; that she had to talk it over with someone; that there was no one with whom she could talk it over because no one knew about Lukas – except Dr Cerny, to whom she could not turn with this piece of news because he would fulminate against the enemies of the state and read her a lecture about the responsibilities she bore towards her son without realising that it was precisely those responsibilities that were making her hesitate. But all the time – Hana sat in bed, breathing heavily – all the time the doctor would really be afraid that she had brought this problem into his house lest someone come in and find out and he would be compromised.

Suddenly, sitting alone in the stillness of her bed, Hana said aloud, 'Shit!' She had been stupid, too kind to that scowling, self-preserving old communist fool. Milan got on his nerves, she had thought. Too old to mend his ways and warm to a child, she had thought. No way. He had wanted them out because he was already scared to have them there at all. It was just the same as when she was a child. He hadn't changed at all. Oh, if only she could get away from them all.

Waking next morning, convinced she had not slept, Hana set about making that getaway.

Dear Mrs Cerna,

Thank you so much for your presents to my son. He is looking forward to the summer when he can go swimming again. We hope you are well. My life is the same as always, which means that Milan is at home with me most of the time because he is feverish. I think it must be the air here that is so bad for him and I was thinking of paying you a visit in England when I have saved up enough money, if they let me have a foreign currency account.

How is Peter? I wonder what he looks like these days, we have all changed so much. When I see some of the people I used to know and I think of Peter, I wonder whether he still has his curly hair. If he is bald, please don't tell me. I don't want to know . . .

Hana printed her letter, as she would for a child. Rereading what she had written she saw that she had even used a child's stilted language, like Milan's letters to his 'Grandad'. Well, there would be no more of those. She would stand Milan between her knees and hold his hands in hers, rub his upturned wrists with her thumbs as she did when she had matters of principle to explain to him. But what she would explain she did not know. 'Your Grandad has only been pretending to like us.' Then Milan would ask why. 'Because he's one of them.' Milan would ask what she meant; and she would be unable to say because to say more she would have to tell Milan who his father was – that she had confided this secret to Grandad. But Grandad didn't like Milan's father so he had sent them away just as he had sent her away when she was a little girl because he didn't like her father either. And what would be the result of that? Milan would not understand but there would be more nightmares if he believed her, or he might not believe her. No more letters from Grandad. She'd say, 'Well, perhaps he's too busy.' No more letters to Grandad. 'Why waste your time on someone who can't be bothered to write back?' If she could bring herself to say it, that is what she would say, but she would have to turn her back when she said it, and with Milan between her knees it could not be said.

Seventeen

It seemed to Dr Cerny that the days were longer than they should be, that the hours stretched further than their allotted time, that there was no particular reason why he should continue to apply himself so conscientiously to his work. These thoughts, however, so appalled him that in a spirit of self-defiance he worked harder than before, so that it would be already dark when he returned to his flat – and he would be tired enough to be able to sleep without turning over in his mind ideas which served no purpose but left him weakened and depressed.

It was very nearly Christmas. As he would be alone he would not celebrate it, for what, indeed, was there to celebrate? He had thought of buying some carp, preparing the potatoes and surprising Hana and Milan with another invitation, but of course they were young. They would have their own friends to keep them company. All the same he had packed a gift for the boy, cut-out cardboard puppets, and had posted it well in advance to be sure the parcel arrived on time.

In the ground-floor hallway he looked for letters in his mailbox but found only the newspaper, and shook his head. They should have received the gift by now. She could have acknowledged its receipt. He trudged up the stairs and opened his front door. Inside, his ancient cat was already removing itself limb by limb from his slippers, leaving behind a pad of matted hair and a small pool of some secreted liquid.

'Oh dear, oh dear,' said Dr Cerny, pausing for a moment to allow the cat to stalk stiffly in a figure of eight around his legs, while he himself bent equally stiffly to touch the creature's dry head with his fingertips. Then he went into the bathroom where he poured disinfectant on to a twist of newspaper and began scrubbing at his soiled slipper. He kept his face averted and breathed through his mouth.

The boy. He could not get it out of his head that something had happened to Milan, something that Hana felt unable to tell him in a letter. He was seriously ill somewhere in hospital. Or worse. And yet Dr Cerny could not bring himself to believe that. There was something else. In the weeks that had passed since their visit, she had written to him only once, coolly rebuffing his services. The only communication had been Milan's pictures and letters, which the doctor kept in his study, filed in date-order. He had marked each letter, on the back in the top left-hand corner, with the date of its arrival. And on a separate sheet he noted his comments on the remarkable progress in the boy's handwriting. He was proud of him. He had sensed a striving, an urge to impress, and he had been impressed. He had been able to imagine the angle of the boy's head bending over the table, the thin hand pressing the pencil into the paper. 'Dear Grandad . . .', a form of address that, in itself, became a term of endearment despite the formality of the childish messages that followed. 'I am well. How are you? I am enjoying school. I hope your cat is well too.' Every letter, since it told him so little, had made the distance between them seem all the greater, so that Milan's efforts had not brought him the joy that the boy intended, but instead a terrible regret.

If only Hana had appended comments of her own; she was a good letter-writer, he remembered. She would have been able to say everything that Milan's childish endeavours still could not. He would have been able to piece together their daily living, how the boy looked, what he played at, who his friends were, whether they came from the sort of family whose children would make desirable companions. Milan had drawn his bedroom, and the doctor had deciphered a bed, a cupboard, a chair and a door. He could not tell if this was indeed the room or the boy's vision of how a room ought to be. But Hana had written nothing except, at first, the address on the envelope. Later even that had been laboriously copied in the characterless hand of a seven-year-old. Peter's handwriting had been the same at that age. But Peter had been so indolent, unwilling to be taught, his eyes everywhere but where they should be, as if he knew it all already and was waiting for something else. That was Peter, egged on by his mother, with her deliberate disdain for application, for effort of any sort. 'Do you imagine,' Dr Cerny's father had said, ten foot tall, 'that your mother or I or

141

anyone else will wash your clothes when you come home like this?' And Dr Cerny, at nine years old, had been made to stand at the kitchen sink and wash and wash his muddied socks until they were clean, while his father ladled soup into a tin-lidded container so that *his* patients might at least have something to eat. 'Medicine is what they call me for,' he had said, 'but food would take care of most of their ills.'

And it seemed now to Dr Cerny, scrubbing at his reeking slipper, that the success of the system had been to provide so much soup that the people who ate it forgot immediately how it had been provided but only wanted something more. They were all like that, this ungrateful generation. They took for granted the roof over their heads, their four walls, the hot water they washed in. And when you tried to tell them that it was the privilege of their times, that their grandparents had had no such comforts, they merely shrugged as if to say, 'Well, I'm not my grandparents.' Dr Cerny pegged his sodden slipper on to his clothesline and set a plastic bucket underneath to catch the rank drips. Perhaps he should get himself another pair of slippers.

Milan would not be like that; he couldn't be blamed for his father, no matter what the man had done. That was one of the mistakes they'd made in the past, blaming the children. He would explain all that to the boy, in good time. If only the child would write.

Christmas passed without a letter from Grandad, not even a short note to say how much he liked the present Milan had made him. It had taken so long, too, the best thing he had ever done. He had carried it down to show Auntie Alena and Uncle Josef before he gave it to his mother to send off. They had all said how good it was, a picture of his house and the forest behind, a collage of material and twigs and pieces of pine cone. His mother had mixed up flour-and-water paste for the glue but Uncle Josef had said that would never last and given him a pot of real carpenter's glue. 'Can't have it falling apart before the old man gets it, can we?' he'd said. 'But make sure you cover the table with lots of newspaper first or your mother will never speak to me again. Isn't that right, Hani?' His mother had smiled and said it was true, but it was a funny smile, like the ones she tried to put on for him when he knew she wasn't feeling well. And when he was making it, every evening for

142

more than a week, she kept saying, 'Why don't you get the boys up to play? You don't want to be sitting here all by yourself all the time, do you?' He had thought, how strange. She was usually so fussy about things being done properly, making him copy out his homework again and again for the teacher he heard her saying rude things about to Auntie Alena. Surely she knew that an important thing like his present for Grandad had to be just so. Grandad was even fussier than she was. And he had packed it so carefully. Auntie Alena had given him some soft paper to wrap round it and some cotton wool because his mother said she didn't have any, and then some parcel paper and lots of string round it with knots. He had glued the knots, then waited and waited to see what Grandad would say. But Grandad hadn't written at all, hadn't sent him a present either, although he hadn't minded that so much.

They'd had Christmas Eve dinner all together with one of Uncle Josef's geese because there wasn't any carp – 'Aren't you pleased? After all, you never did like carp.' But he hadn't wanted to eat it. The lady Nora in England had sent English sweets and his mother's friend Peter had sent more Lego and a toy London bus. The Frantiseks had laughed at it and told him to drive them to Piccadilly. Uncle Josef, who'd been singing in a very loud voice, kept asking his mother how to pronounce 'Piccadilly' because she was learning English from the radio. Auntie Alena said, 'What's the matter, don't you like the goose? Aren't you hungry?', and his mother had felt his forehead and said, 'I think he's sickening for something', but it wasn't true.

They'd gone home early then – she was going to get him to bed just to be sure. But when they got home she lit a fire, opened Nora's sweets for him and said he could eat as many as he liked, then kept saying to him, 'Aren't they delicious? You're such a lucky boy to have such good friends over there.' And she had got out her box of photographs to show him the lady Nora and said, 'Look, that's me and that's your Uncle Honza. You look just like him except he was a bit of a cry-baby. You're not, I'm glad to say. And that's Nora. Isn't she big!' But he had seen Grandad in the photograph. He looked cross; probably he didn't like his picture being taken.

Eighteen

Installed in London in a flat of her own, bought by her son, Nora sat in front of her television set, her hand on the remote control. They looked so nice in their white shirts and shiny black waistcoats, their hair so sleek she could smell their pomade just by looking at it. They moved, in that almost-silence, bending and swaying till their eyes were on a level with the snooker table, like dancers, all their motion choreographed. There he was, her pretty boy, squinting along the line of his cue.

'Come on, my little one,' crooned Nora and extended a pudgy hand to stroke his strawberry hair. He raised his eyes from the tip of his cue, left the table and stepped out, took her fingertips and lifted them to his lips, holding her eyes with his. Returning to the table, he winked briefly over his shoulder before clicking the blue ball neatly into its pocket. Nora clapped. 'Oh, well done, my darling.'

Down the corridor Mrs Taylor, wearing the pink rubber gloves she brought with her every week, stacked dishes on the draining board. And she thought, as she thought every week, that if these were all the dishes Mrs Thing used in a week she didn't eat a proper meal. Mind you, if these were all the dishes, why couldn't Mrs Thing wash them herself? But who was she to worry about it? She wasn't paying. That was all set up by young Mr Peter, though money was all very well. What the old lady could do with was a sight of her son. Shouldn't be on her own so much, not that she wasn't difficult. There she was now, shouting for something.

Mrs Taylor wedged her elbows into her waist and, like a doctor in an operating theatre, raised her pink-gloved hands in front of her face to keep the soapsuds from marking the walls of the narrow corridor. When she pushed open the door to Nora's room with her knee the heat took her breath away. You could suffocate to death in that room, that gasfire on all the time, and you could smell how long it hadn't been cleaned. You'd have thought Mr Peter would have come in and told her to get the place done over, but he was no better by all accounts. Just do the dishes and make sure there were no mice or rats, he'd said – and laughed. It wasn't funny. Rats and mice. Well, there could be, for all she knew. And the room all dark now. Mrs Thing wouldn't have the lights on.

'Did you want something, dear? I'll get you a cup of tea, shall I?'

'Oh, Mrs Taylor. Here you are. Not tea, no thank you. Wait.'

Nora leaned over and made scrabbling movements by the side of her armchair, gasping aloud as she did so. With a final resigned groan she hauled herself upright and sank back in the chair. 'It's no good. I can't do it. You'll have to, Mrs Taylor.'

'What is it? What you got down there?'

'My bag. I want my handbag.'

Made wary by experience, even though she was wearing her rubber gloves, Mrs Taylor poked the floor with a shoe. Encountering an obstacle, she spread her legs and bent to the floor, clutching at her back with a soapy hand. She straightened, still holding her back, and dumped the bag in Nora's lap. Nora plunged in a hand and left it to forage inside. There were wisps of used, dried tissues; scraps of paper on which she had written names and addresses; tiny tight silver and gold balls rolled from chocolate wrappings; an unfinished piece of knitting, to be a tank top for Hana's boy one day; finally, her purse. Nora pulled it out and beckoned to Mrs Taylor to stoop once more.

'I want you to do something for me.'

'What's that?'

'If I give you five pounds, will you go out and buy me some fish and chips?'

Mrs Taylor stepped back. 'Oh now, Mrs Thing, you know I can't do that. You know what your young Mr Peter says, what the doctor says.'

Nora crowed in a high curve of amusement and exasperation. 'Oh, them. They talk and talk. But what do they know about life? After all I've been through I need a reward: a consolation for the years of neglect, the years of suffering. Privations. Starvation. Imprisonment. Rude men in badly made boots, Mrs Taylor. Did I ever tell you? Did I never tell you?'

Mrs Taylor hastily snatched the five-pound note. 'I'll do it, but I shouldn't.'

'I knew I could rely on you. There are so few reliable people left these days, don't you find? And please keep the change.'

Mrs Taylor's shoulders stiffened at the affront. 'I shouldn't dream of it,' she retorted, and waded towards the outline of the door.

'Mrs Taylor. One more thing.'

'Yes?'

'Don't forget the salt and my pickle.'

Then Nora folded her hands over her stomach and snuggled back against one high wing of her armchair to wait. By her side the gasfire hissed steadily. The television drew her into its light, to the small neat figures of the preoccupied men, prowling around the green-baize table, stalking the elusive trajectory. Her favoured ginger head bent towards her, so close she could make out a fine strand of dissenting hairs crossing the frontier of his parting. She held her breath as the cue glided back and forth in the outstretched V of his finger and thumb. Any minute now. Yes. Plink! The red ball sped to her. She backed away to allow it an unhindered path to its welcoming string bag. There was a flap of applause. 'Who else would have had the audacity to try that one!' mused the whispering voice of the commentator. 'What a talent! Where is he going now? Will he really? Can he? He is. He's going to try for it. Quiet now, carefully does it . . .' But she knew her boy. She wasn't afraid for him but tightened her interlaced fingers none the less.

Mrs Taylor stumped back into the room.

'You've got a letter,' she said reproachfully. 'Don't you never look at your letters?'

'Nobody writes to me,' Nora complained, annoyed at the interruption. 'Shush! You'll put him off!'

'Yah!' observed Mrs Taylor. 'Kids' stuff, playing down the pub dressed like fancy boys. Do you want it or don't you?'

Nora, keeping her eyes on the screen, extended a soft wrist round the wing of her chair and tweezered the letter.

'It's from there. Foreign,' said Mrs Taylor. 'Shall I switch on the lamp?' She snapped on the standard lamp behind the armchair. Taken by surprise, the young man on the screen muffed his shot and straightened up, disappointed but expressionless.

'Oh, Mrs Taylor.' But as the opposing player moved to the table Nora examined her letter. 'Oh yes. It's from my little girl.'

'Your little girl?'

'Ah now!' Nora shook the letter at Mrs Taylor, teasing,

reproving. 'You don't know everything. I have my secrets. Maybe even you have your secrets – who knows? But I have mine and that's for sure. However.' She ripped off the top of the envelope, tearing across the stamp.

Mrs Taylor sighed. She'd have asked for that stamp for her grandson. She sidled closer and looked over the back of the chair, over Nora's shoulder. The letter was printed in capitals, like a child's writing.

'She very young then, your little girl?'

'What do you mean?'

'Well, that writing. It's like what kids write.'

Nora looked down at the square black lettering. Hana's effort to be legible and clear for her untutored foreign reader.

'My dear Mrs Taylor,' she said patiently, 'there are some languages that are so complicated they have to be written like this or no one would understand them. I mean, look at this carefully. Can you tell me what it says? Can you?'

Mrs Taylor bent her nose to the paper Nora held over her head. The words wore a dancing row of hats and dashes and meant nothing. She shook her head.

'There you are. Now think how much worse it would be if it were written the way we write in English. After all my years there, my immersion in that alien and strange culture, I can read it; but, believe me, that's not a gift God gives to everyone. Now be off and fetch those fish and chips.'

'It's pissing down out there.'

'Then take an umbrella. Surely you brought one with you.'

Nora returned to her letter. She held it down with one hand and placed a fleshy fingertip under the first word. As Mrs Taylor navigated a path back across the carpet, Nora's lips moved.

Dear Mrs Cerna,
    Thank you so much for your presents . . .

Nora wondered whether Hana's boy might have grown out of the swimming trunks she had sent. They had looked so nice, so bright, enough to cheer anyone up on a dark day. And the days were dark. Perhaps she should hurry and finish that tank top and get it off to him before it was too small as well. Maybe he would be proudly sporting it when they came to visit. But Hana said she needed to save money. That wouldn't be easy, so Nora must help if she were to get Hana over in time. In time

147

for what? She squealed a self-mocking peal of laughter. She might be at death's door half the time, as she told Peter, who showed no interest, but that didn't mean she was prepared to cross the threshold yet. Not until everything was sorted out. Peter didn't understand what she needed. He hadn't wanted to accept the position she'd had over there. Here, what did she have? Whom did she have? Mrs Taylor, with her bad-tempered prattle, and a weekly visit from her son. She could tell he only came round because he felt he should. Sons were like that, but a daughter-in-law – a capable, reliable girl like Hana, who had a reason to be grateful – that would be quite different.

Hana would wear white; no one minded virgins and colours these days. She might even run up the dress for Hana herself. No, not white. Too dull. A brilliant primrose yellow with a garland of rust chrysanthemums. Peter would look best in black, of course. Nora stretched out her feet and moved her toes in her slippers. As for herself, she would start with the best. Her hair was still exceptional. She would twirl it high upon her head around the wicker construction she would make for the purpose. The base would be clipped to her scalp, and her long tresses would wind up and up and form a plume at the summit. On it she would pin a yellow chrysanthemum. Let the others wear hats, whoever wanted to attend.

She began to hum the Wedding March, holding her head high, in stately procession, then suddenly stopped in mid-phrase. First things first. She had to bring Hana over. And how was that to be done? This would need planning. Nora's breath came faster as she warmed to the difficulty.

She had willed Hana to England, she knew that now. The power of her will had exercised itself across that bleak continent to reclaim ownership of the pharmacist's daughter, but the willing wasn't enough. It didn't allow for the financial aspects, and here was the rub. She must get Hana over. She *must* get Hana over. How? Hana had no money. Nora had no money, only her bit of pension and the little allowance from Gerald which she forwarded to Hana, which he had forgotten about, which he must have forgotten about: he was too mean to go on paying if he remembered. Peter had pots of money, as far as she could tell; but turning to Peter in this enterprise would be foolish.

She put her hand up to her throat in a gesture of alarm and her fingers closed on her pendant. Her great-grandmother's. It was passed, according to family tradition or in line with her great-grandmother's will, one or the other, from mother to daughter down the generations. But she had no daughter. The nearest would be a daughter-in-law. And to procure that daughter-in-law she would have to sell the object intended for her. That was not the way it was meant to be. However . . . Again Nora exhaled in triumph. But careful. People were schemers. You couldn't trust them to do what you wanted. You had to put it down on paper.

Where did she have paper? There must be some in this house, if it could only be found. There on the floor, maybe among the pile of magazines, under that big book of Gauguin Peter had brought her from the library. Nora banged the arms of her chair, and sank back to wait for Mrs Taylor. She could hear the key in the front door. There had never been anything wrong with her hearing. Some of her faculties, the finer ones, were not dulled by time.

'Here we are, then. I'll just get you a plate.'

'Don't bother with the plate. They serve it in a bag, don't they? I'll have it out of that.'

But Mrs Taylor had already stumped out to the kitchen and was returning. 'Much nicer off a plate, Mrs Thing. Now I'll just lay it out for you and then I must be getting back. He'll be wondering where I am.' Accusing her. 'Here's your pickle.' She held it up. 'Chips with salt on, and no cod – they'd run out. But I got you a nice piece of skate. Knife. Fork. All neat and tidy.'

'Have we got any paper in the house, Mrs Taylor?'

'Paper everywhere, dear. What's it for?'

'I've got to write an important document, and I need you to help me. It's a secret. Between the two of us.'

Mrs Taylor backed away. 'I don't hold with secrets.' What was the old bag dreaming up now?

Nora beamed at her, wheedled. 'It's a good secret. It's to help someone. My little girl.'

'Oh yes?'

'She's got a little boy of her own – a very nice little boy – and he's ill. We've got to help them, Mrs Taylor, because if we don't no one else will. You know, the sort of thing I told you about. Medicines and so on. We have to send them hush-hush, so that their government doesn't know.'

'It's not going to be anything illegal, is it? I don't want to get involved with anything like that.'

'This will be an act of humanitarian kindness, Mrs Taylor. A Christian act. Mr Taylor will be pleased.'

'So it's not that secret, then. I can tell him.'

Nora frowned. 'Well, maybe. But no one else. Now, what about finding me some paper?'

Mrs Taylor searched through the magazines on the floor, through the leaves of the heavy book from the library Mr Peter had brought. She'd never so much as glanced at it, Mrs Thing, when the young man had made that effort, too. But no paper. There was none in the kitchen, that much she knew. Nothing in the bedroom neither.

'Then you must pass me my scissors.'

Must, always must. How's about a 'Please would you mind', once in a while? There were scissors in the kitchen. Mrs Taylor fetched them with bad grace. 'And what did the old bag do then, do you think?' she said later in her own kitchen, over tea and a Penguin biscuit. 'She cut up the bag the fish and chips was in. All down the side. Irons it on her lap. And then it's "And now I need a pen." And off I have to go looking for a pen. She had one in her handbag all the time.'

Nora searched for the right form of words but failed to find it. She wrote: 'May it hereby be known that I wish my great-grandmother's pendant to be immediately sold for the largest amount of money possible. The proceeds are to be sent directly to Hana Masnikova, 64 Bytlice, 76321, Czechoslovakia.' She signed her name in large, curlicued letters. Underneath she printed 'witnessed by:' and Mrs Taylor, still in her coat and outdoor shoes, bent over Nora's chair and signed. Then, impatiently, she handed Nora the plate of fish and chips. All cold. Well, that was just too bad.

'I'm off now, Mrs Thing. I'll see you next week.'

Nora ate like a child, choosing the best bits first. The pickled onion was large, moist and greenish-grey. She held it up above her head, tilted her head back and bit into it with outstretched teeth like a horse. The outer skin slipped away and one half of the onion was propelled into her mouth, while the other fell into her palm. She crunched the half in her mouth, her chin puckering with pleasure at the vinegar. She swallowed and slipped the rest of the onion on to her tongue, wiping her palm, on her skirt. Next the chips. One by one, between her fingers. The salt stung her cuticles and a raw patch inside her lower lip. She sucked her fingers and her lip, swilling it with saliva. The irritation did not detract from her enjoyment. Life had so few sharp sensations. Finally the fish. They made it with too much batter. If she could only get out, she'd tell them. She'd show them how to fry a fish. She peeled the batter off, exposing the white flaky flesh, and sucked her fingers again. Cod would have been better, but beggars and so on.

With very little fish left to eat, Nora choked to death on a bone. She knew it immediately. An iron bar rose through her chest from below, guided by a hand pressing on her gullet. Her chest twitched. She knew what one should do in these circumstances. She had taken a first-aid course from the St John's Ambulance people before opening her boarding-house, in case one of the guests should need her. They had not. You put your arms around the victim from behind and squeezed violently. Who would ever get their arms round her? Someone – only there was no one – would need very long arms. She pressed her own ribs and pushed feebly at them. It was ungallant that there was no one. Pretty boy had vacated the screen, deserting her. Her nose hurt terribly. She saw her fingers fluttering ridiculously on her lap like fins. People were dreary. They had no sense of colour. They let you down – now, for instance, when she could feel her entrails swelling, preparing to explode from her body. At least she had eaten the pickle first.

This final reflection provoked a last guffaw that surged through her with such violence it dislodged the fishbone and sent it flying from her strained and gasping mouth. Nora looked down to identify the culprit which lay disingenuously among the remains of the fish on her plate. She drew in a long, heaving breath and died a second time, conclusively, of relief.

Nineteen

The strange wet winter gave place to an uncalled-for bitter spring. It was as if the pages of the calendar had been reshuffled in the printing and the seasons had unthinkingly obeyed their instructions. Behind the house the plantation of young pines spiked motionless at a frost-bitten sky too bright for the month; buds were postponed. Only the slowly lengthening days betrayed the season's camouflage.

Hana's breath, when she woke, steamed from her nostrils as if she were an overworked horse. No matter what she did she could not heat the house, although, thank God, the cold air was still. Unaccountably Nora's last remittance had not arrived and Hana wondered whether the old woman had, for some reason, been frightened off by her intended visit. Nora had not replied to that letter. Hana had written again, tentatively, but had thrown the letter away. Her tone, on rereading, sounded whining. But she was whining. She had every reason, and under the covers in bed she whined herself to comforting, self-pitying tears – at the cold; in a panic that without Nora's money she wouldn't get by; at the knowledge that, in twenty years' time, all that would be different in her life would be the size and temper of her son and the ache in her bones. 'What's happened to you, Hana?' she rehearsed; and answered, 'Nothing. Nothing's happened. Why should anything ever?'

However, for Milan there was change, glorious change. It was no longer so dark in the early morning so he was sent to school by himself. At first he had been afraid and felt foolish because of it. I shall get lost, he had told himself, and wondered how he could think so. The path down was steep and treacherously covered in lead-grey ice. A few yards to the left along the road was the bridge over the railway line and then over the Berounka – the bridge whose planks carried cars and laden

152

lorries but threatened to tip him into the freezing shallows. From there it was straight into the village between the super-market and the post office, past the butcher's into the school. He had walked this road with his mother every day of his life, tagging behind her, hanging back when he was smaller ('You're a mountain goat, you're not afraid of the hill'), leaping ahead these days, when they descended into the village, so how could he possibly lose his way? It was impossible. He knew it but was still afraid at first and then, when he did not lose his way, triumphed as unreasonably as if he had, uniquely, mastered a rare and difficult skill.

As his path wound down among the houses he gathered classmates in their gaudy woollen ski-hats and giant satchels, shouting. He felt years older. He bought a small square of chewing gum on the way home. He played follow-my-leader in the snow, and the boy in front who was bigger – everyone was bigger – bounded from one deeply crouched knee to the next like a mad hare. Milan was meant to place his feet exactly in the boy's footprints but his legs weren't up to the stretch. The bigger boy laughed but it was not unkind. Milan was content. By the time he reached home, always before Hana's return from the collective, his face was crimson from the biting air and from his joy in it.

Now he dropped his satchel just inside the door and slithered back down the track to the steepest point, where, when he was younger, he had always stopped to draw breath and complain, skidding on the rutted ice until he dropped into the crusted snow under the trees where he was building an igloo. He couldn't believe how long it was taking. The walls were still only a few inches high, although they were good and thick, as Uncle Josef had told him to make them. Every morning he awoke afraid that the thaw everyone was waiting for might have arrived and destroyed his work. He imagined his igloo finished, visitors dropping in. Auntie Alena would be offered beer. His mother would ask for coffee. Uncle Josef would have brought his own rum. Tea for Grandad.

Forced by the weight of snow into attitudes of contrition, the branches bent dismally to the ground. You had to double up to see anyone hidden behind them, but from his frozen fastness Milan recognised passing legs. The feet of their neighbour, Mrs Kralova, skittered in tiny terrified steps over the steep ice. She seemed to have no weight, no solidity to hold her down. Milan restrained the greeting that came to his lips for fear the woman would fall. The postmistress, wearing spiked boots, was pushing her bicycle up the hill. Milan wondered why she didn't leave it at the bottom. She assaulted the climb at each step with her toes, jabbing at the incline with a grunt of effort and displeasure.

'Good day,' Milan sang out, raising his voice to an eerie squeak.

The postmistress stopped and bent down, peering into his front door. 'Oh, it's you. Well, since you're here, you can take your letters up to your mother. Then I won't have to struggle up this damned hill.' Milan crawled out. She sounded as if she were blaming him for the climb. 'Don't drop them, mind. Nor the newspaper.' His mother had said that the newspaper was only good for wiping your arse; but he was old enough not to say so out loud. 'This one's your mother's and this one's yours, of course.'

'Mine?' Milan looked down at the envelopes in his hand. Grandad had written at last. He hopped fearlessly on the ice. 'Look! Look! It's my letter.'

'Yes, we don't get so many from there.' The postmistress tapped curiously on the English stamp on the other letter.

'No,' insisted Milan. 'Not that one. This one.'

'Well, I don't know what you're so excited about,' grumbled the woman. 'You get one of those every week. Every week – Tuesdays, like today.'

'What?' Milan stared at her dumpy figure, red-faced, wrapped round and round in scarves. What was she talking about? But it didn't matter. He had what he had been waiting for.

He skipped home, hugging the letters under his coat. As soon as he arrived he put his mother's letter and the newspaper on the table, looked at them, took them out again and posted them both in the mailbox by the gate as the postmistress would have done. He climbed up to his bedroom and on to the chair by the window to see if his mother was coming up the path, but saw no one. All the same, he tiptoed back across the room and sat on the floor, pressing his back against the door, knees bent up. He had no key. His mother always said, 'We have no secrets from each other.'

Dr Cerny had continued to write to Milan every Friday evening, no longer expecting a reply. It was, he reproached himself, a wasted activity, but it sat well between cleaning his shoes at the end of the week and totting up his accounts.

He covered the paper in his meticulous and diminutive writing, seeming to have forgotten the limited abilities, even the age, of his reader.

My son Peter has informed me that my wife, Nora, has died in London. I found the news disturbing, not knowing the circumstances of her death. She was, of course, rather older than I am, but when you reach my age and people you have known begin to die you are brought face to face with your own mortality.

I cannot honestly say that I am sad, but I am saddened, for hers was a wasted life. She achieved nothing. She has left nothing behind her and it is my belief, Milan, that when the time comes to take stock we ought to be able to look back and acknowledge that we have been of some use to mankind. I can at least say that the community I have served as a doctor has to some degree benefited from my efforts, although I would not pretend to have brought about the changes in child-rearing practices that I hoped for. That is profoundly frustrating. When you know, as I do, what people should do to improve their health and that of their families, it is very hard to understand why they do not do it. It was much the same with Nora, who would not learn, who was not even interested to learn the simplest principles of running a house. She seemed only to want to live for the moment, although her favoured moments were lodged in the past. She had no concept of the future and was impatient whenever I broached the responsibilities on the present generation that the future implies. It distresses me all the more that she was not alone in this grasshopper attitude. All around me, it seems, there are people who despise the efforts of the hard-working ant. She had beautiful hair, I remember. It was her best feature.

I am certain that my cat will not survive the season, which is not a bad thing. She is not a happy creature and gives no pleasure any more, but I think I may miss her. I cannot decide whether I will replace her. Do I really want another living thing in this flat?

Milan could not read his letter. The writing was so small and all joined up. He pored and puzzled over it, line by line, and picked out his name scattered through the pages. So it *was* his letter. He struggled to make out other words and worked out a few of the short ones. He noticed, in the top right-hand corner of the first page, a tiny number 14 in a circle. He folded up the letter and tried to put the flimsy pages back into the envelope but his fingers were too clumsy. What was that number? He was hungry. His mother should be home soon. He went down to the kitchen to look for a piece of bread already sliced off the loaf. She wouldn't let him touch her knives; they were too sharp. She had left two slices for him, wrapped in a cloth. He would take them out to the igloo and eat them there while he buried his letter in a hollow in the earth under one of the trees. The postmistress had said he had a letter every week but she was lying. He hadn't had any letters at all. His mother always said the postmistress was a prying cow.

Suddenly he stopped short, his stomach as cold as his fingers. That number. Grandad always put labels on things. It meant that he had sent fourteen letters. Milan turned and scrambled back to the house and into the kitchen where they kept the calender pinned on the larder door. He found Tuesday and began counting backwards. March, February, January. The calendar went no further but there were still two weeks to go and Christmas was at the end of December. He counted on his fingers, lost count and started again. His counting took him back before Christmas, before he had made his collage of the house and packed it with Auntie Alena.

He would waylay the postmistress every Tuesday from now on and hide his letters where his mother wouldn't find them.

Hana chafed her gloved hands together, rubbing joint on joint, her newspaper and her letter clamped in her armpit.

'Christ, it's cold out there. And in here. Bloody hell. I'll make a fire and we'll have some soup, too.' Milan looked a bit pale, but she wouldn't say anything. Wait and see. Maybe it was just cold and hunger. He'd not been down with anything all this cold spell.

'I'm not hungry.'

'You must be. Anyway, you have to have something. I made a soup this morning.'

'I don't want anything. I don't want your soup.'

'Milachku, you have to have something in this weather. If only a little bit.'

Well then, he'd have to. But he wouldn't enjoy it.

156

Hana, on her knees, unfolded the newspaper and rolled its pages diagonally into thin tubes, coiled the ends together and laid them in the fireplace. She banked up the shards of kindling and stacked a circle of logs around the base. She lit a match and sat back on her heels, still banging her gloved hands together, then she leaned forward and blew into the base of the fire. Her face steamed. If they sat close by they'd be warm. She brought in two bowls of soup and the pieces of bread Milan had already unwrapped.

'Come on. Just a bit.'

Milan made a face. But he was hungry and the soup had smelt good as it was heating. He took a small spoonful and one bite of bread and laid down his spoon, staring defiantly at his mother. Hana did not notice. She was reading Peter's letter, her soup untouched.

'Oh, poor old thing!'

'Who's a poor old thing?'

'Nora. The lady in London. She's died.'

'Was she very old?'

'No. Well, yes, you'd think so. She ate something, then she had a heart attack.'

'What's that?'

'It's when the heart stops working.'

'Will my heart stop working?'

'No. Not now. Not while you're young.'

So the lady Nora had died because she was old. But his mother was quite old. 'Are you as old as lady Nora?'

Hana laughed. 'No, sweetie. Not by a long way. You don't have to worry.'

He wasn't worried. He'd be able to look after himself, but was seized with panic.

'Good God!' said Hana.

'What?'

'She's given us some money.'

'She was always giving us money.'

'No, but real money. A lot of money.'

'Was she very rich?'

'I don't know. I don't think so.'

'Where is the money. Can I see it?'

'It isn't here. It's going to be sent to the bank. I'll have to get an account. I'll have to think.'

'What are we going to buy?'

'Buy? We're not going to buy anything. We're going to go.'

'Where are we going to go? I don't want to go anywhere.'

Hana finally called herself to order. She looked across at her son, still so small, crouched by the fire, drinking his soup, his face glowing orange on one side. It would be as always. She would have to do this all by herself; but for the first time she thought she was not all by herself. Poor Nora. Maybe she had died in her sleep with Peter by her side. She hoped there had been no pain. Hana wore a small silver cross round her neck. She touched it apologetically. There was a purpose in this.

'You see? You *were* hungry after all. Do you want some more?'

'No.' Yes.

'Oh well, then.' She picked up the bowls. 'Look, I'm going to be busy this afternoon. Can you amuse yourself?'

And when didn't he? 'I'm going to be busy too.'

'That's good.'

While his mother was on the phone trying to reach someone called Alex who knew about money and passports, Milan was in his room writing to Grandad. He was making an igloo. They said he was good at maths. The lady Nora in England had sent them a lot of money and they were going somewhere.

Later, when Hana was sleeping in front of the fire, Milan stole just a little bit of money from her purse for the stamp.

The cold spring yielded to a still, heavy summer. Below the forest the nights were stuffy and close. And now Hana sat cross-legged in her sitting-room, drinking whisky and sorting through photographs. It was quite likely that she would not be able finally to confer greater significance on one picture than another, so she would take them all. She had packed and repacked, torn between the demands of her subterfuge and the disinclination to leave behind serviceable clothes for which she had paid money. A bag of sanitary towels, which she had to pay for in foreign currency, leaned bulkily against one of her suitcases. She presumed that sanitary towels could be bought over the counter in any English pharmacy but she was loath to leave them behind.

She decided to bequeath the sanitary towels to Alena; she would wrap them in her winter coat and skirts in a bedsheet and then hide them in the cellar behind the boiler. She could leave a note for Alena, and Josef could come up for them under cover of dark, with his torch.

She was jumpy. She suspected (without very good reason)

that her absence would bring opprobrium on those who were close to her. She remembered her classmates, those other children of the condemned men who had infected their offspring with their crimes. In his cell, she was still convinced, her father had died under a heavy boot. Decades had passed since then, methods become both more elegant and more weary, but she thought at that moment that she was important enough to be a risk to others. Perhaps she was. Perhaps not. Her problem, like everyone's, was not knowing.

Because she had drunk too much whisky – nearly finished the small bottle – she lurched as she tried to fold the clothes for Alena, grazing her arm against the rough-cast plaster of the wall. It left a flaky white dappling on her upper arm which came off on her fingers when she rubbed the sore spot. She sniffed her fingertips without knowing why, and through the vapour of her own breath faintly detected a dry chalky odour. She wondered, near to sentimental tears, whether this was the last and most penetrating memory of the house that she would have, whether some time in the future, in someone else's home (would she ever have her own again?), the smell of chalk might summon up to her the chicken house at Number 64. Her azaleas would surely droop. She found the notion that they might ever flower again atrocious. Not for the first time she prayed, literally, that her chickens would be devoured swiftly and painlessly by the fox. And may he prosper. She regretted that she was leaving before the plums ripened.

Upstairs Milan was sleeping uneasily, excited by the forthcoming holiday at the spa, where the food was said to be delicious, the doctors kind and the distance from Grandad's flat none too great. Grandad had said so in his last letter. He'd already looked up the timetable, he wrote, and found a convenient early-morning bus for his 'surprise' visit. The surprise was to be all Hana's; he and Grandad would come together like two old conspirators – said Grandad. If it weren't for that, Milan would have cavilled at this trip to the spa – his health had never been so good. His mother, always thinking about money, shouldn't have wasted it on him when he didn't need it. He felt guilty for not saying so.

Always a light sleeper, Milan was aware of his mother's movements in the room below; a distant and comforting scraping, the padding of her feet, a single cough, a door closing in the draught, all registered on his unconscious mind but did not really disturb him.

Hana feared Alena would never forgive her for running away without a hint as if she did not trust her. And later, when the time came to write and explain to Alena why, she would be twice offended that in all those years of girlish confidences, shared weeping and coarse asides Hana had deliberately and studiedly refused to give up her most precious secret.

She had to go to bed now, here, for the last time. She had to go to sleep. She had to be alert tomorrow but could not be. She had drunk too much, she knew, and her head would be heavy, her temper fouled. She would have to disguise that and smile, as one would, however one would, but not excessively. Too much smiling would suggest over-eagerness and nerves. And what should she be nervous about in front of her friends? Josef, giving her the promised lift to the station tomorrow, had to be smiled at as one smiled at Josef, warmly, gratefully, but with that reticence that kept him at a distance, a metaphorical and playful tap on the wrist to stop him thinking there'd be something in it for him later on. Give over, Josef. Behave yourself. You know I wouldn't. Never would he have been so taken for granted, so unfairly used for his generosity. But after dropping her off he was going up into the forest with his mates for a day on the bottle and would enjoy that. Maybe he wouldn't think too harshly of her when the penny dropped.

And the officials in the airport would have to be smiled at as a mother would smile, taking her child for their first holiday trip to the West (all paid for in the right sort of money). Excitement in the smile, not the dread of discovery, the dread of departure. Above all, she had to smile at her son, betraying him to save him, lying to him so that he might have the privilege in future of telling only ordinary lies. She, who had been the self-proclaimed enemy of falsehood, cheating her friends, conspiring alone, defrauding her child of the holiday he had been expecting. And she knew, although he did not know she knew, what else he was expecting; for she had – and the devil would spit on her – searched through his things when the boy was at school and found, oddly, not the old man's outpourings (wherever could they be?) but the tentative first drafts of the letters Milan had been sending out in reply.

Twenty

The morning sun fell directly on Milan's upturned face and woke him early. His mother was still asleep, he could tell. There were no noises in the kitchen downstairs, the radio was silent, no smells. He padded to her bedroom in his bare feet – his slippers were packed – and gave the door a tiny push. It swung open and he saw her sleeping. Often, when they had shared a bed and he had woken before her, he had glanced into her face and, thinking no further, slipped away; but today, for some reason, he was held in the doorway staring at his mother's powerless features, spying on her.

Her face was pale and puffy and looked tired even in repose. He thought she looked like someone acting being asleep, her eyes screwed up at the corners, jammed tight shut to show how fast asleep she was. The little vertical lines running up from her top lip made her look like a crumpled hankie. Her clothes were lying on the floor and he thought how pleased she'd be if he picked them all up and folded them on to her chair. As he moved forward and reached out for her clothes, the floor creaked and she opened her eyes. See, she wasn't really asleep at all.

Milan stood there holding her underpants and T-shirt and looking like a thief. A reproof nearly escaped her but was restrained in the nick of time. Her head was heavy, her mouth tasted as if it were full of old metal. She must get going and quickly.

'Come on and give me a kiss, my darling. I'm going to have a bath.'

Milan dropped the garments on to the bed and crawled up to his mother but drew back puzzled and repelled. Her breath smelt sour, like Uncle Josef's sometimes did. She didn't smell as she should.

'What's the matter?' She was hurt.

'Nothing.' And he kissed her quickly on her cheek but turned his face aside to receive her kiss. Usually, ritual would have had her take his face between her hands and kiss him on the forehead, on his nose, on the lips and on the chin, to set him up for the day. Today he was rejecting the old ritual.

'Oh well, then.' She rolled on to her side and pushed herself up. 'We'll have breakfast in a minute. A big one and no non-sense. I don't want you telling me you're hungry later when there isn't anything to eat.'

The room swung and swayed. She was still drunk and getting drunker, the whisky working its way into her system. She blundered down to the kitchen and drank glass after glass of water, leaving the tap running as she refilled her glass, gulping. The skin on her face was dry and crusted as if she had been sleeping in the sun.

She lowered herself on to the toilet and looked out at her favourite view. The sun was still rising behind the plantation of young pines, casting long misty shadows. Through the open window she felt the motionless warm air of a morning promising the sort of heat that would have directed her day. By midday she would step into the house, across the discarded clogs they wore outdoors in summer, into a cool darkness in which she could breathe. The chickens would be crooning somewhere under the bushes, complaining of thirst but too stupid to seek out their water trough. Vera Kralova, sweating under her breasts, might drop round for a glass of tea, reeking of that sweat as she fanned herself. 'Jesus,' she'd moan, not unhappy, 'but Christ it's hot out there. When was it ever as hot as this? Do you remember?' Hana wouldn't remember. She'd climb down to the cellar to find a jar of pressed raspberry juice from last year and come up wiping the grime from the glass on her skirt. 'Here,' she'd offer, 'have some of this. With ice, if I've got any', and they'd tinkle out to the table by the azaleas with their drinks to swelter in the shade. Milan would have gone to the Frantiseks', scrambling in the outreach of the forest where the murky twilight of the trees in daylight held no terrors. Josef's caged birds would mewl from time to time, from habit, dazed on their perches. Alena would be pouring beer and glistening around the slight creases of her midriff, 'well oiled', as Josef would say, slapping her thigh. An old and tired joke from which Alena would recoil.

But Josef was outside, standing by his car, leaning in through the window hooting his horn. Perhaps he thought they weren't up yet, playing embarrassed. She saw Milan skipping out.

'Hallo, Uncle Josef.'

'Hallo there, Twiglet. Your mum out of her bed yet?'

'Sort of.'

'Ho! What's she been up to, then?'

So she hung out of the bathroom window and waved a whole arm. 'I'm up here!'

'Stop piddling, will you? You've got a train to catch, haven't you?'

No. What a sweet face he had, bearded like a fairy-tale forester's. His trousers hung below his waist because he wore them loose; 'Got to put the bottle somewhere,' he always said.

'Give us a chance, Josef. We haven't had breakfast yet.'

'Then have it quickly. I've got to be going.'

His mates were waiting for him already, then, wanting to be up in the hills before it was too hot. They wouldn't make it, and all on her account. 'I'll just make us a sandwich. Do you want one?'

'Me? Come on, kid. I had my breakfast at dawn.'

Bet he didn't. Just showing off.

He tramped in and out of the house, scrupulously shedding his shoes at the door. She was tempted to tell him not to bother.

'You've got enough stuff here,' he called. 'How long are you away for? A week? You could have fooled me. I know you. You'll be out dancing with some heart-breaker every night. I know you.'

He was loading up. He was in a hurry and she had to comply. She put a sandwich and a glass of milk in Milan's hand.

'Come on. Drink this up. You can eat the sandwich as we go. Uncle Josef wants to be on his way.'

She bundled the boy out, sucking the crumbs from the cracks between her teeth, closed the door behind her, returned, grabbed her cook-book and crammed it into her handbag, then closed the door again. She locked it, nearly throwing away the key but sensing that Josef and Milan had twisted round in their seats and were watching her.

'Okay,' she said.

Briefly his wheels spun on the dry grass and for a moment she imagined the fates holding them back – the car wouldn't make it back up to the gate and she'd be able to stay. Only she didn't want to stay. They rocked down the rutted path, Josef cursing the damage to his undercarriage.

163

Suddenly she said, 'Josef, sorry. I left something behind. I won't be a minute', and leaped out before he could demur. She ran back up the path, her legs sluggish from the previous night's drinking, pulling her keys from her pocket. Into the house. Behind the door her axe leaned against their muddied winter anoraks, the axe Lukas had taken from her hand so he could casually demonstrate how you really chop logs and then raise his glass to her and she could wipe the sweat from his face. She felt almost nauseous. She shouldn't have drunk that whisky. She took the axe, raised it high above her head and brought it down on Aunt Veronika's antique inlaid table. Damn them. Damn the Bolsheviks for killing her father, exiling her lover and making her run away, and damn them for making her double-cross her son and laying suspicion between them. They were not going to get it, when they came looking for her. Not a single valuable thing. The axe bounced off the polished surface leaving a searing scar.She raised it again and again until the table was irrevocably split, then turned towards the chaise-longue. She had to smash it all, but she could not, had left it too late, for Josef was waiting. She dropped the axe on the floor and ran out, forgetting to lock the door. She scrambled back down to Josef.

He was tapping his wedding ring against the steering wheel and looking at his watch. 'For Chrissake, Hani.'

'Sorry.'

'Did you get what you wanted?''

'Yes.'

He didn't ask what it was.

Josef drove with panache, proud of his car, which he kept spotless, proud of his skill behind the wheel. It gave greater pleasure to him than to his passengers, who were flung from side to side as he swung the car nimbly out of one bend into another. Milan was pale. He tended to be car-sick. Hana put an arm round him and drew him to her, as comfort, and because she feared he might be projected against the door and hurt his head.

'Did you finish your breakfast?'

'Yes.'

'And your milk?'

'Yes.'

'That's a good boy.' And a relief. She inspected him again

but he looked much the same. No change yet, and perhaps that was just as well. For the first time she understood Milan's queasiness and herself swallowed repeatedly, her mouth filling with unwanted saliva. It was still the whisky, she knew.

'Josef.' She leaned forward. 'We've plenty of time. Could you slow down a bit? Milan isn't feeling very well.'

Josef twisted round in his seat. The lad *was* looking pale, even for him. So was Hana, for that matter. Nerves, probably. He wouldn't go to a spa if you paid him, all those flat-footed hags in white headscarves telling you were to go, and fat old women with arthritis and flatulence. He slowed down. She had forgotten that he was in a hurry to get back to his friends, who would wait only so long. No matter. He knew where to find them, where they'd be.

Sometimes, up in the forest in the early hours after a day out, the carcass of a deer well hidden, the pheasants under his coat, he dreamed of spending the night by the embers of the fire, not with his companions, whose rum-laden snores he knew of old, but with Hana. He had never mentioned it to her, because it would get back to Alena – those two were so thick. Time was, he'd have wanted his wife up there under the trees with him, between a layer of coats. But you got to know people too well and Alena had a thing about beetles. Funny that she'd never got used to them. He couldn't imagine Hana worrying about anything like that; he could imagine Hana without her clothes under the trees, the dim orange light of the fire settled on the line of her hip and shoulder. He'd never been one of the lucky ones to surprise her at her exercises but he had seen her body basking on the veranda with Alena, but wearing those silly triangles of cloth that always seemed to him, by hiding the tips of her child's breasts and her furry cunt, to conceal the rest of her. If she would only stand before him, just once, completely naked, her arms and legs and neck would also be revealed to him for the first time. It remained a dream and not one that was going to be realised today. But another time, who knew?

At the station he pulled up, switched off and sat unmoving. Hana also sat in silence and Milan said not a word. For some reason Josef was loath to get out of the car and unload Hana's things, as if there were a secret finality in the action that could be prevented simply by leaving her luggage in the boot, as if a week's break in the spa threatened to return her so altered they would have nothing to say to each other. He sighed, shook his head at his womanish romancing, and opened his door. Christ, it was hot already and the city smelt foul. One of those two great clumsy fountains they'd put up had given up the ghost, dribbling from its central nozzle. Probably been like that for months. He took out the two bulky suitcases. She'd be lucky if they lasted the journey.

'Did you reserve seats?'

'No. Should I have?'

Josef was busy with her luggage, so Hana slipped a sealed envelope down the back of her seat and pushed it in. It would be days before he spotted it.

'Dunno. You may have to sit on your cases. You want to be careful they don't burst on you.'

'They'll be all right.'

Hana got out of the car and they stood facing one another, embarrassed.

'Well, there you are. I'd best be on my way,' he said. Milan was leaning against his mother, looking properly peaky, as if he wanted his bed. And they were only saying the other day that the kid had seemed really well this year, didn't need a cure. Josef mussed the boy's hair. 'So, Twiglet. Off on your great trip, eh? Don't forget us in your sanatorium, will you? Send us a card and look after your mum. Women can't manage on their own, know what I mean?' It was a tired old joke they had and Milan responded accordingly, only raising his lashes to Josef's face. 'Go on, then. Off you both go.'

Josef wrapped his arms round Hana and squeezed her. She leaned against him and thought she could sleep standing up, propped up by his massive solidity, like leaning on a wall. He kissed her cheek and suddenly, again, on the lips, putting his tongue into her mouth. She was too surprised to object. In fact, she didn't object but clasped him tighter. Then they both put their arms down and stepped back, astonished at themselves. Hana bent at the knees, grasped a suitcase in either hand. She had forgotten her shoulder-bag still on the ground and Josef picked it up for her, hung it over her head, across one shoulder like the postmistress's canvas bag. A book stuck out of the top and Josef tipped his head to see what it was. He straightened abruptly, his eyes distant with distress. Her recipe book. Why had she got her recipe book? Who took a recipe book to the spa? He touched her arm and spoke in a tight voice:

'Taxis are over there.'

'What do you mean, taxis?'

'Hani, where are you going? Really, where are you going?'

'Be quiet. Please be quiet.' She looked down at Milan, who stood with his head bowed, who hadn't heard, she hoped. 'Please, please be quiet. For my sake, for your sake.' His mouth, behind its beard, was trembling at the corners. He had turned grey, the high colour bleached from his skin like a sun-washed photograph. 'Look, your friends are waiting for you. You'll be late and that's no way to treat them.'

She had given him a reason to be angry and he took it gratefully. 'Don't you tell me how to treat friends.' He flung himself into his car, slammed the door and drove away, revving up, wrenching the car round so that its tyres screeched on the hot tarmac. Heads turned.

Milan was slumping on the pavement.

'Come on, sweetie. Put your hand through here and hold on. I don't want to lose you.' She shuffled with her heavy cases, slowly trailing her son, whose limp hand she clasped against her hip with her arm, towards the taxi rank.

How was she to get Milan on to the plane before he fell asleep? He had obediently drunk the glass of milk she had pressed on him, and had only complained gently – 'It tastes funny. Like medicine.'

'Tastes of plastic, I expect. Never mind. Drink it anyway. It's my fault. I forgot to pour it out of the bag yesterday.' When would she be able to stop lying? But there had been no choice. She had to have him quiet and compliant – asleep.

Milan's head lolled in the taxi and the driver kept eyeing him in his mirror.

'What's the matter with your kid? Is he ill?'

'No, he's fine. Just tired.'

'Kids!'

The driver turned his radio up. Someone was talking about a new nursery school in Bratislava. '. . . and so, once again, our families can rest assured their children are always in good hands.' Two pop-eyed gaudy creatures in green and yellow fur dangled from the mirror. Glued along the dashboard were the photographs of three tumble-haired young blondes blowing kisses between their fingers at the camera. They had signed their names for the driver. Actresses maybe, or pop singers. There were all sorts of advantages in the airport run, Hana supposed.

If she had been a foreigner, he would have got out and helped her with her luggage, but she would be paying in crowns so it wasn't worth his while. He sat in his seat, his elbow at shoulder level, palm cupped to receive her fare.

'Keep the change.'

'Thank you,' he drawled emphatically, and reached round to open the door for her, but still didn't stir. A trio of tourists – an elderly woman with crisp yellow hair and two men in check shirts and light trousers with peaked baseball caps – were emerging from the airport building with their luggage on trolleys, turning their heads left and right helplessly. They had cameras round their necks. Americans! The driver was in luck and sprang out to meet them.

Hana dragged her luggage from the boot and waited by the car. She would take one of the trolleys. Milan was still lolling in the taxi nearly asleep. She began hauling him out, appalled at the weight of his unwilling small body.

'Look,' she said to him in a harsh loud voice – he mustn't sleep yet – 'we're going to get you a drink. I'm thirsty as hell. You must be too, it's so hot.'

Watched by the driver and the Americans, she slid Milan on to the suitcases and wrestled the trolley round towards the terminal door. One of the wheels was jammed and the trolley kept skewing round and tipping. Milan toppled like a corpse. Hana turned the trolley and backed towards the doors but at that moment a stream of Vietnamese jostling trolleys piled high with cardboard boxes came gabbling out. All were men, in dark cotton jackets and trousers, thin as monkeys, clustered together. Hana pulled her trolley back.

Inside the building she had to leave the trolley and push her cases along the floor with her feet, one arm round Milan holding him up, through passport control, where for whole minutes the official, enthroned high in his kiosk, flipped back and forth through the pristine pages of her passport, looking at her, at Milan and back at her photo; then along to customs where again they read her passport as if it were a poem. They prodded her cases but waved them through. She was simultaneously relieved and annoyed. If that was all, she could have taken more things. She had some English notes in the waistband of her trousers, just in case, but was hoping desperately not to have to use them. Nora's money had dwindled, the cost of the tickets as nothing beside what Hana had had to pay, first to the local man, then to his buddy in town, to get the passport and the exit visa. The rest of her cash crackled in her knickers.

Once the suitcases had been labelled and bumped out of sight, she had been able to take Milan in her arms and carry him, his arms wound round her neck, his legs dangling off her hips. She had sat with him on her lap in the departure lounge on a black plastic-cushioned chair. A bar, beaded with high round stools, jutted from the back wall. Libyans in their shirt-sleeves propped their elbows on the counter, tapping the ash from their cigarettes into empty coffee-cups. A group of Russians, with money to spare and surly as Brezhnev, were picking over a presentation box of cut-glass. The saleswoman watched them bleakly, attentive but openly rude. The rows of seats by the plate-glass windows that gave on to the tarmac were crowded with a party of Cubans. There were only one or two women among them, sitting with their plastic carrier bags propped upright between their feet. They carried bouquets of plastic flowers. Their men strutted between the seats in high-heeled shoes of sand and tan, wide sombreros on their heads, their pale jackets unbuttoned. They had high, tight, protruding buttocks and walked like women, but with a demeanour Hana had never seen. They shouted to each other although they were pressed close and she pulled Milan's doped head into her chest. She would have liked him to be more alert so that he could see all these strange people; yet she was glad he was not.

None of these people could be flying to London. Where were the London passengers? She panicked, staring about her. They had gone. She had missed her flight. No one had told her. Deliberately they had let her miss her flight and then they would come and start asking questions. She cowered into her seat but the tannoy tinkled twice and a woman's voice called all passengers on flight BA 515 to London to go immediately to gate A.

Milan's weight dragged her down as she struggled to get up. A man beside her steadied her under the elbow but she neither looked at him nor thanked him. Staggering slightly, she followed a small group of dark-suited men with briefcases. There was a family, carrying posters rolled in wrapping paper, the man with his arms round two cardboard carriers of the bottled beer people had been buying from the bar. The cardboard handle had already given way and he was muttering as the bottles clanked and slipped. They were English. The woman wore an anorak and crumpled corduroy slacks. She had ginger hair and protruding teeth. Hana followed them. She would follow them everywhere. They would lead her. They had two boys, older than Milan but not much, who chased headlong up and down, skidding in their trainers and leaping to catch each other. Their parents didn't seem to mind.

They passed through another narrow doorway with a picture of a gun crossed out in red to one side of it. There was a silence as they waited, all of them, gathered together in their specialness. A young woman in a red and blue uniform walked briskly past with the confidence of one to whom the world belongs, who knows where she is going and what to do when she gets there. She had a clipboard and a key.

Suddenly, Milan moaned – a long deep animal cry of despair. The waiting people moved towards her and the uniformed woman stopped and came back.

'Is everything all right?'

Hana, fearing she was about to be discovered, fearing she had overdosed her son, was white and sweating. She did not understand what the woman said but turned upon her a face of such terror that the woman stepped back before asking, 'Is your child ill?'

One of the dark-suited businessmen came forward. 'She is asking if the boy is ill.'

Hana did not want to speak to this man. She did not know who he was, what he was doing there so close to her, following her, but she had to answer – the people were waiting, watching her. 'No, no. We're fine.'

The uniformed woman smiled but appeared to take no notice. 'If he's ill it might be better not to travel this time. Or we can arrange to have a doctor or an ambulance waiting in London.'

The man translated.

'No, I promise he is quite all right. He slept badly last night, that's all. It happens sometimes.'

The woman raised her eyebrows and turned away. She had other things to do. She unlocked the glass door and the passengers filed down the stairs and across the tarmac. One by one they overtook Hana, whose legs began to buckle under her. She felt a trickle of urine run down her leg and could not stop it. She would not make it up the stairs: she needed her hands to haul her up but her fingers were clenched together around Milan as his body sagged lower and lower.

'Here, let me.' An official from the aeroplane came down the gangway stairs. He plucked Milan from her arms and carried

170

him up as if he were a baby. The uniformed woman took Hana by the hand and led her to her seat. The man laid Milan in the seat next to her and both officials retreated.

Sitting in the plane, her heart thumping, she gasped audibly, aware that across the aisle a man and woman were leaning forward staring at her with horror on their faces as if they feared she was having some sort of attack. She feared it too and gulped air, ordering herself to calm down. She began counting in her head rhythmically and by twenty-three, although her heartbeats were still shaking her ribs, her breath was almost normal. A stewardess patrolled the aisle, glancing from side to side. When she reached Hana she stopped, leaned over and fastened the seat-belt for her, fastened the belt round Milan too. Milan was asleep, unconscious, drugged by the sleeping pill Hana had put into his milk.

Hana looked up at the stewardess and smiled her thanks wanly. The stewardess regarded her doubtfully and briefly passed a hand over Milan's tousled hair. 'I don't know,' she said to herself.

All the passengers on Hana's side of the plane stretched their necks for a view as the aircraft tipped down, flying low over London. It was not quite dusk and the city was not yet lit up. From this height it seemed quite flat. Hana saw rows of trains criss-crossing one another into the distance. She sat back puzzled. London houses, from above, looked like trains. Why?

PART III

Twenty-one

'Why can't she stay in a hotel?' Melanie's response to the news of Hana's impending arrival had been ungenerous. She admitted it, but her own words rang in her mind long after she had finished speaking them. She would not pronounce them aloud again, not so much for fear of antagonising Peter but because she knew that he had decided she must move out of his house, that his childhood friend, if that was indeed all she was, must move in, and that this temporary ejection might serve as a dress rehearsal for a final expulsion.

Contemplating this possibility Melanie was outraged. Not that she particularly wanted to stay with Peter. He had begun to pall, to embody his success and security. His daytime suits she grudgingly accepted as a necessary obedience to the expectations of his clientele. That he had taken to wearing them in the evenings too marked him out as a man who was selecting middle age without a struggle.

Or such was Melanie's view. But then Peter would quickly offer the corrective that Melanie had many views. Too many.

He was not looking forward to this visit. Hana would expect to be taken on outings: the sights of London, Oxford, Cambridge, Stonehenge and the sea. And he would have to forgo the cataloguing of his beer bottles. He wished she didn't have a kid in tow. He didn't know what to say to children and avoided the offspring of his acquaintances. He hoped she wouldn't read him a litany of complaint about shortages and oppression. He knew. He remembered. He would have to get that over to her as quickly as he could, forestall her. But he doubted it would work.

Above all he feared the undertow of the past sucking at the stability of his Englishness. He had given up the tussle with the remnants of his accent but at least it had become unplaceable, and he had done everything else required. He had made a success of himself by the standards that appeared to matter. He had made money, had bought and sold houses, never the loser. He had kept himself to himself and drunk his beer flat and tepid. And he had his bottles in all their stillness, their submissive silence. To them a man could give himself, alone.

Was Hana going to disturb him?

Melanie rolled her skirts and T-shirts into a holdall and swept her moisturiser from the bathroom shelf. She was, it seemed, dispensable – suddenly not needed at all because there wasn't room for her. And why? Because that great huge room upstairs was given over to Peter's damn bottles, to which she was the also-ran. How many hours did he spend each week gathering them, labelling them, tracing the provenance of their makers, arranging them in such a way that their combined architecture complemented their chronology? Every time she put her head round the doorway of his 'museum' – she dared not venture further – she was reminded of the evenings she had sat alone while he hared about the countryside in his fast, elegant and, she insisted, wasteful car in pursuit of nothing more life-enhancing than empty containers. It was such a handsome space overlooking the street, a room in which people might ordinarily have sat in armchairs and on sofas exchanging words and drinking from chunky tumblers. But the new beige Berber carpet was reduced to paths between glass cabinets carefully placed to allow the setting sun of summer to illuminate the fabulous collection, throwing giant shadows, elongated and bulbous, on to the opposite wall. It was not a room where you walked with impunity, but one whose inhabitants silently proclaimed their superiority. Shouldn't the nation benefit from what he had amassed? Shouldn't he donate the collection to some municipal exhibition where curators, like antique naval officers in grey jackets and gold embossed buttons, could patrol these upstanding, narrow-shouldered ratings and feel proud to do so? Melanie's suggestion, expressed more frequently than served her cause, had each time been brushed aside. And now it turned out, far from the bottles going into exile, it was to be herself.

Peter would pay for her to stay in a hotel while Hana was in London. Crazy. She had tossed the offer aside, feigning insult but in reality amused. Could he really be as clumsy as he seemed? She was moving in with a woman friend with whom she had long considered sharing a flat. They had discussed it often but never got round to it. Now it looked as if Peter was getting them there.

She wondered whether Peter would introduce her to Hana, and if he did how he would describe her. 'My live-in girlfriend' or 'my erstwhile live-in girlfriend'? Or – and this was the most likely – 'Melanie'. He avoided words implying possession, with the exception of his bottle collection. On that he bestowed the full force of his attention, dubbing it proudly 'mine'. Good luck to it. She did not want to be 'his', but she was riled that he took her so lightly at her word.

'I'll give you a lift. It's on my way,' he suggested, ushering her from the front door.

She noticed, with irritation, that he had cleared the kitchen table of the remains of last night's takeaway and washed up their breakfast tea-mugs. She rejected the offer – it was a nice day, after all – and strode out, her wrap-around skirt clinging to her legs.

Peter was at the end of his tether, unprepared for what was happening to him and seething at the injustice. He had taken the day off, Friday, to meet Hana; and booked a restaurant for dinner, not too late, bearing in mind the kid. Next he had carefully made up the bed with clean sheets, replenished his booze and bought a stock of good strong coffee and a tin of assorted biscuits. But how was he rewarded? How indeed. It was made worse by the fact that he could not expect to complain to Melanie without conceding to her the right to gloat. As he paced his kitchen, his hand lingered over the phone; he touched the receiver, picked it up, replaced it. Pride held him back. A burst of sobbing upstairs spurred him on. He dialled.

'Hallo? Is Melanie there, please? It's Peter. Would you tell her?'

A pause, and he could hear, through the distant echo of the receiver laid on some surface at the other end, Melanie's friend Sandra calling, with laughter in her voice: 'Melanie! Melanie! It's Peter.' There was a longer pause than he liked before Melanie came to the phone.

Her voice was bright. 'Peter, hallo' – as if they hadn't spoken in months. 'And how are you? How goes it?'

He could have kicked himself but jabbed at the wall with his toe instead. 'Melanie, could you come round? Take a cab. I've got a crisis here.'

'What sort of a crisis?'

If he could only make her curious. 'It's too complicated to explain.'

'Can't you cope?'

'It needs a woman.' A woman. He could hear her thinking it, but you couldn't always choose your words carefully. He steeled himself. 'I need your advice. It could be serious.'

'But it's late. I was going to have a bath. I was going to go to bed.'

'You can go to bed here.' He accepted her shrill epithet in silence, but flinched. 'You'll see what I mean when you come.'

At last she agreed, driven by something other than compassion, without a doubt, but she agreed. And arrived so soon afterwards, carrying her holdall, that he thought perhaps she had never even unpacked it.

'So? Where is she? What's your famous crisis?'

Peter had a story to tell. He had arrived at the airport exactly on time. The plane too was on time, but he had waited for one and a half hours for Hana to come through customs, waited helplessly, not knowing whether she had missed the plane, been detained the other end . . . or what. There was no one he could ask. They wouldn't tell him. 'Passenger lists are kept at the point of embarkation, sir. I'm sorry, we have no way of verifying if your friend was on the plane.' So he waited, needing to pee but afraid to move lest Hana emerge at the very moment he was away. Then she came, among a crowd of Whitsun holiday-makers returning from Majorca with their flip-flops, suntans and Union Jack T-shirts. She was pushing a trolley with the kid draped across her luggage like a dead cowboy over a horse. Her face was grimy, her mouth pressed tight as if she had been slapped. She looked younger than he had expected, still slender – this he did not tell Melanie. She stopped in the middle of the concourse causing a pile-up of people with trolleys behind her, cast about, then saw him and pushed her trolley at a run. People were staring at her and pulling their children back, she looked so wild.

She stepped up to him, held out her hand formally and pecked him on both cheeks. Then she burst into tears. Some people came closer hoping to hear something ghoulish. He took the trolley from her and headed for a corner behind some telephone kiosks. She was hysterical. He hugged her but she just went on shaking and bawling, so he shouted at her and some woman appeared from the other side of the telephone kiosks and planted her feet like a policewoman. He said to this woman, 'She's upset by something and I don't know what. I can't find out why.' The woman edged closer and peered at Hana, made off, and returned with a glass of water. 'She won't drink that,' Peter said, but the woman threw it in Hana's face. It worked, but Hana was drenched. She didn't seem to mind. She kept repeating, 'I'm sorry, I'm sorry', and the woman left because she couldn't understand what Hana was saying.

They had held her up at immigration. Where was she staying? Who with? She had barely understood but repeated Peter's name. They had said they would ring. She had said, 'He is here, he is here', but they hadn't listened. They had asked about money. How much money did she have? She had thought they expected a bribe. They had wanted to see her money but she had hidden it in her knickers. They wouldn't let her go into a private room to get it out. They had asked where it came from. She hadn't been able to make herself understood. They hadn't noticed the kid. She had been surrounded by Turkish families with hundreds of children and a woman who covered her face with her veil, wailing and wailing. It had made Hana wail too.

In the car on the way home Hana had fallen asleep, sitting bolt upright, as if she'd been shot. When they arrived he had had to shout at her to wake her up. He had carried in her luggage, carried in her kid, carried her in. The child wouldn't wake up but slumped on Hana's lap on that chair like a rag doll. He asked if her son were ill. She said no. He started patting the kid's cheeks but she told him to leave him alone. He said he was going to call a doctor and she shouted, 'No!' He made coffee and she drank it off in one go, then puked up on the table.

She had burst into tears again, apologising, and he had taken her upstairs to bed, but she had said this was his bed and she couldn't sleep in it. He had said he was going to sleep in the spare bed next door but she had insisted she would sleep there with the kid, in that tiny bed. Now she wouldn't come down.

'She smells awful. What am I to do?'

Melanie shook her head with that knowing, capable expression that usually set his teeth on edge but not this time. She pulled her wash-bag from the holdall and went up to the bathroom. She ran a bath and poured a generous measure of pine oil into it, went to the spare room and tapped on the door. Someone was breathing heavily on the other side. Melanie felt

179

as tight in her throat as someone who has been charged with breaking bad news, but it was her role to put things right. She opened the door.

The room was in darkness. Melanie said very slowly, 'Hallo, Hana. My name is Melanie. I am Peter's friend.' She turned on the light.

By breakfast-time next morning things were better. Hana was fragrant again, sluiced off by Melanie's pungent bubbles and smelling confusingly like Melanie.

She had been apologising. She didn't know what had come over her, she said; she remembered only fragments. Splintering wood, Josef's tongue in her mouth, a strutting Cuban, a ginger-haired woman with protruding teeth. The memory's tricks are selective, she had once read, to protect its owner, but she didn't know whether she was being spared distress or embarrassment and suffered both.

Her face was strained, pale, drawn but still impish. Cleaned and wrapped around in Melanie's kaftan, too wide and too long, she was reduced to child size.

Her son was sitting next to her, dead white but alive, so silent one couldn't hear him breathe. For the first time Peter took a look at the boy's thin face and was shocked. Hana seemed to have brought with her not her child but her own younger brother Honza, suspended in time, petrified in marble. Hadn't Honza looked just like that when Nora had hauled him helplessly down the street, calling, 'Coo-ee! Coo-ee! Look what I've got'? Peter's nostrils filled with the smell of the dusty grass outside the block of apartments where he had stood with his father; he saw again Engineer Tvrdohlavy's feet poking out from beneath the mayor's car, felt by his side his father's contained and speechless fury. That night Honza had whimpered in his sleep and Hana had sucked her thumb.

'Come along, come along,' Nora had said in English, and pulled the pharmacist's two children up the stairs like bags of heavy shopping. As she was yanked past him, the girl had stared straight into Peter's eyes with a look of such defiance he had stepped back against the wall. Honza's eyelids were lowered: he was looking nowhere and unseeing. Things were being done to him that he could not prevent, so he had, Peter now imagined, fixed reality by keeping his eyes on his feet.

This kid was the same – staring at the table on which Peter

had laid two plates, one for Hana, one for the child. There was a knife by each plate, and a mug.

For his guests' sake Peter had popped round to the corner shop and brought back ham, garlic sausage, Edam, and gherkins in a jar. He was slitting open the sealed plastic round the cold meats, laying the slices in circles on a platter around a flower of the gherkins he cut lengthwise. It was nine o'clock on Saturday morning – early for Peter, very early for Melanie; but Melanie, assuming she might be needed again, had shaken herself downstairs, resentful of the imposition but buoyed also. She stood in the doorway observing Peter's culinary arrangements.

'Good grief. Lunch already?'

'It isn't lunch. It's breakfast.'

'Breakfast!'

'Just to make her feel at home. Do you want some?'

'Don't be silly.'

He'd made tea in a teapot, and wrapped a towel over the pot; all the same, she sat down opposite Hana and the kid. Hana was buttering a slice of bread, laying on the butter in slabs, crunching the slivers of gherkin. She had put ham on a slice of bread for the child but he wasn't eating it, just sitting there with his hands in his lap. He hadn't looked up since Melanie came down, hadn't looked her in the face.

'Peter, what did you say his name was?'

'Milan.'

Hana beamed at Melanie and nodded, hearing her son's name. The boy himself didn't react.

'Hallo, Milan,' said Melanie.

'Milachku' – Hana's voice was nearly chiding – 'say hallo to the lady.'

Melanie understood that the boy was being told to be polite. 'It's all right,' she said, but appraised Milan over the top of her mug of tea. There hadn't been a sound from him, not in the night, not this morning. She wondered if there was something fundamentally wrong with the boy, opened her mouth to say so, then closed it again.

Peter leaned across the table and selected a circle of garlic sausage, wrapped it round a gherkin and ate it. 'Mmm!' he said, almost as if he were surprised, and took more.

Hana watched Melanie nursing her mug of tea and turned to Peter. 'Doesn't Melanie eat breakfast?'

Melanie turned to Peter. 'What? What did she say?'

First to Hana, 'No.' Then to Melanie, 'She said, don't you eat breakfast?'

'No, never, tell her I don't.'

'I have,' Peter said.

Hana was asking, 'What did she say?'

'She said to tell you she never eats breakfast.'

'Why not? She should. It isn't healthy going without breakfast.'

'She doesn't get up in time. By the time she wakes up it's time to get to work.'

'When does she have to be at work?'

'I don't know. It varies. Nine, ten, that sort of time, when she chooses.'

'We have to be at work by six.'

'I know.'

'What was that?'

'We were talking about why you don't have breakfast. I said you don't get up in time; she said she starts work at six in the morning.'

'Milachku, eat up.'

'That's not true, I do get up in time. I just don't feel like eating in the morning. Anyway, what time does she go to bed? I'll bet it's earlier than we do.'

'I expect it is.'

'What did she say? What were you saying?'

'Nothing.'

'I'm in the West!'

'So you are.' Peter leaned across the table, with his hand bunched like a microphone. 'And how do you find our country?'

Hana laughed. 'I don't know yet.'

'What was that?'

'Well, what d'you want to see? Buckingham Palace? The Tower? Piccadilly Circus? Soho?'

'Yes. Everything. And I want to go shopping.'

'Oh, but of course. Oxford Street.' Then he said in English, under his breath, 'Better still, Brent Cross. That'll teach you.'

'What?'

'What?'

Hana cleared away the plates, made as if to wash them but was forestalled by Melanie. The child was still sitting at the table, his piece of bread and ham in front of him. In obedience to Hana's command he had eaten one mouthful.

'Stay there, sweetie,' Hana said. 'I'm just going up to get dressed and tidy up a bit. Melanie will look after you.' But Milan slid away from the table and followed his mother, holding on to the flowing kaftan like an elephant in a circus.

Peter called after him, 'Milan. Aren't you going to finish your breakfast?' Receiving no answer, he shrugged and ate the bread and ham himself.

Melanie, returned to her seat, nibbled on a slice of gherkin. There was a side to Peter with which she was not familiar, a person hidden in a language she could not understand and had never heard until today. Even the quality of his voice was changed, more resonant, seeming to fill the space from wall to wall. The novelty attracted her, the mystery offering her a man she was no longer sure she knew. But she was unnerved. There was something that he shared with Hana, quite separate from the sounds, and the gestures the sounds brought with them, the grimaces and movements of lips and eyebrows: a language, she realised, that rested on something other than words and therefore could not be learned.

Twenty-two

On Saturday Peter took Hana and Milan on a tour of London in his car. Melanie, who did not much want to come, decided she would. Peter sat Hana in the front passenger seat so that she might have the best possible view, and opened a rear door for Milan. But Milan climbed on to his mother's lap and would not budge. Nobody attempted to move him, for some unspoken sense had passed through them all that to do so would be fruitless, unwise, possibly embarrassing. Hana relinquished the front seat to Melanie and gathered Milan to her in the back. He lay down, putting his head in her lap, and slept. Once again he refused to be roused.

As Peter drove he delivered a competent lecture on what could be seen to the left and to the right, and Melanie, demanding a translation, was impressed. She didn't know he knew so much about London. She didn't know half the stuff he was going on about. Or was it all bullshit? Peter bridled. Had he never told her that he'd had a spell as a tourist guide? No, never. Well, there you go, then. Foreigners always knew more about other people's cities than they knew themselves. They looked things up in guidebooks and learned them. Peter had never referred to himself as a foreigner before, Melanie reflected.

Hana swivelled her head obediently as Peter pointed out the sights but she saw nothing. She did not greatly care where the Queen lived, or indeed how. These sights, these places, could all be explored later, with Lukas. She had come to find Lukas and until she had him the city he had made his home did not interest her. Under her hand she felt the warm sleeping body of her son. Perhaps Milan, too, was merely marking time, willing it to pass as quickly as possible, sensing that the questions, the confusions of his life were about to be resolved. She wished she could bring herself to believe it.

Peter decided to take his duties as host to a foreign tourist seriously. He fed Hana and Milan from McDonald's, ignoring Melanie's snort of objection.

'Cheeseburgers'n'chips and a strawberry milkshake. That's what it's all about, isn't it?'

'Well, it shouldn't be.'

'That's another matter. It is, and that's what she's come here to see.'

'What? What are you saying?' Hana asked.

They took their meal to sit on the summit of Parliament Hill where the grass was criss-crossed with kite strings. The breeze was sharp, and high above them a giant kite cracked like washing hung out in a storm. There were dogs everywhere, chasing, snapping, stalking each other with stiff legs and raised hackles. Families processed up and down the steep path; a young couple in jeans and bulky pullovers overtook them, the man carrying a baby strapped against his chest in a cloth sling. One bench was nearly free but for two old women in windcheaters and flyaway grey hair who were conversing in German with wide wet mouths. They edged closer together to make room for the newcomers.

Hana bent her head close to Milan and whispered instructions in his ear. He turned his head away but took a chip from her and pulled a long suck at his milkshake. Hana took a large bite from her cheeseburger and nodded vigorously, chewing. She drew on the straw and her mouth filled with a thick foaming sweetness, shocking her as it mixed with the burger. She swallowed, drew on the straw again and turned to Melanie.

'Very good,' she pronounced in English.

On Sunday Hana left Milan sleeping and crept about the house. Her hosts were still in bed and would not be up early, Peter had warned her.

She looked down into the garden below. It was small. On either side and backing on to it were similar gardens of houses just the same. On the lawn to the left there was a swing; to the right a climbing frame – but no children in the gardens on this fine morning. Each had a wall round it. She thought, if there were a child playing on his swing or on his climbing frame, it would be a sort of solitary confinement. The other gardens were planted with flowering shrubs and the lawns were mown. Peter's was unkempt, which she did not understand. Peter had said his friend was a gardener.

She sat on the divan in the next room and watched Peter's collection of bottles as if she were expecting it to move. She got up and slowly circled the glass cases, bending to read the minutely typed labels stuck on to the glass in line with each bottle. 1697 Exeter Ale. Aloysius Baker, Bury St Edmunds 1811. James Hamble or James Hamble Son. The words meant nothing but the glass gleamed. She put out a finger and touched the cold surface, wondering. She thought of Peter's father and his catalogued lists of books and records.

The house was silent, breathing in the rhythm of the breathing of its sleepers. The street outside was silent too. Last night she had said to Milan, 'Listen, sweetie, we're in England, do you understand? Where the lady Nora was. You remember, she sent you clothes. And Peter sent you your Lego for Christmas. I can't tell you yet but there's someone very special here. You wait, you'll see. You'll be really pleased.' Milan had stared at her with an expression she had never seen before and could not fathom. It might have been hatred, distilled hostility, but there was in it, something that shook her. Something blank behind the eyes, as if Milan had heard but not listened, as if Milan had not heard and could not hear, as if Milan was not there at all. 'You liked that drink, didn't you?' she had asked, and he had liked it, she had seen it from the way he had sucked and sucked at the straw. Milan had not even turned his head towards her. 'Give me a kiss,' she had said and held out her arms. He had crept into them on to her lap but then sat motionless and formal, as if she were a stranger on to whose lap he had been commanded. When she went to the lavatory he followed her and calmly pushed his way into the narrow little room with her, without a word, and again there was something about the way he did it that took her breath away and she dared not gainsay him. He did not speak to her, but he did not let her out of his sight. She thought, what have I done? But she clenched her teeth. What she was doing had to be done and it was as much for Milan's sake as it was for hers, even if he couldn't, as yet, understand. In time she would explain; perhaps she would not need to; if only he would speak to her.

She went to look at him again, sleeping the sleep of complete exhaustion, the sleep that renounces life itself, replaces it. She knelt on the floor beside the bed and laid her head next to his to listen to his breath, as she had when he was newly born and home from hospital. So she stayed, bent over and twisted, knees on the floor, her head next to her son's head on the pillow, and prayed.

But, not used to such a late start, her stomach rumbled. She must not help herself in someone else's house where customs were unknown, where she couldn't tell what food was meant for which meal. Even so, she would at least have a look. She went to Peter's strange sparkling kitchen where all was black and red, metal and moulded plastic. She opened the fridge and found it quite empty but for a carton of milk, a tub of margarine and some beer. She didn't understand. She lit a cigarette standing at the sink, tipping the ash into the plughole and dripping water on to it, guiltily, afraid to be caught. She soaked the stub-end and looked about her for a bin but could not find one, put down the dead cigarette, picked it up again and put it in her pocket. There was a clock on the wall with thin black hands on a numberless disc of glass. The hands suggested quarter to ten. When would they wake up?

She went upstairs again, less worried by her hunger than by the aimlessness of being a guest in a house of sleeping hosts. Their door was ajar and she positioned herself so that she could see in without, she hoped, being seen. Peter was sleeping on his back, his thick hair more startling in his sleep on his pillow than when he was awake. He was handsome really, maybe, but she could not separate these heavier, harder male features from the still soft contours of the adolescent student, the plump child. Melanie, on her stomach, face turned sideways towards the door, wore nothing in bed, just as Hana did when she was at home. But of course, Hana remembered, Melanie was, perhaps, at home. Peter had not made this clear. Hana admired Melanie's long fair hair and wondered how she wore it when she was working. Melanie had held her hand that first night, led her into the bathroom, into the scented steam. But there was something sharp about Melanie that Hana would have liked to understand better; it troubled her. How she was to understand it she didn't know. She thought instead of Nora, blundering about in the language, how funny that had been. Only it wasn't funny any more. How much had Nora really not understood? Hana felt herself diminished in this place, where she was helpless. She wanted urgently to do something, it didn't matter what.

Just inside the door of Peter's bedroom was a bulging pillow on the floor. Hana knelt again, edged the pillow-case gingerly towards her and found it filled with men's socks. They looked brand new. She sniffed them: dirty. Now she had something to do.

She opened every door, every drawer in the kitchen, in the bathroom, searching for a container that looked as if it might be washing powder. In the end she washed the socks, fourteen pairs of them, with the bar of soap in the bathroom, hanging the socks, squeezed almost dry, along the rim of the bath. Halfway through she sensed Milan standing beside her, very close. She said, 'Hallo, did you sleep well?' And Milan said nothing at all.

Later that morning, when she had observed that breakfast was not kept in the house but bought for the occasion, that Melanie did eat breakfast although perhaps only on Sundays, and only if Peter had been out for croissants and blackcurrant jam, that Milan had enjoyed his croissant because he was blotting up the crumbs on his plate with a saliva-moistened finger, she heard an argument between Peter and Melanie. She couldn't follow what was being said but she knew that she was the subject of their quarrel.

Peter, entering the bathroom to shave, had encountered the row of twenty-eight socks along his bath, neatly laid there in pairs, smelling of toilet soap.

'Bloody Hell!' he said with such vehemence that Melanie, fearing he had injured himself, came running to his aid, anxiety wrinkling her face, but burst out laughing.

'What's so damned funny? What is this? What's going on here?'

'She was trying to be helpful, for Chrissake, Peter. She's only done your washing.'

'Nobody does my washing. I don't have washing. When I need clean socks I'll buy them!'

'I know that but she doesn't.'

'She doesn't have to know anything. Why can't she keep her paws to herself and not interfere?'

'Why are you so angry? She probably wanted to do something for you because you invited her.'

'I never did. I didn't invite her. She invited herself.'

'Well, you said she could stay here and she wants to do something for you.'

'Typical. Same as always, nosing about after people, tidying up. She was like that before.'

188

'You said. But she's trying not to be a trouble.'

'Well, she is a trouble, and that damned moronic kid.'

'He's not a moron. Don't say that.'

'Look, where are we? Sunday? Two days and he hasn't said one thing. Not a peep.'

'I should have thought you'd be glad. You don't like children.'

'Nor do you.'

'I never said I did, but this isn't my house, not my things, not my bottle collection. That's what you were so worried about. That the boy would tear the place apart. Well, this kid isn't going to do that, is he?'

'How do you know? He's obviously retarded.'

'No, he isn't.'

'Well, what is he, then? You don't call that normal, do you?'

'Nno.'

'So?'

'I don't know. There's something wrong but I don't know what it is.'

'Ask her.'

'How can I? She can't put two words together. You ask her.'

'Not me. It's no concern of mine. I'm going out. For a walk.'

Hana heard the slamming of the front door. It seemed her presence caused friction here too. Dr Cerny and Nora had sounded just the same.

The tall window was open at the top and at the bottom, it was so hot outside these nights. Hana lay on her back staring at the night sky, tinted orange in the distance. Melanie had kindly pulled down the blind for her but Hana, waiting until she heard their bedroom door click to, released it again. Blinds, curtains – they seemed to add solemnity, power even, to the walls. She preferred the black oblong, the hole into the outer world.

She must make herself pleasant, become a wanted addition to their lives for the short while she was to be with them. She had done it before. Dr Cerny, irritably bedridden with his flu, had scowled at her saying, 'What's she doing here?' Or had he not said it? She could no longer remember. And Nora had almost rubbed her hands in anticipation of the care she expected to receive.

Hana would look upon Peter and Melanie, busy all day, as invalids, lavish upon them the total solicitude in which Milan

189

had made her so practised, cause the house to sparkle in the hard testing sun of the season. She would devise delicacies they would never trouble to prepare for themselves. No, she would cook for them as if she were cooking for Lukas, she would cook as she had never cooked before. She would devote herself to a special meal, and the preparing of it would use up the long hours of another day, bringing him nearer.

'I buying,' she announced to Melanie after breakfast. Peter had already gone to work. Melanie was watching Hana polishing at the cutlery with a tea-towel.

'What? What do you want to buy?'

'Eat.'

'Are you hungry? Oh, I'm so sorry. You're quite right, there's never any food here. We always eat out or takeaways.'

Hana shook her head, less in disagreement than in incomprehension. 'I cook you and Peter.'

Melanie stared at her momentarily, giggled, but immediately understood what it was Hana intended to do and foresaw disaster. Hana must be stopped or Peter would lose patience and sling her out. And so what? Would it matter? She looked down at the small woman standing there with the foolish smile of the suddenly inarticulate on her face, hand in hand with her unnerving, wordless child. His round eyes gazed back at her and briefly she imagined they registered her presence. Melanie's considerable conscience offered her a warning prod. If Hana were to leave unwillingly, it promised her little peace. Besides, she was intrigued. Was the boy *compos mentis* or wasn't he?

'No. No cooking. We go restaurant tonight.' She winced at the contagion of the flawed, accented language but Hana didn't notice the unintended pastiche.

'Yes, I like give. You show shop? You say me where is shop?'

Defeated, Melanie slung her handbag over her shoulder. 'Come on then.'

They walked with Milan between them. Melanie held out a hand to the boy but he slid his behind his back, edging closer to his mother.

Melanie led Hana to the High Street, indicated for her, with much energetic mime, which butchers she must avoid, pointed out to her the vegetable market, showed her the supermarket, pressed the front-door key into her hand and leapt for a bus. Twisting in her seat to see where they would go first, she saw Hana and her mute son motionless where she had left them, while around them the people to whom the city belonged seemed to be performing the steps of some frenetic dance.

All that morning Melanie discussed winter foliage with a client who had bought three barnacled urns for a patio and wanted to see them instantly resplendent. However, at the back of her mind and nudging forwards was the image of Hana lugging her shopping and adrift in the back streets; mugged or cheated of her money; made tearful by some appalling piece of rudeness; or tightly aproned, chopping onions with streaming eyes, stirring and frying for Peter, and Peter exasperated out of all courtesy, scowling, shouting, opening the front door and, positioned like a Victorian martinet on the threshold, thrusting out his arm with index finger extended. Hana cowered, waiflike and shrunken, with her child in her arms.

Melanie was torn. She was impelled to rush home, leaving the glass of iced tea her client had given her, to interpose herself before the damage was done, to make the incredible excuse – 'I asked her to cook tonight'; she was impelled to stay away, go out for the evening by herself and leave them to it. Half-measures. The iced tea, not quite drained, remained on the white-painted wrought-iron garden table. The client saw her to the door. She mooched home.

The front door was propped open, releasing a succulent aroma, and Peter's car was parked outside. On this day, of all days, he had to choose to come home early. Melanie heard voices in the kitchen sharing a lilting cadence that did not suggest discord.

'Hi!' Peter came out to meet her, his face glistening from the heat, a tall misted glass of beer in his hand. 'We're going to have such a meal tonight, Melanie, you just wait. You should see what the silly woman has been up to.'

On a steaming summer's evening – soup. Meat in a sauce. Dumplings. Bowls of preserved morello cherries. Cakes like cushions filled with poppyseed. On a summer's night. The table had been laid with everyone's bowl of cherries already placed above their plates. Melanie would have settled for a salad. Peter had eaten to a state of immobility. Hana ate like someone in a canteen, in a hurry, starting on her cherries before the others had finished their first course.

Peter was laughing at something Hana said; elbows on the

table, sleeves rolled up, empty beer bottles. Melanie stood up and brusquely cleared the table.

'I'll wash up, then.'

'You must do as you like.' Dismissing her; don't interrupt, Melanie, we're busy, we've got so much to say. Why was he so pleased when he was so angry about his fucking socks? And what was he laughing at, laughing from the depths of his belly as she had not heard him laugh before? They were cutting her out.

'Oh, Hani. For God's sake, don't tell Melanie that story. You'd be out on your ear before the washing up's done.'

Melanie responded to her name. 'What was that?'

'Hana was telling me about her shopping expedition.'

'So where do I come into it?'

'I was just telling her she shouldn't tell you.'

'Why on earth not?'

'Because you'd freak out.'

'What do you mean? What did she say?'

'Well, she went into this shop, which just happened to be an Indian one, helped herself to some celeriac and ran away without paying.'

'Why?'

'Because it was an Indian one.'

'What?' Melanie stared at Hana, who had followed enough and was nodding, delighted. 'Why?'

'Disease.'

'What disease?'

'I don't know. Disease you get from Indians.'

They were making fun of her, surely. Her face hardened. It wasn't funny.

'Like what?'

Peter translated and Hana launched into a long explanation which set Peter laughing again.

'What did she say?'

'I can't tell you. Really, I mustn't.'

Melanie dried her hands and sat down. The table separated them.

'Tell me what she said.'

'Well, worms, for starters. You see, if you sit next to a Vietnamese in a bus you get worms in your teeth. They have these worms which don't affect them but do affect you.'

'You're joking.'

'Yes, I am. But she isn't.'

Grimly Melanie returned to her washing up.

'She's offended,' Peter told Hana, cocking his head at Melanie's stiff stance at the kitchen sink.

'Why? There are some things people don't know about. She should think about it.'

'Oh, she will, she will.' And Peter shook with the deep chuckle of a more convivial man. 'But tell me, Hani, how's old Honza. What's he doing these days?'

Hana spat theatrically. 'Pffui!'

'Oh. That bad?'

'Listen, Peter, I'll tell you.' Their heads moved together and they did not notice Melanie leaving the kitchen. 'That bastard' – Peter raised his eyebrows – 'he's got it all nicely sewn up. Nice wife, two kids, a three-room flat, a video, a music centre, a stack of records from the West, a car, an automatic washing machine and a passport. And all because his arse warms the biggest chair in the Institute of Economics.'

'Well, he always was a clever fellow.'

'Oh come on, Peter. He sold out.'

'Unlike the rest of the population.'

'And who are you to talk?'

'Leave me out of it. I'm English, through and through. Didn't I ever tell you? Just as Mummy wanted.'

'Don't talk about Nora like that. You should respect the dead, especially your parents. Where would I be if it wasn't for her? How would I have made it here without her money?'

'I wasn't putting her down. I'm not kidding, though. Why would I have gone back once I was here? Why would I? It wasn't a question of selling out, because I was never asked to stick my neck out.'

'Well, aren't you lucky. And aren't you bitter?'

'You mean you were. What were you asked? Were *you* asked to sign something?'

Hana shrugged.

'And what did you do?'

Hana shrugged again. Perhaps Melanie forgot to wash the saucepans. Melanie. Where was Melanie?

'Peter . . .'

'I've been wondering, though. Have you any idea why my mother sent you that money? I mean, not that she shouldn't, of course.'

'Peter . . .'

'She damn near got buried in that pendant, you know. She

193

was wearing it when she died. I don't know what made me suggest they take it off her. Thcn we found this note she'd left, saying she wanted it sold and that you were to have the money.'

Hana shivered. Nora's mountainous body, pale as cheese, poured on to a slab with the pendant round her neck and someone fumbling at the clasp, stripping jewels from the dead. And now she was carrying the proceeds in her knickers. The meal they had just eaten was Nora's pendant, the aeroplane they had flown in was Nora's pendant. Yes, why had she wanted Hana to have the money?

'Peter. Melanie's not here. She's gone out.'

'So she has.'

'Yes, but where? Did she say she was going?'

'Can't say I was listening.'

'Don't you care?'

'Not really.'

Could that be true or was he pretending? His face was handsome in the candlelight but he had been making fun of her, making fun of Melanie. She got up from the table and instantly a small, silent shadow followed. She called up the stairs: 'Melanie!'

Melanie lay on her back in the garden, the uncut grass as sharp as straw through the flimsy cotton. It kept her awake when she might have fallen asleep and she didn't want to sleep. She couldn't hear their voices out here. She couldn't hear them laughing.

Hana searched the house calling constantly as if Melanie were a missing child, her voice rising in pitch, becoming shrill, almost angry. Come out, the game's over, we're not playing hide-and-seek any more. But fearing the child is gone for good. She lost her enthusiasm for this chase in the bedroom where she slept with Milan (Milan standing beside her, holding her hand) and leaned her hot head against the cold glass of the window. There below in the grass was a shape, a body, light against the dark, motionless as a grotesque doll.

'Peter!' she was shouting again. 'For God's sake, quickly. I've found her.'

But Peter had fallen asleep sitting at the table, his head on the square of his folded arms.

'Let her be all right, Milachku. We never do the right thing, do we?'

She knelt in the warm grass by the inert body. Melanie's head was turned sideways, her arms spread wide like a lowered crucifix. The fingers gripped the grass, the eyes were open, staring stonily up at Hana. Hana took one of Melanie's hands and pulled at it but Melanie tensed her arm, pressing it against the ground. The grass ripped.

'Melanie. Please. Soon I going. I am not clever.'

No, you're not, but you've turned the tables on me. Hana lay down beside Melanie and the two women looked straight up into the orange-tinged sky. The grass smelt dusty. What the hell was wrong with that kid? Melanie dropped the handful of torn grass on to Hana's stomach and sat up. Her nails were tight with dust and grass seed. What she wouldn't do with this garden if she were let. She flicked Hana's thigh.

'Come on.'

But it didn't alter the fact that Hana was up to something, forehead to forehead with Peter, and if Peter couldn't see that then he was as blind as a man. Look at the way she fed him, what she cooked for him, solid nostalgia, and didn't he put it away? Was that what she should have been doing all this time, kneading dumplings and stirring sauces? You have to be joking.

On the landing between the two bedrooms Melanie suddenly stepped back, bowed dramatically and with a flourish indicated the open door to Peter's room. He had taken himself to bed and lay naked on top of the tousled sheet.

'All yours,' she said.

Hana burst out laughing and put her arms round Melanie to hug her. 'Listen, if you only knew who's waiting for me.'

Melanie, stiff as a Christmas tree in Hana's embrace, couldn't understand a word.

Hana knew that gratitude must be expressed but dreamed of a time and a circumstance in which it would no longer be necessary. That time was not yet with her and once again she was aware that she was indebted to these people, who were putting themselves out for her – it was no good pretending otherwise – whose unfathomable relations she had somehow disturbed. When she looked back she could remember only one short period of her life when she was not beholden to someone else. Only the first years of her childhood remained untarnished by the burden of gratitude, but Hana, grown sceptical, examined her own musings with a raised eyebrow. Nostalgia, she had been heard to say, was for the elderly. Yet there was no getting away from it. Thanks be to Nora, thanks be to Aunt Veronika, and how can I thank you, Peter and Melanie? She would thank them most sincerely but without profound enthusiasm, for she was not enjoying herself; only biding her time, ticking the days off on her fingers, sensing the weakening of her will.

She had planned. She had planned to present herself to Lukas on the last day. She had intended to be an ultimatum but she was not going to be able to hold out.

Peter and Melanie had been so very kind, so generous, laying open to her their city where she had plotted so long to be. They had taken her to a shopping emporium where fountains played and distant music tinkled somnolently, they had called out to her feel the softness of bright wools, to sniff at perfumes, eat a cake. They had offered her museums, the Houses of Parliament, a trip up the river to Greenwich, but her distracted mind slithered over the city's surface, finding no toehold, lacking the commitment to seek one.

She could not hold out but she must. Every evening they asked her what do you want to do tomorrow and she had no answer. They thought her dull, but she had no answer none the less. She would accept what they proposed but had no wishes. Let them only suggest something, anything that would last from morning until evening. What about the zoo, maybe Milan would like the zoo? Glances were exchanged. But yes, why not? Yes, let's go to the zoo. Hana did not like zoos, nor yet did Melanie and Peter, but no one said so. Milan was given an ice-cream with a stick of chocolate in it. He ate it slowly, methodically, staring before him as if unaware that he was eating an ice-cream. They stood, the four of them, bunched together; and around them ran children whose parents were somewhere else, and shouting. So what shall we go and see? Melanie chose the children's zoo because they had come here for the kid, after all. A fat cinnamon pony plodded the outer perimeter of a circle of bales of straw. On its back a small girl wedged her feet into the loops of leather that held the stirrups, which dangled below her short legs. She slumped, both hands gripping the horn of the saddle. Her mother walked beside her, an anxious hand on the girl's back. A dejected young man in wellingtons preceded the pony trailing a leading rein. Other children were waiting their turn in a queue that broke and re-formed. Boys fired imaginary guns across the bales of straw. Would Milan like a ride? Who could tell? It was hot. Peter bought cans of Coca Cola with striped straws and they all stood drinking. Let's show him the small animals, the guinea pigs and rabbits. You can pick them up and stroke them. Look at the brown one, isn't he soft? Melanie selected a plump, quivering body and placed it in Milan's arms. The boy started violently and grasped the rabbit so tightly that Hana had to leap forward to rescue it. Returned to the patch of grass, the rabbit crouched, its ears flattened along its humped back. The Frantiseks kept brown rabbits.

Twenty-three

The house was quiet. Peter and Melanie had both gone to work today, the last day, and Hana had announced she was going to wander around taking pictures. Instead she ran a bath, and added to it a pearly-pink ball of bath oil from Melanie's jar. She watched it dissolve in glutinous ribbons, tested the water and shed her clothes. She had lost her appetite in the waiting and grown as scrawny as the child she had once been. She ran the fingers of both hands up and down her ribs, elbows out to the sides, her shoulder-blades protruding like wings. This was no good. One wall of the bathroom was a mirror, floor to ceiling, and through the steam she judged her outline, a young boy's body. Womanhood seemed to have fallen from her as if it had never been more than a veneer, just when she needed it most. She clambered into the bath, dipping her buttocks cautiously in the water. She felt them reddening and held her breath as she forced herself to sit down, lie back. Around her the oily pink water drifted into question marks. Her breasts were even too small to float any more. If only she had Melanie's body, on loan, full-breasted, round-hipped . . .

Milan sat on guard on a stool by the bath, a wizened dwarf in the steam, keeping his counsel. What price would have to be paid later she could not tell. If Lukas rejected her a second time, if he rejected their son, she would have to account for herself. But not yet. She must not even consider that yet.

She had an address dictated to her by the man at the BBC. Oh yes, he said, no problem. You'll find him at the Czech club, he's mostly there.

In the sunlight Milan held his mother's hand. It was sweating.

Dr Cerny disembarked from the early-morning bus and rubbed his eyes. He had slept well, as he knew he would, having taken the precaution of swallowing a sleeping pill before setting out for the bus station. He wore his haversack on his back and already his shoulders ached from the weight. He was as skilled at packing a haversack as a soldier – it only required a little thought and well-folded clothes. The sun was rising high, the sky perfectly blue and promising to remain so, but it was unwise ever to rely too completely on promises. Therefore Dr Cerny had included in his luggage an oilskin, his heaviest walking-boots and a groundsheet to sit on when he took Milan up to picnic in the mountains. So perfectly had he arranged these items in the bag that he had had room enough to include a large-scale map of the area and a magnifying glass through which they would examine local fauna.

He knew of old that he must sit in the open air for a few minutes to clear his head from the lingering effects of the sleeping pill. He was anxious to make as lively and youthful (he shook his head) an impression as reality would allow. He rotated his aching shoulders one after the other, got to his feet, pushing down on his knees to lever himself up, and stretched up, to the sides, down, in obedience to the memory of boyhood callisthenics. His fingers tingled, the blood had run to his head; he considered himself fully awake.

In the reception, a woman in white cotton with a white cotton cap tied around the top of her head sat by the open door fanning herself with a newspaper. Her wide forearm moved up and down with the regularity of a sluggish piston. Her eyes were closed. Dr Cerny remembered that in establishments like this you could not tell who was a doctor, who a nurse, who the cook, who the masseur. All dressed in white cotton and all displayed ill-temper. The ill-temper of this woman was concealed by her closed eyelids and the temporary pleasure she was experiencing from the fanning newspaper. Dr Cerny's request required her to open her eyes, to get up from her seat by the open door and to persuade him physically, because he seemed not to be willing to accept her assurance, that there were no people such as he described at this spa.

'Nor will be. See for yourself.' She pushed towards him the book in which present guests were inscribed in ink and future ones in pencil.

'Well, perhaps they have used another name?' Dr Cerny's natural diffidence of manner was, for once, put to one side. He

199

had come a long way and for all this woman's rudeness, red and ugly as she might be, he would not be easily deflected.

'Are you looking for criminals? Who would use another name? What's wrong with the name they've got?'

Dr Cerny felt bound to agree. He could not imagine why Hana should reject her name, nor which alternative she might choose. Still he persisted:

'Never mind about the names. I'm looking for a woman of about this height' – he held out his hand, palm down, level with the top of his ear – 'and slim' – with both hands – 'short brown hair, grey eyes, with a little boy of seven. Very thin and pale.'

'They're all pale when they come here.'

'And rosy and robust when they leave, I do not doubt.'

This woman, however, was not to be placated. Frankly, she couldn't care less what colour they were coming in or going out. She had not seen any short-haired grey-eyed woman with a small thin boy.

'Perhaps one of your colleagues?' suggested Dr Cerny. 'This is a large place. You are obviously kept extremely busy. It's possible, isn't it, that there might be clients here whom you have not yet met?'

'Are you doubting my word? Isn't my word good enough for you? Well, all right then, I'll get the Comrade Director. But he won't like it one little bit. He doesn't take to being disturbed. But that's your problem.'

The Comrade Director was, indeed, only a little more affable than the woman. She had taken up a position behind him, at his shoulder, like a bodyguard, an expression of expectation on her face. Dr Cerny, making an effort to feel charitable, told himself that most of the time she was doubtless bored and that, contrary to appearances, she was now possibly enjoying herself for the first time that day. He did not wish to curtail anyone's pleasure.

The Comrade Director wiped his mouth on the back of his hand. 'Yes?'

'I'm enquiring about two of your clients. A woman and her child.'

'Why don't you look in the book?'

'I have. Their names aren't there.'

'Then they aren't here.'

'I feel certain they must be. They are booked to be here for a week. Today is the sixth day in that week. How many clients do you have at the moment?'

'Full house.' A flutter of doubt creased the Director's forehead. He lowered his voice and pressed a smile from his lips. 'You're not from the inspectorate, are you?'

Dr Cerny did not understand. 'My name is Cerny, medical doctor from the Department of Paediatrics at Merunkov.'

'I can show you our books. Receipt of medical equipment, everything.'

'I would be very interested to see them. But later, if you don't mind. At the moment I would prefer to sort out this matter of the two people I am looking for.'

The result was a guided tour, through steam bathhouses, massage rooms, the mineral bathing pools, canteen, exercise room, gardens. It took a long time. The Director led Dr Cerny along a complex and twisting route with the intention, entirely successful, of so confusing him that he could not take note of how many available rooms there were or how many clients actually occupied them. They bypassed altogether the outhouse at the back where the allocated provisions, which had turned out to be in excess, awaited collection by the Director's brother-in-law. Dr Cerny noticed only one thing, and that was that Hana and Milan were not there, had not been there, would not be coming, were not expected, had never been heard of, did not exist, for all the Director knew.

They walked, stopping at every intersection for Hana to consult the map she had taken from Peter's car. She imagined Lukas running towards her, arms flung out, the light in his eyes and in his hair. She saw him on a platform, caressing his guitar while people on an endless bank of seats sat in rapt silence, alternately disturbed and amused. But then – and a surge of terror swept over her – she pictured him standing, head on one side, gazing down at Milan's upturned face and shaking his head. 'Sorry, Hani. Not my child. Don't recognise him at all. Try someone else and get off my back.'

Traffic roared; cars threaded on a necklace along the road, glittered under the sun. It was on a bend, indistinguishable from its neighbours, a grey-brick double-fronted house. The front door was black and dusty, and closed. Hana looked for a bell, placed the flat of her hand against the door and pushed. The door swung open. Inside it was cool, smelling like home.

Someone was cooking. A wide staircase curved up opposite the door, a short hallway ran past to the back. A door off the hallway seemed to be the source of the smell. She opened the door and gasped on to a flight of stairs, steep as a ladder, plunging down into a basement. By the sound of it, someone was hacking meat with a cleaver. She recognized the sound and visualised the squat blade rising and falling. Somebody was swearing and there was laughter.

'Excuse me,' she called. 'Is Mr Vratka here today?'

'Who's that?' A man's head, flattened like a frog's, peered up the steep stairs.

'I'm looking for Lukas Vratka.'

'Out the back.' The man shooed her away with his hand, like wiping crumbs off a table. 'Left-hand door.'

She stopped at the open doorway, on the outside, the safe side, and gripping the door-frame with both hands for support bent her upper body through. A long room with brown-lino floor, wooden tables with wooden chairs tucked in – no guests yet, nor expected – and opposite was the bar, high, formica-topped. Empty. Someone had been through, for the surface glistened, recently wiped with a damp cloth. Hana stepped in. At the far end another door was propped open. It led on to a small concrete landing with a single rustic wooden table and benches on both sides and hanging flower baskets on iron hooks lurching from the wall. Concrete steps, rough-cast and flinty, propelled down to the garden. An immense wide lawn, cut grass but spotted with weeds and bare patches. At the further end two great rusted swings for children, with no children. And behind them some dusty, dark-leaved shrubs.

'Do you want a go on the swings?'

Milan didn't reply.

Footsteps behind her. She turned her head, offering her profile.

'Well, and I wasn't wrong. It is Hana. I thought I knew that arse from somewhere. How are you, girl? What are you doing in this hell-hole?'

The sunlight still seared her eyes, blinding her. She couldn't see. Now she could. He had a white apron strapped tight over the hips.

'I've come to see you.' She swallowed. Not what she intended.

'Great! Really? Well, let's sit down. Do you want a drink?'

'No thanks.'

202

'Czech beer. Good stuff. No? Well, I will. Coffee, though?'

'Yes, all right.'

He rose, padded to the inner door, feet in flapping faded-blue canvas. His buttocks nudged one another. He called out the order, shouted something to an answering bark.

'They'll be along. He makes good coffee, that one. One thing you can say for the place, the beer and the coffee. So you've come to see me, all the way from Bytlice?'

'No, don't be silly. I just heard you were here. Someone mentioned it.'

'I'm astonished anyone knows.' Did he sound bitter? 'So, how've you been?'

But she had nothing to say. 'I'm fine. I got given some money by a woman I used to know when she died here. So I thought I'd travel.'

'A lot of money?'

'I thought so, only it goes so fast.'

'You're telling me.'

The man from the kitchen was in the doorway, clapping one hand against the frame to attract their attention. He held out a cup. Lukas collected it.

'You know' – setting it down – 'sugar? They're stingy beyond belief here. I tell you. Do you know how much they give me? Two pounds an hour. That's eighty pounds a week. You'll get tips, they said, but you know these bastards. If anyone's meaner than the English it has to be the Czechs in exile. Tips! Don't make me laugh.'

'What do you do?'

'Well' – vigorously rubbing an imaginary surface – 'mopping up, pouring out. Some of it goes down me, mind you; there has to be some compensation, they owe me that much.'

'But I thought you were having concerts. I heard you.'

'Yes? On the radio? I always wondered if there was anybody out there. I'm glad it was you.' Leaning forward he covered her hand with his. 'But there's not much going on in the music scene here, not at the moment. And the record people are no damn help. It's either finance yourself or forget it. They said I was too old for the scene, I said I wasn't into that sort of music. They said there wasn't a market for mine. A market! They want to make a market out of national destiny. But that's these people all over, they don't give a damn. Find yourself a place to stay, find yourself a job, find yourself this, find yourself that, then this chap I met gave me a bit and said did I want to do odd-jobbing for people, so I say yes, why not, got to do something to keep body and soul together to make it to the evenings when I can write. But even there, people with big houses, videos, hi-fis, dish-washers, everyone his own room, and they stand back and look at you as if you were a gipsy and they say, oh yes, and what can you do? And you say, well, I can do you a bit of painting or digging or something, and they say, well, we'll start you off on one pound fifty an hour, and then we'll see, if you're any good we might up it. And I thought, no bloody thanks, I didn't come here to be exploited.'

His wrists were puffy and the line of his jaw had blurred.

'Anyway, how are you? Is that your kid? I didn't know you'd got married. Though, come to think of it, how would I have known? I haven't seen you in ages. It must be seven years.'

'It's eight.'

'Is it? There you are, then. I got married, did you know? It didn't work out, though. I don't know why. I did think sometimes that if we'd had a kid it might have been different, but she didn't want kids, and I always wanted a kid so much. I told you that, didn't I? And now here we are, you're the one with the kid and I'm stuck here pulling beer for people with a handful of war medals and memories between them, all second class, dreaming of the First Republic. I did a couple of concerts but it's always the same forty people, very sweet sad exiles and so on, turning up so I don't end up singing to myself, but you can't go on like that. And they haul in their English buddies but you have to explain everything. And Hani, you know, I can't write songs any more. Not new ones. I sit there and try, I strum a bit and find a tune and that's okay, the tune is there but I can't find any words. Literally. No words at all. I think it's this place. It was a mistake coming here. I should have gone to Germany or Holland, or Canada perhaps. There's something about these people, I don't know, you can't put your finger on it, but they're so self-centred you wouldn't believe it. Here I don't know who to write for except the émigrés and what's the point? They're so stupid, most of them, they get me down. I can just see them in twenty years. They'll be like the old ones.'

'Why don't you sing in English?'

'What about?'

'I don't know. There must be things to sing about here too.'

'Yes, but I can't make head or tail of it. Sometimes it's fantastic, and sometimes they make me mad, they're so clever and so ignorant. And anyway I have to be careful. They didn't say,

Oh yes, Mr Vratka, do come in and take refuge with us and, incidentally, you can go ahead and do anything you like. They wouldn't. I've got to watch my step.'

'You didn't worry about that before.'

'That was different. It was worth it at home – I could make a difference, or I thought so. You can't do that here. Nothing makes any difference because everybody's shouting and screaming at once. It's too much. They'll never achieve anything because they all want something different. At least we knew what we wanted. Are you sure you don't want a beer?'

The wings of his nose were moist. He drank steadily from his glass until it was nearly empty and looked at her across the rim, his face noticeably cheered.

'Tell you what I'm going to do, though. I'm going to write my autobiography when I get out of here. I'll have something to say. Hey, you remember' – he stretched out an arm and laid a finger on her cheek – 'we had some times, didn't we? You were a good fuck – oh, sorry.' His eyes turned towards the child, who was staring at him unblinking. 'Different now, though, I expect. With the kid.'

'Who'll read it?'

'What?'

'Who'll read your autobiography?'

Lukas dropped back in his seat, a childlike expression of hurt on his face. 'What do you mean? You think I can't write?'

'No, of course you can write. I mean, who'll be interested?'

'They will. People will be interested. Why shouldn't they be interested? I'll make them interested.'

Hana nodded acceptance, bestowing upon him the reassuring approval she had, so far, saved for Milan.

'What about my petition? How are they doing with my petition? Have they got many signatures? Hani, you must know. Did you sign? For old times' sake?'

'No, I didn't.'

Again Lukas was crestfallen. 'Why not?'

She pushed back her chair. 'Because I didn't think we were that close.'

'Oh, Hani. But you were one of the best.'

She nodded again, this time dismissive as a teacher.

'How long are you staying?'

'I'm going back tomorrow.'

'Well, look. Let's spend the evening together. I'm sure you could park the kid somewhere. We could have a meal. Only you'd have to pay.' He laughed awkwardly. 'Siliy, isn't it? I'm the one who made it out and you're the one with the money.'

Hana felt in her waistband and pulled out a ten-pound note. She passed it across to him.

As she left she turned in the doorway. Lukas sat at the table holding his note and watching her with a frown of bewilderment between his beautiful eyes. She thought of her chickens and the pity she used to feel when she selected one to wring its neck. And she had thought she would be looked after.

'Mummy?'

'Yes? Oh, Milan. Yes?' Hana dropped to her knees and held his face between her hands.

'Who was that man?'

'No one, sweetie. No one special. Let's go home, shall we?'

Dr Cerny's legs were buckling. He had taken so many wrong turns on this maze of tracks and now yet again the path forked. The straps of his haversack were biting into his collar-bones. If he didn't find her house soon he would have to discard the bag under some trees and hope to find it again. If only there was someone he could ask. His mouth was dry. He had not been prepared for this, the late-afternoon heat; he needed to drink something, to wash – his face was unshaven and the stubble humiliated him. The house was right at the top of the hill with trees, only trees behind it. That's what Milan had said. He stood at the forking of the path, assessing the two tracks, both of which wound up between the trees to be quickly lost from sight. The steeper one, then.

He set off again, bending deeply forwards to ease the weight on his back, pressing his hands on his thighs. It seemed to have been the correct decision. The track climbed and climbed and now he had to stop again to draw breath. He was getting too old for this sort of hiking. He looked back along the way he had come. Below him he could see the main body of the village and the line of the river Berounka glinting like a shard of glass. Somewhere above him in the trees people were playing tennis. If he could follow the sound he might get directions, but he had to lay down his haversack. He feared ill-health, he feared the strain on his body. Slowly, his heart pounding with discomforting violence as if it would batter an escape from his chest, he slid the haversack from one shoulder, then the other. He looked into the trees for a suitable place to hide it. There was a hollow off the track under the overhanging branches of an old spruce. He nudged the haversack to the edge of the track with his feet and all of a sudden it tumbled into the undergrowth but lay in full view, wedged against a protruding root. He must push it behind the tree. His breath was uneven, tense with the worry that he had undertaken too much. Backwards he clambered down into the hollow. His hands were shaky. Don't be afraid, he ordered himself, there have been steeper places than this before. On all fours now, grubbing among the roots, unkempt and unpresentable. It was no way to be seen. Please let no one take this track until he was on his feet again. He hauled the haversack around the tree, propped it against the pungent trunk and made to climb up to the track once more.

He had to find a toehold, a handhold, something solid that could be trusted not to give way. There was a rocky crevice in the bank above his head and he felt for it cautiously, his fingers prodding, clawing, grasped a small ledge of stone. He pulled at it, both feet still firmly planted, tugged it. It held! He thrust his hand into the crevice and locked his fingers on to the stone. There in the dry depths he felt a package. He stood on tiptoe and scrabbled for the package, pincered a piece of paper and drew it out. The package, only a bundle of paper, came tumbling out and slipped down between the bank of earth and his legs. He pressed his knees into the earth and pinioned the papers, leaned panting against the bank, retrieved the papers. He smoothed the crumpled sheets, covered edge to edge in fine, meticulous writing, the ink blurred with damp. He raised the papers to his eyes. His spectacles were in the haversack, but he could see enough to recognise his own handwriting. Each sheet had a tiny number encircled in the top left-hand corner.

He did not understand. There was a great deal he did not understand but he could not work it out now. He must get to the top, get to the house and rest. He folded the papers carefully and tucked them inside his jacket.

A spatter of applause from the tennis court urged him on. One side of the court was deep in shadow, the other in the glaring sunlight as if the court had been divided in two and painted black and red. Two boys were playing, while a further group sat at small tables in front of a clubhouse. As he approached them they looked up at him and he saw one of them gesturing towards him and whispering something to a companion. They both laughed. He did not want to have to speak to them. As he wiped his face with a dusty hand he saw above the court, set against a backdrop of young trees, a small wooden house. Grimly he bade the youngsters good day and passed them by.

The tall narrow gate into the bottom of the garden was ajar and he couldn't close it behind him. Half a dozen chickens came creaking and squawking to meet him, springing from foot to foot in a wild extended frenzy. They grouped themselves behind him and followed him up the steep garden, excited and expectant. He paused, clapped his hands sharply, and they scattered in screeching disarray but regrouped immediately. He looked for the door, found it closed, pushed on the handle. It was locked. He hammered. Hammered again. Maybe if he could look through the windows. He circled the house but the ground dropped so abruptly he could not see in. There was a terrible stillness.

Then he heard a scraping. Someone was there, someone was moving.

'Hana? Hana?'

The scraping stopped. He waited. A woman backed out of a low doorway under the house, dragging something after her. Her neck and cheeks were smeared with coaldust. She stood up.

'Hana!' But it was not Hana. It was an unknown woman taking something from Hana's house. Dr Cerny forgot his appearance.

'Who are you? What are you doing here?'

The woman looked at him over her shoulder. 'Who are you?' she retorted.

The doctor ignored her question and, filled with rage for which he could find no reason, barked at her in a voice of awful authority: 'Answer me. What are you doing here?'

The woman shrank back. 'I'm collecting something.'

'What are you collecting. Who gave you permission?'

'Hana. The woman this house belongs to. She said I should take this. She left a note in my husband's car but we've only just found it. I can show you.' Dr Cerny pushed her aside and bent over a bulky parcel wrapped in brown paper, tied with string.

'What's this? What's in here?' He pulled at the string and it slipped off the paper. A packet of sanitary towels spilled on to the grass. A winter coat. Skirts. Shoes. 'These are Hana's things. What's happened? Where is she? Where's the boy?'

The woman had covered her face with her hands but lowered them now. She was afraid but the panic in the voice of this stern, grizzled old man restored her courage.

'Do you know Hana?'

'The name is Cerny, Dr Cerny,' he said stiffly.

Her eyes were on his grimy beard. 'Dr Cerny? My God. I know who you are. You're Grandad. But you're too late. She's gone. She's gone away.'

'Away?'

'She told us she was taking Milan for a cure. She would have been back tomorrow but she went away. My husband told me, but now they've found out. How did they know? How did they find out so soon? She hasn't outstayed her visa yet, so why did they have to come in and do that, as if the place was theirs already?' The woman was crying and angry.

'I don't understand. What are you talking about?'

'Look inside. They left the place open.' Dr Cerny frowned but did as she said. In Hana's sitting-room there was a large desk, a chair at an angle as if she had just been sitting there, a chaise-longue. And in the centre the shattered remains of an inlaid table, smashed to pieces as if some vengeful fury had been at work. Somebody had left an axe lying among the pieces.

Twenty-four

They sat with their elbows on the table in a sudden and spontaneous silence that was, nevertheless, without awkwardness. They had eaten well – even Hana, who, Melanie had whispered to Peter as soon as she saw her, looked sick.

'Let me take you all out tonight.' Peter, expansive, had wanted to crown Hana's English visit with something lavish, something memorable; but for the second time it was not to be. She had walked too far, taken too many pictures, exhausted herself on her packing – but it was all done. Milan fed, early in bed for an early start.

'No thanks. I'm too tired to enjoy that. I'd disappoint you. Let's stay in. I'd prefer it with just the two of you.'

'I don't mind. It was for you anyway. So what's it to be? Chinese? Greek or Indian?' Not Indian. They had laughed at that.

Hana had accepted a single small glass of wine and, raising it solemnly to Peter, then to Melanie, sipped twice and put it down. She was fidgety. She wanted to get up and move about. She felt partitioned from herself, as if she had been turned inside out and scraped bare, like someone just bereaved. She was bereaved and, as the bereaved are, angry with the object of her grief for causing her such sorrow. She couldn't wipe from her mind the picture of Lukas staring after her holding his banknote and looking so much like an admonished child. She couldn't clear her ears of his petulant and rattling speech. If he had stayed at home, she thought, he would have gone to prison. So he had come to London and was imprisoned. And fate had so arranged it that she, too, had to come to London to see that incarceration. She did not want to be like Lukas, pitiable, and carping at the people who had given him refuge for continuing to live, unchanged by his arrival. Losing his

210

public he had lost himself. 'Did you sign my petition?' he had asked. No, she had not, too frightened and still hoping. But now – and anyway, Lukas, it isn't *your* petition, it's young Ondrei Sedlak's – now she knew what she would do, and having decided couldn't wait to get home to do it. Lukas had asked her, 'Did you sign?' In his ignorance Peter had as good as asked and she had shrugged him off. She did not want to be like Peter either, pretending to be English with his money and his bottles and his strange unpeopled perfect house. In a closed corner of her memory she smelt again her brother reeking with shame and realised that the stench was all her own, saw the spitting child, ugly in his contempt, with his running nose, who had made her so angry because she couldn't answer him, wouldn't sign. Well, she would answer him now. She would go home and write her name in large letters at the top of a page where everyone would see it; add her address – and in so doing release herself from the burden of indecision. So she was elated too and the two torn parts of her tussled over her peace of mind.

She looked across the table at her hosts. They didn't make a good couple, she thought, and was sorry. Peter had been generous but it was Melanie whom she might miss, a Melanie she had not come to know, beyond the reach of language. But that would have been rectified in time. Now she would have to content herself with invention, create a Melanie and commune with her creation.

The phone rang.

Dr Cerny emerged from Hana's house and lowered himself to sit on a log, the woman holding him under the arm.

'Thank you. I can manage,' he said gruffly, and removed his arm. 'I don't know what you were implying. But that's the work of hooligans.'

'Hooligans! What hooligans? Here, in a place like this? It's them, I don't care what you say. Even Josef says so.'

'Who is Josef?'

'My husband. And he should know. He carries the card. I always said, there'll come a time when you'll be ashamed of it, and he is now. You should see his face! Oh, where is she?'

Dr Cerny's head was swimming, from the heat, from his thirst, which would not now be quenched. He looked at the woman's pinched face. Its features seemed to be moving from one expression to another in slow motion. He thought he could answer her question. Nora had left, taking Peter with her; fled the country or, maybe, run away from him. No doubt she had had her reasons. But now Hana had done the same. Why did she have to go? Why did she have to choose that road, taking the boy with her, just when the child was learning? It would all have been all right. He would have explained so much to Milan, but the child had been as good as kidnapped to be handed over . . . What could Hana have been thinking, going that way? Now it would all be such a mess, such confusion. And how would they manage without him?

'Where is she?' He hunched on his log and repeated the woman's question bitterly. 'I can tell you where she is, I think. She's gone to her lover.'

But the woman gawped at him, threw out the derisory finger of a fishwife and laughed. 'Hana's got a son – have you forgotten? A son she dotes on, who's been all her life to her. She never had time for a lover. What lover? What on earth are you talking about?'

'Sons have to have fathers.'

'I'll get it.' Melanie reached for the phone.

Hana was tracing a spiral on the table-top with the fingertip she had moistened in her glass. Peter had begun to work out when he could next afford to take a few days off work to start on the cataloguing of his bottles.

'What? Wait . . . please . . . Peter, I can't follow this. It's an overseas call and a terrible line.'

Peter could barely hear. 'It's from Czecho,' he announced in English and returned to shouting. 'What? What? I can't hear you. Give me your number and I'll call you back.' He put down the receiver and immediately began dialling. 'Some woman called Alena, Hani, something about you. I couldn't hear.'

'Alena? How does she know I'm here?'

'You must have told her.'

'I didn't. I didn't tell anyone.'

Peter paused in his dialling and looked at her. She flushed. 'Hallo? Hallo? Is that Alena? This is Peter. Peter Cerny. Hana is with me. Do you want to speak to her?'

He turned into the room, fixing Hana with incredulous eyes, while Alena spoke to him and would not stop. Hana got to her feet, hand extended to take the receiver; but Peter had already replaced it.

'Hani. What did you come here for?'

'For a visit. To see London with my son.'

'Is that all?'

'Yes, of course that's all.' She was not meeting his gaze. 'I'm all packed to go back.'

'Well, you'd better unpack. You're not going anywhere. Your place has been smashed up. And we all know who by.'

Hana's mouth opened. 'What . . . ?'

Peter put an arm round her shoulders to steady her, thinking she might fall. She stood firm but he led her back to the table, sat her down and poured her a large glass of whisky. His hand was shaking and some of the spirit spilt on the table. Hana shook her head but picked up the glass and drank. The taste repelled her. Why would they do that, and so soon? Or had they found out about Lukas? She drank some more, feeling herself floating in whisky, the smell of it all around her. She closed her eyes and thought she felt someone's tongue in her mouth, heard the sound of splintering wood. Where were her house keys? What had she done with the keys? The whisky. There was something she ought to remember. She drank some more. She needed time, only a little more time, a little more whisky, then she would remember.

Peter was still talking. 'Incidentally, my father's there. He told her to ring me. He said you had come to be with your lover. Who is it?'

Melanie's voice was frantic. 'What's going on?'

'I haven't any lover.'

'They've been in and smashed Hana's house up. Alena says they think she came here without meaning to go back. And now she can't. She's going to have to stay here. Oh shit, what a mess. Now what do we do with her?'

And Melanie, who had downed all the wine that did not go into Hana's glass, spread her arms like a prima donna taking the final curtain, elegant wrists, long silky fingers beckoning Peter, embracing Hana, hiccuped and proposed:

'I think the two of you had better get married.'

What? What did she say? But Peter's reply was inaudible, buffeted aside by a piercing, twisting scream from upstairs. 'Grandad!'

'It's Milan. He's having a nightmare. Help me, Peter!'

He trod gingerly, craning his neck over the unfamiliar body

of the child in his arms, step by step down. There was no more screaming but the boy's eyes were wide open, seeing nothing. What's the matter with him, Hana, for God's sake? It's all right. It's only a nightmare. We have to walk him round, we have to talk to him. Now, Milachku, look, this is the table where we eat our meals, can you see it? Nod your head. Right. And this is Melanie with the lovely yellow hair. Say Melanie. Me-la-nie. Good. Now, who am I? Mummy. Say it again. Who am I? Mummy. And this is Peter, look at him. Who is it? Peter. Who is it? It's Peter.

Milan opened his eyes, already opened. 'Where's Grandad? I want Grandad.'

'He can talk! But who's Grandad, for God's sake?'

'Grandad's what he calls your father.'

'Mummy?'

'Milachku?'

'Who is Peter?'

Her voice was flat. 'Peter is Grandad's son, Milachku.'

Milan unravelled his mother's fingers, sidled, crablike, to the tall man with the curly black hair and put his hand in the man's hand. 'Are you my father, then?'

Peter looked down at the narrow spiky head of mousey hair, and across it at the child's mother.

'No,' she said and was taken aback by her own peremptory tone. Peter's eyebrows formed into question marks but she could give them no other answer. Milan was still holding Peter's hand. He should have been holding hers but her hand did not deserve his fragile fingers, fingers that had once clamped themselves round one of hers with sharp nails so tiny that she had been too frightened to trim them. She had felt vulnerable because of him then and had forgotten how defenceless he was – most of all against her. She had done it all for him, without consulting him because you did not consult a child.

Milan looked up at his mother. She had answered so quickly. She was bending down towards him, kneeling on the floor in front of him so that they were face to face, holding him between her knees, rubbing his wrists with her thumbs. He had never seen her crying before but her face didn't look sad.

'It doesn't matter about your father, Milachku. All that matters is you and me. I'm so sorry, sweetie. God, I'm sorry.' She reached out for him, drew him to her and spoke into his hair. 'If you like, tomorrow we'll write to Grandad together. Shall we do that?'

Jiří Weil

Life with a Star

(with a Preface by Philip Roth)

In 1942 Jiří Weil, the Czech novelist, was summoned for transportation to a concentration camp with the rest of the Prague Jewry. The experience of living in hiding during the Nazi occupation furnished the inspiration for *Life with a Star*. It is the intensely moving story of Josef Roubicek, an unemployed bank clerk, who lives in isolation, subject to the physical, emotional and psychological barbarisms of the Nazi regime. *Life with a Star* tells of the gradual stripping away of his possessions, his relationships, his human dignity, until a point is reached when he finds the spiritual courage to resist.

'Few books have kept me from sleeping at night, but this one has. It is like a pulling tide, like some kind of terminal book whose words turn one into an outcast from human society. And strangest of all it opens out on a vision of earned hope – to choose, it says, is to master death and to live. A profound work.'

Arthur Miller

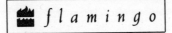

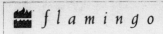 *flamingo*

Flamingo is a quality imprint publishing both fiction and non-fiction. Below are some recent titles.

Fiction
☐ News From a Foreign Country Came *Alberto Manguel* £4.99
☐ The Kitchen God's Wife *Amy Tan* £4.99
☐ Moon Over Minneapolis *Fay Weldon* £5.99
☐ Isaac and His Devils *Fernanda Eberstadt* £5.99
☐ The Crown of Columbus *Michael Dorris & Louise Erdrich* £5.99
☐ The Cat Sanctuary *Patrick Gale* £5.99
☐ Dirty Weekend *Helen Zahavi* £4.50
☐ Mary Swann *Carol Shields* £4.99
☐ Cowboys and Indians *Joseph O'Connor* £5.99
☐ The Waiting Years *Fumiko Enchi* £5.99

Non-fiction
☐ The Proving Grounds *Benedict Allen* £5.99
☐ The Quantum Self *Danah Zohar* £4.99
☐ Ford Madox Ford *Alan Judd* £6.99
☐ C. S. Lewis *A. N. Wilson* £5.99
☐ Into the Badlands *John Williams* £5.99
☐ Dame Edna Everage *John Lahr* £5.99
☐ Handel and His World *H. C. Robbins Landon* £5.99
☐ Taking It Like a Woman *Ann Oakley* £5.99

You can buy Flamingo paperbacks at your local bookshop or newsagent. Or you can order them from Fontana Paperbacks, Cash Sales Department, Box 29, Douglas, Isle of Man. Please send a cheque, postal or money order (not currency) worth the purchase price plus 24p per book (maximum postage required is £3.00 for orders within the UK).

NAME (Block letters)_____

ADDRESS_____

_____

_____